DRIVE

TAMARA LUSH

DRIVE

The **PRETENDERS** Series

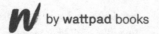 by **wattpad** books

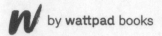

An imprint of Wattpad WEBTOON Book Group

Published in Canada by Wattpad Books, a division of Wattpad Corp.
36 Wellington Street E., Toronto, ON M5E 1C7

www.wattpad.com

First Wattpad Books edition: March 2022

ISBN 978-1-77729-001-6 (Trade Paper original)
ISBN 978-1-77729-002-3 (eBook edition)

Library and Archives Canada Cataloguing in Publication information is
available upon request.

Printed and bound in Canada
1 3 5 7 9 10 8 6 4 2

Cover design by Laura Mensinga
Image by CJC Photography
Typesetting by Sarah Salomon

To Marco, who still makes my heart race.

CHAPTER ONE

DANTE

"I will not allow a girl to change my tires. Absolutely not,"

Jack, my chief engineer and oldest friend, shot me an acerbic look that indicated he wasn't in the mood for my attitude. We were the only two at a twelve-seat conference table, where team principals normally met to discuss engines, tires, and race strategy.

My Italian accent turned thick with derision. "What the hell, man? I'm not going to dignify your laughter with a response. This is serious. This is world-class auto racing, not some reality TVshow."

Jack, an intense and sardonic Australian, finally sobered and turned his gaze out a window. My eyes rested on the vibrant green grass flanking the smooth asphalt of the Maranello test track. In the distance, the turret of a Renaissance-era palazzo peeked over a cluster of trees. I could practically smell the eucalyptus and lavender mixed with the burning rubber of tires. It was the scent of home. Of motorsports in Italy.

"Look here, mate. I know you don't want a woman on the team. But it's boss's orders. Might as well get used to it. She's part of us now. That's what I'm hearing, at least. And apparently she's quite competent."

Boss's orders. A woman in the pit crew was a responsibility I didn't need. A distraction I didn't want.

"There's never been a female tire changer in the history of Formula World. She'll ruin the team. And where the hell is Bronson? He called this meeting and now he's ten minutes late. You know how I feel about being late. Or coming in second."

Jack plucked a small model of our team's Formula World car off the conference room table and turned it around in his hands. He set the little white car back down and ran it back and forth on its toy wheels, avoiding my stare.

"Just because your sister—"

"This has nothing to do with Gabriella," I growled.

Jack pushed the little car across the table toward me. "It has everything to do with her. I've known you since before she . . . before the accident. And you didn't use to be so against women on the teams."

Slapping my hand on to the rolling car, I halted its journey. Jack was my savior on the track, my wingman. We'd worked together my entire dozen-year career. He was one of the few people on earth who treated me like a regular guy and not a racing superstar. But he knew how—and when—to poke at my tender spots.

"Gabriella shouldn't have tried to be a mechanic. She should have gone to school to be an engineer and gotten involved in the behind-the-scenes of racing. Or taken a job in the corporate offices of a motorsports team . . ."

"We've had this conversation a thousand times. But hey, we can have it again, I don't mind. I was on the track the day it happened six years ago." Without the car to fiddle with, he drummed his fingers on the table, unable to be still. "She didn't die because she was a woman. She died because of a faulty design in the fuel-rig. She happened to be the unlucky soul who was draining the rig after your practice lap."

The familiar feeling of sadness churned in my gut at the memory of my older sister, and the flash of terror I'd felt when I'd staggered out of my car, screaming her name. Every time I walked into the pit, the smell of gas reminded me of that day. Reaching into my pocket, I touched the silver medallion she'd given me for luck the year I started racing, back when I was twelve and into go-karts. "And you never listen. Or agree with me. She didn't have the upper-body strength to wrangle the hoses on the fuel rig. Which is my point. Women don't have the capability or stamina to be part of this."

Good God. How difficult was it for people to understand?

"Also, a woman will be distracting. Can you imagine how the guys will react to her? It won't matter what she looks like, someone will want to . . . you know." I waved my hand dismissively.

"Screw her?" Jack offered.

What a disaster. It was difficult enough to stomach that Brock Bronson, the team's owner, barely knew an open-wheel car from a junker in a demolition derby. He was a Silicon Valley billionaire with a fascination for speed. But he'd offered me such an astronomical amount of money to sign with Team Eagle—had assembled such an incredible car, drawn such lucrative sponsors—that it was impossible to say no.

Eagle was new and risk taking, my agent had said. *Sign the contract*, my agent had said. Six world championships in, I had been looking for the ultimate challenge. To win a seventh in my final season with a rookie team would be the biggest conquest of all, and it would bring both visibility to a new team and plenty of retirement sponsorships my way.

Good karma and a ton of cash, my agent had said.

"All I want is to win and stay drama-free. Can you imagine the headlines if she screws up?" I said.

"Really? Will she distract us? How will we even know she's a woman? She'll be done up in coveralls and helmet during races, like the rest of us. Surely you can control yourself. And look, Rolf is gay, and he's on the pit crew. We don't worry about him being distracted by other blokes." Jack reached across the table to grab the little car.

Hell. His logic was solid. "This isn't about controlling *my* libido. Like I would be interested in a tire changer when I've got models and actresses and that singer . . ."

What was the name of the pop singer I'd hooked up with last season in Malaysia? I couldn't recall. Women were among the many perks of being a driver, and I hadn't ever felt the need to settle down with only one.

"A lone girl around a group of men will always be a distraction to someone. And it's our championship and my safety on the line." I threw my hands in the air. "And what does she know about tires and cars? She won't have the hand-eye coordination needed to change a wheel in seconds. *Porca miseria.*

"Oh, we're trotting out the nonsensical Italian swear words, are we?" Jack asked, annoying me even more. "She's starting at Monaco. And testing with us soon here on the track. In a day or two."

"We'll see about that. She can't waltz in now and begin a week before the season," I snapped. "I'll meet with Bronson and try to knock some sense into that stupid American. He thinks he knows everything because he made more money than God with his computer chips, but he knows nothing about cars, tires, or racing. He's a—"

"Who's a stupid American?"

It was Brock Bronson. In all of his friendly, casual glory. Regarding him with a surly smile, I decidedly ignored what he'd overheard. Other drivers would have quaked in fear had they insulted their team owner. But Bronson needed me, so I smiled. Fuck him.

"*Buongiorno*, Signor Bronson. We were just discussing the team's new hire."

Bronson took a seat across from me at the conference table. To my ears, his thick American accent sounded like syllables scraped against a cheesegrater.

That's one of the reasons I wanted to sit down with you two. I knew it would get some of you boys in a snit. But first, I wanted to update you on our other situation, in private."

Jack and I straightened our spines in tandem. This was far more interesting than any woman.

"The Praxi steam is still considering going to the FIA World Motor Sport Council about Max and his engineer," Bronson said. If the Fédération Internationale del'Automobile got involved, it could lead to terrible press and even worse morale for an organization as new as Eagle.

Jack stared at me as if to say, *I knew coming to this team was a terrible decision.* We'd had a bit of a quarrel over whether to sign the contract when we'd found out that Max Becker, a hot shot young German who'd been in the sport only a year, would be the other, junior driver.

"So they're serious? They think Max and his engineer stole the technical information on the chassis last season?"

Jack sat back in his chair and folded his arms. There was no love lost between him and Max's crew. We'd competed against them last season on opposing teams, and never trusted them. Now we were on the same side, but apparently Max's past slippery nature was catching up to him. And we could be collateral damage.

Bronson held up his hands. "Look. Max assures me that his guys are clean. No one stole anything last year, he said."

"Was he or was he not in possession of the Praxis chassis information?" I asked.

"I'm still looking into that. He claims no."

The way Bronson evaded my question was concerning. "I didn't sign onto a rookie team and bring my trusted crew with me to be embroiled in drama. I wouldn't have signed at all had I known you were bringing on that kid."

"Max is no rookie. He's been driving for three years and isthe future of the sport. People are saying he's the next . . . you," Bronson said.

Max was only twenty-four, and as hungry as I once was. A fact I didn't like to be reminded of at my age. "Still. I don't enjoy the scandal."

"There's no scandal. No drama. Don't worry, dude. We've got this. I know the press is sniffing around, but I'm confident everything will turn out fine. I'll make sure of it."

Figures. Bronson was the kind of guy who thought money could fix everything. Admittedly, it usually could in Formula World, but I liked to think that talent always rose to the top.

"When will we find out whether Praxis is taking the case to the FIA?"

"A few weeks. A month, maybe."

We'd be in Montreal by then, perhaps Belgium. "Fine." I sighed. "Let's try to put it behind us, especially before the first race in Monaco. And what's this about the girl? Please tell me it isn't true."

"Oh, right. Savannah." Bronson chuckled. "You'll meet her soon. She's doing onboarding with HR as we speak. I spoke with Max earlier, and he said he doesn't have an issue with her."

He spoke with that kid before me? "Then assign her to his pit crew."

Bronson tilted his head. "Nah, I think that would be a little too obvious. As if we were purpoocfully trying to distract the public from the chassis info situation."

"Max would definitely try to sleep with her," I muttered.

My German teammate was as legendary on the party circuit as he was on the track. The two of us made quite the tabloid fodder, actually. Two months ago during a promotional event in Chile, he'd had a threesome with two flight attendants after the exhibition race that somehow got leaked to the press, and I'd gotten a speeding ticket the day after.

On a Vespa. With a soap opera actress riding behind me. Later, back at the hotel, she'd ridden me. Then proceeded to divulge everything about our night together to a gossip site.

The media never ceased in their attempt to stir the pot, whether it was with the drivers' on-track problems or their off-track escapades. "Terrible Twos," the tabloids had recently dubbed me and Max. We were the biggest celebrities in motorsports and could pretty much do anything we damn well pleased.

And now, with Max's crew and the accusations of possible

stolen technical information, Eagle was in the press every day. Hell, every hour on the blogs, which I tried not to read.

"With all due respect, I need to tell you there's a million reasons why it would be disastrous to have a girl on the pit crew. What if she becomes involved with someone?"

"Not a chance in hell. She comes highly recommended by some of the top IndyCar executives. She interned there. And at NASCAR too. Pretend she's a guy. She's one of three hundred people on the entire Eagle payroll. Ignore her. Your only job is to win."

Bronson reached across the table and clasped my muscled forearms with his smooth, chubby hands. "With the car we've put together and your skills, you've got a serious shot at a seventh championship. Then you can retire in glory, bro."

Nothing was more irritating than that man calling me bro. A man with his wealth should be more formal, less crass. But the American was right: if I won a seventh championship, I'd be remembered as one of the greats of motorsports, alongside Hamilton, Schumacher, and Andretti.

"Have you told the guys?"

"I'm making it clear to everyone, including Max, that they're not to harass Savannah. I'm telling you the same thing, and that's why I wanted to sit down with both of you today. I want you to welcome her and turn on that Italian charm of yours when you meet her in the coming days. I think it looks good to have a woman on the team. I'm not going to lie: it'll help our image, given Max and his alleged 'espionage' controversy."

"Espionage. I'll strangle him myself if it's true." I swore under my breath.

"And Savvy will practice with us next week."

"Savvy? What kind of a girl name is that? It sounds like the moniker of an exotic dancer."

"She's not a girl, she's twenty-four. She's a woman, and you should respect her as such. And Savvy is short for Savannah. As in Georgia, USA. Which is where her father, Dale Jenkins, the owner of Jenkins International—one of the largest parts distributors in North America—makes his home and his corporate headquarters. I'm surprised you don't know her, he's such a high-profile man in the industry and all."

Hearing the name of Jenkins International sent a frisson of awareness through my body. Of course I'd heard of her father and his company. The brand was known the world over.

"Why does *she* want to be on the team?"

Bronson guffawed. "It might have something to do with the fact that her father is now one of our sponsors. She asked her daddy if she could work with us, and I couldn't say no. He and I met at a party in the States—he's a stand-up guy. It was too good a PR opportunity to pass up. But you can always ask her yourself. Maybe she's got her own reasons."

I leaned forward, gesturing by turning my hand upward, pressing my thumb against my four fingers, and flicking for emphasis. "Let me get this straight. Our new tire changer is the daughter of the man who owns one of America's largest auto parts companies? The outfit that sponsors NASCAR teams?"

"What are the chances of that?" Jack and I stared at each other.

Bronson stood up. "Sounds like you two will have a lot to talk about."

So much for a drama-free season.

CHAPTER TWO

SAVANNAH

Showtime. Well, not exactly. It was only practice. But every practice needed to be perfect, at least for me. This was the final run at the test track before the season opener in Monte Carlo, and my heart practically raced in time with the RPMs coming from the gleaming white car.

I pulled on a white helmet and adjusted the strap under my chin until my head was safe and snug inside. Snapping the visor into place, I knelt between two men, one of whom was holding a tire. I picked up the pneumatic wheel gun, and it was heavy and comfortable in my hands.

Finally. It felt amazing to be in the pits, the roar of the engine echoing in my head. I'd spent the last three weeks here at the Eagle headquarters, mostly doing boring onboarding with Human Resources during week one. Life had gotten more exciting in week two, when I'd shadowed crew members from the team's other car. After all this, I was assigned to Dante Annunziata's crew and had recently learned the fascinating—and highly confidential— technical aspects of his vehicle from the engineers.

Fun fact: The steering wheel for the car on the track cost close to a hundred grand. It was made of carbon fiber and silicone and controlled up to forty functions for the vehicle.

And now, it was time for me to control my own destiny.

Everyone was clad in identical white, fire-retardant jumpsuits, with heavy black gloves and boots. Not to mention the white helmets, which made us look like aliens. Even the most ardent of racing fans wouldn't be able to tell I was a different gender—the other tire changers were also trim, small, and nimble. Sure, maybe I was a bit shorter than the rest, but I didn't feel like I stood out.

Giorgio, the tire carrier next to me, gave a thumbs-up, and I responded in kind. He flipped up his visor.

"*Che calor,*" he yelled, and I recognized his words as Italian, something about the heat, because I'd been studying the language for the last month in preparation for my first practice with the team. I wanted so much to be accepted by them, and each time anyone talked to me, I tried to be superpleasant. So far, everyone had been respectful and kind, and I was grateful.

It didn't feel hot outside to me, not after a lifetime spent in the steamy south of Georgia. This heat had nothing on my hometown, where palm trees, moss, and people visibly withered in the summer months. I grinned wide inside my helmet.

Girl, you've got this.

I'd signed with Eagle to show everyone a woman could break

barriers in racing's most glamorous sport. I'd also wanted to prove something closer to home.

My mother assumed I'd choose something genteel, a branch of the motorsports profession with a whiff of glitz, like public relations. She'd gone along with the engineering diploma from the University of Georgia and the internships with NASCAR and IndyCar. But my traveling the world with a race team for the better part of a year had been a bridge too far.

"You're going where, to do what?" Mom had asked a month ago, during our weekly bottomless mimosa brunch at a place not far from home. Her incredulous tone had caused many of the well-heeled Southern women at nearby tables to turn in our direction. "But what about that assistant public relations job with the racing team in Atlanta? Or something with our family's company? You'd be close to me and Dad, and you'd be able to find a nice Southern boy to settle down with."

Then came the inevitable guilt-trip. "How could you leave *me*?" she'd wailed.

The emotional manipulation had become too much to bear, and for the first time, I stood up for myself. "I don't want nice, I don't want a Southern boy, and I don't want Atlanta," I shot back. "I want international travel and fast cars and Formula World."

She'd fixed her hard blue stare on me and doubled down on her toxic tactics. "You'll never succeed in that world, Savvy. That's a rich man's game, and you have no business sticking your nose into places it doesn't belong. Don't even bother. You'll fail."

That conversation, and no small measure of satisfaction, raced through my head as I stood there, waiting for the car to pit. I was here in Italy. I was succeeding. *Thriving*.

Crouching into position again between the two men, I sent a

silent thank-you to my unconventional father, who had always encouraged me to follow my dreams. It was Daddy who had introduced me to the world of motorsports, and who had been the only one to know my secret dream: to help run our family's company, alongside my brother, and sponsor my own racing outfit—an all-female team in one of the top circuits, proving that women could be successful athletes and equals in motorsports. First, though, I needed *experience.*

"Get in place!" yelled a voice.

With a high-pitched roar, the powerful machine whizzed into the pit. The guy standing at the hood—the lollipop man—held up a sign to signal to the driver to keep his brakes on during the pit stop.

I moved fluidly, pressing the gun into the middle of the tire, unlocking the single lug nut at the center of the wheel. I eased back. The man to my right slipped the tire off, and the man to my left slid a new tire on in one seamless motion. I moved forward and quickly locked the lug nut with a fierce blast of the wheel gun.

Zip. Whoosh. Zip.

It was an intricate dance, albeit one that happened in a few blinks of an eye. The twenty-one strong pit crew that hovered around the car stepped back with uniformity. The lollipop man at the front raised his sign and the car sped off. With that engine, it would eventually reach its peak of fifteen thousand revolutions per minute—up to two hundred and twenty miles per hour.

Faster than a hot knife through butter, I thought.

I thought something else too: *You're a beautiful girl, Savvy, which means you have to work harder and smarter than everyone else to be taken seriously.* That's what Daddy always said, and I'd reminded myself of his words a thousand times during my first weeks with Eagle. It was a mantra I repeated every time I was asked to do something new.

Work harder.

Work smarter.

Don't show any fear.

The team practiced the pit stops four more times, each one more efficient and faster than the last. The pit crew manager took off his helmet. "Three point one seconds on the last stop. Nice work. Let's take a break and recap the day."

One of the tire carriers who'd stood nearby during the pit stop clapped me on the shoulder as we all walked into the pit garage. After a few moments, a hand firmly eased me aside. From the specially tailored uniform, the uniquely decorated helmet, and the swagger, I knew it was Dante Annunziata, our driver. I'd seen him earlier when he'd climbed into his car for the test laps.

Pulling off my helmet, I watched as the team parted for him, a king given the privilege of entering the air-conditioned garage first. Drivers, even the most decent of guys in any semi-pro contest, usually displayed a hint of entitlement and brashness off the track, and an exacting, calculating iciness behind the wheel. He was no different, from what I could tell.

I followed everyone inside. Although the team was American owned, the headquarters were in Italy because the owner loved it here, I'd heard. The Team Eagle operation was like nothing I'd ever seen in other circuits back home. The place was a vast motorsports complex that had been recently built with an eye for detail. Everything from the polished concrete floors to the mahogany conference room tables to the tools with their surgery-theater-level gleam screamed money.

Owner Brock Bronson had spared no expense for the building

or the cars. This was how I'd explain the place to my dad next time I called: cleaner than a bar of soap, with the added bonus of a catered pasta bar for lunch. Hopefully Daddy would be able to visit during a race at some point later in the season. Making him proud was important to me.

As I started to pull a chair out from the sleek mahogany table, Giorgio tugged on my sleeve and wagged his finger.

"We sit back here during these briefings," he whispered in a heavy Italian accent.

I winced, wishing I hadn't drawn attention to myself. "Sorry," I whispered. He was my dad's age, a guy with salt-and-pepper hair and a handlebar moustache. He motioned for me to sit next to him, front and center in a row of folding chairs.

The team's engineers and computer technicians took their places at the conference table.

I set my helmet at my feet on the gleaming terrazzo floor, mimicking the other guys, and undid my ponytail. Goodness, that cool air felt amazing on my scalp. I combed my hair back with my fingers, letting it fall loose over my coverall-clad shoulders.

My gaze alighted on a man at the head of the table. For a second, everything around me—the two dozen pit crew members, the assistants serving coffee, the strong blast of the air conditioner—fell away, because I was spellbound by a pair of dark, molten eyes.

Dante Annunziata.

My first thought was that it was too bad he wore the foulest, angriest glare I'd ever seen. With his longish raven-black hair tumbling over his forehead and his matching dark brows, it was a waste of a handsome face to look so nasty. My second thought was one of sheer curiosity. Why were his full lips curled into a sneer as if a foul odor permeated the room? Our pit stops had been flawless, and he'd driven as fast as the wind around the track. He should be thrilled that we'd worked so well as a new team, especially since the season opener in Monaco was just days away.

What was he staring at? I glanced to the men on either side of me, then quickly over my shoulder at the two other rows of chairs, which were filled with pit crew members and team staff. I looked again at Dante. He hadn't stopped staring in my direction. And his flashing dark eyes were still unblinking and furious.

Well, that was rude. Surely he wasn't raised by wolves?

As if he'd heard me calling him names inside my head, Dante turned to Jack, the chief engineer, who sat next to him. The two men huddled for a minute until the team's owner ambled in. He was lanky, and wore dung-colored cowboy boots, jeans, a black T-shirt, and thick, black-rimmed hipster glasses. He took up a lot of space when he moved his long arms and legs.

He was followed by Tanya, the team's head of public relations. She was also from the US—Boston, I think, if her clipped accent was any indication. I'd only met her once, and thought she was pleasant in a slightly frosty way. But since we were among the only women employed by the team and both from the United States, I hoped to get to know her better. Being surrounded by all these dudes—and missing my best friend, Kayla, back home—made me crave female friendship.

Bronson passed by Dante and Jack, squeezing both men's shoulders before taking the empty seat next to Jack. "Take it away, Jack. It's your show," he said.

Jack climbed to his feet. "You all looked incredible out there. Bravo, team." He pumped his fist. "Now, let's go over what we could've done better, and talk about the weather conditions for our first race."

I concentrated on his post-practice wrap-up, trying to put Dante's blazing stare out of my mind. Something about him left me with a squirmy feeling.

"We'll likely be starting the Monaco race on soft tires, since they've done so well in practice this week," Jack said, then launched into a long explanation about the weather in France.

I studied Dante. He was a world champion in the sport. A legend. Which meant I needed to be deferential and extrarespectful.

He furrowed his brow. His full lips plumped into a faint pout. He ran a thumb across his jawline, which was sharp as a knife.

I'd bet a hundred bucks that he practiced that brooding, intense look in the mirror just to perfect his sex appeal. The thought almost made me laugh, but I had to admit an uncomfortable truth: he had more sex appeal than his car had RPMs.

It was not something I often thought when looking at a man. Actually, I'd never had a visceral reaction to a guy like this. Not during either of my internships, not in college, not ever.

Guys rarely affected me one way or the other, much to the dismay of both my mother and Kayla. Oh, sure, I thought some were cute, or even handsome. I liked men. I'd kissed a few. But Dante, and his searing, brooding expression, was a different story entirely, stirring in me something both unnerving and unfamiliar. Dangerous, even. I was usually so unaffected by men.

But *this* man was different.

His forehead was high and his nose aquiline, a classic Italian look. He often posed for edgy modeling shoots for various Italian clothing designers, and I'd seen lots of photos of him online.

But in person, he was way different. Rawer somehow, and more arresting. All charisma and attitude. His lips were plush and sensual, which made his sharp jaw seem all the more masculine. He was clean-shaven and I pondered how the olive-gold skin of his face would feel under my fingertips.

Egad. I made a mental note to text my best friend back home about this troublesome thought. She'd probably laugh at me and tell me I was jetlagged or dehydrated.

"And I'd like to again introduce our newest team member, Savannah Jenkins. Some of you met her during this morning's meeting or have had the chance to say hi over the past couple of weeks. Our team's grown so much, though, and we've hired so many new people that I wanted to do another round of introductions, since I know some of the staff and techs haven't yet been acquainted. In case she doesn't stand out, Savvy's the one in the front row of chairs with the long red hair. Savannah, stand up, please."

Oh dear.

I hurriedly smiled and stood, all while being acutely aware of Dante's smoldering eyes. He'd caught me staring, and I watched as his own gaze skimmed down my coverall-clad body. *Just great.*

"Thank you," I said, drawing out the words in my most syrupy Southern accent. I'd been trying to temper that around all these international people, but when I was flustered or put on the spot, my roots bloomed in my voice with a vengeance.

"I'm thrilled to be here in Formula World with all y'all, simply honored to be in your presence," I said. "It's a world away from Atlanta, where I'm from, but I know we're going to win the championship for Eagle. Get 'er done. Shake and bake, and all that. At least that's what we say back home. And Mr. Annunziata,

I must say that was some of the finest driving I've ever seen on a track. You are incredible."

A ripple of laughter and applause went through the room. Except from Dante. He winced. Didn't nod, didn't smile, didn't acknowledge my compliment in any way.

Jack smiled warmly. "We are equally as thrilled to have you. In case you didn't know, Savvy—that's what she likes to be called— has an engineering degree and has interned with a top NASCAR team. She and Eagle are also part of history, because she's the first female tire changer in Formula World. She's a great asset to Eagle, and I hope you'll join me in making her feel welcome."

Bronson stood. "I'd also like to give Savannah a big hello. I know you all got my memo about her, but consider this a formal welcome. Having a woman on the team puts us at the forefront of motorsports. We should all be proud of that. And look at her. She's something, isn't she?"

When everyone again turned to stare at me, I froze. In an instant, my face felt like I'd pressed it into a bowl of jalapeno peppers, and I knew it was turning red. "Thanks, y'all," I replied.

The team applauded, and I sank back into the chair. The guy next to me patted my shoulder. I let out the breath I was holding and pasted on my best pageant smile. Even gave a little wave.

My eyes went from Bronson to Jack to Dante. He wasn't clapping. Instead, he was scribbling on a piece of paper in front of him. Looking like he couldn't be bothered.

What a *jerk*.

CHAPTER THREE

DANTE

Jack and I strolled out of the conference room after the team meeting and stood outside in the bright Italian sun, not far from the garages that housed Eagle's multimillion-dollar cars.

"Those pit stops were perfection." Jack's ruddy complexion was flushed, and he shielded his eyes from the glare. "How did they feel to you? This car really is something impressive. And you know I don't impress easily."

"Seems like we have our act together. It's hard to tell, though. I'll have a better feel for things in Monaco. You know me, cautious until I start winning."

"There's no way we're going to lose with this car. Or with this team. I really sense a great vibe between everyone. All the guys, er, *crew* are hustling their asses off. It's like the old days. Even with a woman on the team. No one even batted an eye when she stood in the pits during practice. I'll bet you didn't even know she was changing your tire."

Admittedly, I hadn't noticed. "Really? Are you bullshitting me? I feel like she's hard to ignore."

"What were your impressions of her, mate?" He seemed to be goading me. Sometimes Jack's incessant questions and chatter set my teeth on edge. This was one of those times.

"She's young. A little brash. Can't vouch for her mechanical skills but my wheel didn't fall off, so there's that. But did you see the way she addressed the team? Seems kind of full of herself."

A few pit crew members left the building and I wondered if Savannah would soon emerge. I waved and they held up their fists in the air. "Looked amazing out there today, Dante," one shouted in Italian.

"*Grazie*," I called back.

"Kind of full of herself?" Jack guffawed, ignoring the guys. "Takes one to know one. I can tell you this, she was great during our test runs. Smooth and quick. She spent a lot of time last week with Max's crew to get a feel for both cars, and I had her observe for some of your stops too. But those final pits when she was working were smooth as silk. She knows her stuff. Maybe we need more women as wheel gunners. Savvy's fast on her feet. I was impressed."

"I heard what you said during the meeting. I know I didn't seem like I was paying attention, but I was."

Jack went on for several moments about how Savannah was well-versed in engines, about her engineering degree, and about the virtues of her excellent hand-eye coordination.

"Enough," I barked, pushing a rock with the toe of my sneaker. Jack reared back. "What? I always talk up our new teammates. Oh, get this: she was a beauty pageant queen."

"She was what?"

"Yeah, Tanya told me, and I asked Savvy about it earlier today."

"Where was I during this conversation?" *A beauty pageant queen turned tire changer? What in God's name . . .*

"You were signing autographs in the marketing office."

"This makes me doubt her credentials even more," I said with a grunt.

Jack's eyes widened. "No, she did two internships with winning teams in the US. She knows her stuff. Her pageant career began when she was twelve and lasted until she was about sixteen. She was a runner-up for the Miss Georgia title. Then she stopped competing. I'm not sure why."

Again he blathered on about her qualifications. I watched as Bronson left the building, his cowboy boots making sharp strikes against the asphalt. He either didn't notice us or was ignoring our presence, because he didn't wave. This annoyed me even more, and I finally held up my hand, hoping Jack would stop talking.

"Fine. I get it. She's got experience in motorsports." I didn't want to be reminded of Savannah and her mane of wild red hair.

"Really, you need to forget she's a woman and move on."

"I expected someone more, I don't know. Like my sister. More strapping and solid." My sister, Gabriella, had been sturdy, like our grandmother. Strong as an ox.

"Oh, Savvy's quite strong. She told me all about how she weight trains and runs. She had no problem using the tire gun."

I shot him a warning look. "Maybe we can reassign her to ordering parts or something. Does she have to be in the pits?"

For some reason, her bright green eyes burned in my mind. *Christ.* Feisty. Bewitching, even. Without makeup and while wearing only a bulky, zip-up coverall, she still looked feminine, with her little nose, her fair skin, and the sprinkle of freckles on her cheeks. Something about her wide, sexy smile and the way she had stared at me with the promise of a challenge had sent an unwelcome surge of blood to the region below my belt. It was all so annoying, though, because this was a situation I couldn't control. She was a wild card. Too wild, by the looks of her.

"You're right, though. I need to forget about her. Enough about Savannah." I clapped Jack on the shoulder. "Are you coming with me in the jet to Monte Carlo tomorrow? We can plan out which yacht parties we're going to hit once we land."

Jack shook his head. "No. Bronson wants me to make sure Savvy's comfortable on the bus."

I swore in Italian. "See, this is what I mean. The girl's a distraction. Why should she get special treatment?"

"You know, maybe if you weren't such an old-fashioned chauvinist, this wouldn't be an issue." Jack laughed. "I'm not a chauvinist. Women are as capable as men. In most things. More capable in some areas, truth be told. You know I love women. But not in this circuit. Remember how I came out against the idea of that eighteen-year-old Brazilian girl becoming a driver in IndyCar?"

"I remember," Jack said. "So listen, old man of thirty-two: Why don't you give Savvy a chance? She seems like a sharp gal with a good head on her shoulders. She actually does know a lot about tires. We had a long conversation about soft compound tires during rainy races."

"Oh, you did, did you?" Exasperated, I shook my head and looked to the garage, where my race car awaited. I needed to inspect an important detail on the vehicle, and this conversation about Savannah was keeping me from the task at hand.

A sharp gal. *Of course.* Maybe that was what had affected me so much about her. During the team meeting she looked like she was soaking up every molecule in the room. Her expression was alert and hungry.

Then I could've sworn she was checking me out. Which wasn't unusual from women, but she did it in such a bold way. I'd even spotted her licking the side of her mouth, like a kitten. A sexy kitten. Arousal from a teammate was a first. It was also unwelcome. What if she distracted me on a race day? What if I distracted her and she failed to lock down my wheel during a race? What if she screwed up and hurt herself?

The thought made me shudder.

I was poised to snap at Jack for calling me old-fashioned, but then I had an idea.

"Get to know her. Might not be a bad plan."

"Exactly. Just be her friend . . . wait. I know that look in your eyes. I last saw it when you invited all those models onto your yacht last year at your Amalfi villa."

"For the sake of argument, what do you think Bronson would do if a driver was sleeping with a team member?"

"If you had asked me a few weeks ago, I'd say he would assert it was a matter between men and let it go. But now there's a woman on the team, I'm not so sure."

I leaned toward Jack and tapped on his chest. "But now there is a beautiful young woman on the team, things have changed, no? And if she falls for her handsome Italian driver, well, there's no way she'll be able to continue with us. Even Bronson would know it's a liability for everyone concerned."

"You're so bad. Stop. Don't mess with the poor woman."

"She's not poor, if she's the daughter of Dale Jenkins. She's probably as rich as I am. Which means she should be at a debutante ball or going to a yoga retreat. Or whatever privileged American women do in their spare time. I'm sure she looks as hot in a dress as she does in coveralls. And even better out of either of them. Maybe I'll find out."

"What, then your plan is to seduce her in hopes of driving her off the team?" Jack scratched his cheek with a finger and looked slightly horrified. "Mate, that's cold."

"It's not like I wouldn't enjoy myself. Did you see her? She's quite striking. But I'll enjoy myself a lot more when she's off the team and out of my life."

"I'm going to pretend this conversation never happened. File this under 'wishful thinking.'"

"Grazie. You definitely can't tell anyone about this." I shot him a pointed look.

"Of course I wouldn't." Jack shrugged. His phone buzzed and he stared at it for a second; then he shook his head and slipped it back into his pocket. "We've been through so much together. Your little fantasy of seducing her is barely a blip compared to some of the shenanigans we've endured."

I smiled, thinking of our second season together, when Jack had the brilliant idea of hiring a photographer with multiple long, expensive lenses to take photos of all the other teams' cars at the season opener. Sure, it was a little like spying, but now everyone did it—although it was Jack who'd pioneered the practice.

"I'm going to miss your sorry ass," I said, my voice gruff. Jack had helped me through those dark days after Gabriella's death, always ready with a party invitation and a crazy distraction—like the clandestine, off-road race in Baja one year—and I'd never forgotten the kindness. As much as the Australian sometimes annoyed me, I knew I'd miss him when the season was over. Jack would continue on in motorsports and I was headed straight for . . . something. Beyond some lucrative endorsements, I still hadn't decided on the direction of my post-race career.

All I knew was that I wanted to leave while at the top of my game. I didn't want to hang on and lose more and more races each year, fading away until I finally retired.

"Let's not get ahead of ourselves. It's a long season, mate, and it's shaping up to be interesting, to say the least." Jack smiled. "On that note, Bronson wanted me to round up Savannah and make a proper introduction between the two of you."

Well. This was fortuitous, if I actually planned on seducing her. Which was probably a shitty idea. Still, I wanted to push back against Jack's eagerness, simply because he was annoying. "Why? It's not like I personally meet with every new hire on the team. I usually get acquainted as the season goes on. I'm not the welcome wagon."

"He wants to make sure it's smooth going between the two of you. After our conversation the other day, I think he sensed a bit of hesitation on your side."

A snort leaked from my nose. "Perceptive, isn't he?"

"Spend fifteen minutes with her to appease him. Maybe you'll get this sorry plan of seducing her out of your head. I'm sure you'll warm up to her once you've had a chat."

I shrugged. "Maybe she and I can catch up in Monaco."

"You know we'll be too busy, between the parties and the

interviews and the actual fucking racing. Suck it up now. It's what Bronson wants. Get it over with and see for yourself that she's a decent person. She's incredibly professional—you'll be impressed."

Yeah, right.

"What are you, scared?" Jack teased.

"Scared? Of meeting her? *Pffft.* Of course not." I pointed to the garage where my gleaming white car sat. "Fine. Meet me in there. I want to check on whether they've added the detail I asked for earlier."

At the start of every season, I had my team paint my sister's name in small, cursive letters on the side of my car. So she'd always be with me on the track.

"Oh, the Gabriella lettering? They were planning on doing it now. Go in and check, and I'll meet you in there with Savvy."

He walked off, and I sauntered over to the garage, thinking about how this would be the last car to carry my sister's name, and the final season we'd race together.

CHAPTER FOUR

SAVANNAH

After chatting with a couple of the pit crew guys after the meeting—it seemed as though everyone wanted to tell me about the time they went to a NASCAR race or visited my hometown of Atlanta—I went on the hunt for Jack, the chief engineer.

I was on a mission.

If I was to service Dante's car in the pits, I needed his trust. Judging from the glares he'd given me during the meeting, it sure seemed like he had a problem with me. I wanted to nip that in the bud and confront any awkwardness right away. That was another thing Daddy had taught me: never shy away from a fight.

Jack could probably set me straight on whether Dante had

an issue with my presence, or if he wore that sour look on his face because he was nervous about the season opener in Monaco. Right as I was walking out the door, the engineer was on his way in, carrying papers attached to a clipboard. We almost crashed into each other, and we both laughed.

"Whoops! You're the man I want to see, Jack. Sorry for almost running into you."

"No worries, mate. This is brilliant because I was looking for you as well."

"Forgive me for being so forward." I smiled. "But between us, does Mr. Annunziata have a problem with me being on the team? I got a frosty vibe from him during the post-race wrap-up. I wanted to clear the air, if so."

Jack smirked. "You certainly don't mince words."

"In fact, I don't. I know my presence here is a bit unusual, and it might take some getting used to, for some of the guys. I didn't expect to have issues with the star driver, though."

To my surprise, Jack looked amused.

"I was actually coming in here to find you so I could personally introduce you to Dante. I'm sure once the two of you get to know each other, he'll be fine and drop his attitude. C'mon, he's in the garage."

Jack gestured for me to follow him. We walked briskly out of the room and into the bright sunshine.

"So my instincts were correct? Mr. Annunziata—"

"Dante. Please. Call him Dante."

"Dante. Yes. Dante has a problem with me? But why?"

"It's not my story to tell," he said as he headed toward the garage bays. "Let's say he has his reasons for being wary of a woman on the pit crew. Dante can be a bit, shall we say, dramatic.

He's hot tempered, says what he thinks, and has absolutely no poker face. He also can be a little grumpy."

"Sounds like we'll get along great," I said, only half sarcastically.

The white of the concrete bay cut a sharp line against the azure sky. "He'll get over it." Jack paused. "And speak of the devil. There's our man. Dante, I wanted you to officially meet our new team member, Savannah. Sorry we couldn't do this introduction before the test runs, but our superstar was pretty busy with marketing earlier in the day, and he's had sponsor meetings all damn week."

Dante was crouched beside his car. He appeared to be studying something on the side, but from this distance and the angle of the vehicle, I couldn't determine exactly what.

He rose and turned to us, fixing those piercing, vicious eyes on me. For a second, I was caught off guard because he filled the room more than I expected him to. Then I gathered my cool and stepped into the garage. I wasn't sure which threw off more masculine energy: the thirteen-million-dollar race car or its driver.

"Hey there." I made sure my voice was as buttery and Southern as could be. "I wanted to get to know you for a spell. It's wonderful to meet a racing legend, Mr. Annunziata, and it's an honor to be on your team."

I extended my hand, knowing it was a bold move. Daddy had always laughed at how his little, confident daughter would totter up to titans of industry and American sports figures as a child and introduce herself, as if she was the most important person in the world. Competing in beauty pageants had taught me to project confidence; getting an engineering degree and being a woman in a man's world had given me inner strength. This ultra-rich, impossibly handsome athlete would not intimidate *me*.

Dante turned, his gaze burning with some imperceptible emotion. His hand claimed mine and I was a little surprised by the strength in his fingers. Although that was silly; he was in top form, all muscle. Why wouldn't he have a solid handshake? I continued to smile as I pumped his hand, but looking at his face made my mouth water, my heart flutter, and my legs shake.

I was uncomfortably aware that our skin was touching. It was as if air movement, sound, even time had stopped in the garage as we looked into each other's eyes.

Come on, Savvy. Really? My own accusatory voice echoed in my head.

This was unnecessary and unprofessional. I hadn't joined the team to gawk at a gorgeous Italian. After swallowing, I reminded myself to inhale. I had to look down at my feet, put my glance out of range of his stupidly beautiful face.

The shrill ring of a cell phone went off. Jack made a sputtering noise. "This is for me, mates—it's the boss. I'll take it outside and leave the two of you to get acquainted."

As Jack loped out of the garage, Dante dropped my hand. My palm felt as though it had been licked by fire. Or kissed by his lips.

"Good to meet you." His accented voice matched his looks: deep and sexy with a heavy dose of self-assured amusement. He cocked an eyebrow.

Truth be told, I had no idea what to say, because my tongue wasn't tied—it was bound and gagged. Mostly because he was so sensual looking but also because of his confidence. And I didn't want to come off as stupid. I always felt that if a person had nothing intelligent to say, they should keep their mouth shut. So that's what I did.

Dante took a few steps toward the hood of the race car, then turned and leaned against the machine. He looked like one of those ads you'd see in a men's magazine.

"I was intrigued when I found out we'd have the first female pit crew member on our team. Jack was telling me all about your prior career, Savannah. I'm going to have to read up on your background, of course, but who wouldn't be intrigued by a beauty queen with an engineering degree?"

He shot me a foxy little smile and my eyes widened. He pronounced my name slowly, every syllable rolling off his tongue. His Italian-tinged English was perfect, yet had enough of an accent to be sexy.

Oh my. He was even more stunning when he wasn't scowling. His hand went to the top of his chest and began fiddling with the zipper of his racing coverall suit as he spoke. He was going to read about *me?* This seemed unusual, if not downright suspicious, and I wondered what he was getting at.

"My pageant career was quite a while ago," I said briskly. "It was pretty standard as those things go. Boring, even."

"A beauty queen," he said, as he lowered the zipper. . . down, farther, over his chest and to his stomach. "Jack told me you were, what? Miss Georgia?"

"Runner-up," I replied, not wanting the memory of my pageant days, and being objectified for my looks, to mar this moment.

"Still, that's quite good. I never thought I'd have a beauty queen as my tire changer. Quite fascinating."

Was he patronizing me? Or flirting? It was hard to tell, and deciphering was even more difficult because he was grinning. How could one man possess so much instant charm? I'd never seen anything like it.

Steady. Breathe. I tried to concentrate on the smell of motor oil and rubber tires.

"There's a first for everything." I tried to regain some composure and not let my eyes drift to where his zipper ended. I decided to study the car's tire instead. The way he considered me, with his mouth turning up at the corners, as if we were sharing a private joke, made my heart flip-flop.

Unfortunately, I lost focus when he shrugged out of the top half of his race suit, revealing a muscular torso clad in a tight-fitting white T-shirt, the kind that wicked perspiration away from skin. The image of his bare chest, slick with sweat, formed in my mind. Eek.

"How did you get into motorsports?" he asked casually, reaching for the bottom of his shirt.

No. Oh no. Please don't let him take off his shirt. As he lifted the hem and pulled upward, I had to remind myself again to think, breathe, and then speak. But of course he was going to take off his shirt. It's what drivers did; I'd seen it a million times during my internships in other circuits. But no other driver had held the appeal of this one.

He paused, revealing a sliver of his bare, ripped stomach. "Sorry, it's too warm in this heat," he murmured. "And I figure, since you're a pit crew member, I need to treat you like one of the guys, no? You don't mind if I get comfortable, do you?"

I shook my head and tried not to stare as he peeled the shirt off. He had perfectly defined shoulder muscles and a *V* starting at his hips and dipping down below his coveralls. He wasn't bodybuilder-muscular but was cut as if carved from Roman marble. Long, sinewy muscles rippled against smooth, olive-hued skin.

"My father," I blurted. Realizing my answer made no sense, I added, "My father owns a parts company in America. Jenkins International. When I was a teenager, after I finished with pageants, I'd go with him to races all over the States. NASCAR, IndyCar, stock car races. I majored in automotive engineering at University of Georgia."

I didn't tell him that I'd wanted to reject everything pageants stood for—the artifice, the superficiality, the focus on perfect femininity. Motorsports made sense. Being a woman didn't. It wasn't that I couldn't act the part of being a girly girl—no, I'd been beautiful onstage, once upon a time. I was simply through with projecting an image of perfection. I wanted people to like me for my brains and personality, not my smile and pale skin and red hair.

Which was why it was so disconcerting, scary even, that Dante was staring at me with big, dark pupils and a seductive expression. Oh sure, men flirted with me often, and sometimes I'd be chummy in return. But I wasn't ever interested in flirtation. Until now.

Which was a pretty big problem, if you asked me.

"You come from impressive credentials." He made wide stretching movements with his arms, crossing one over his torso. The movement sent a little waft of his scent toward me, and even though he'd been sweating in race coveralls, he smelled faintly of lime and spice. And, of course, man.

The man scent was very, very sexy.

"Thanks." I wanted to bury my nose in his chest. "Yes, my family's well known in the American auto industry. My father has a lot of faith in Team Eagle."

He stretched the other arm up and over his head, bending it at the elbow. Transfixed, I watched his muscles ripple. My mind wondered what it would feel like to be lying underneath his chest, to run my hands over it, to arch my own body and feel him against my bare skin. It made me shiver a little, despite the thick Italian heat.

"Your father got you this job, didn't he?" Dante's voice wasn't accusatory, but his words made me bristle.

"He helped, yes. But I have years of internship experience, and excellent recommendations from NASCAR teams in the States."

"I'm sure you do," he muttered.

Without thinking, I toyed with the heavy zipper on my own fire suit and lowered it down. When I realized what a sexually inappropriate message that would send to Dante, I shook my head, as if to clear the tension hanging in the air. The motion caused my long hair to snag in the zipper. Damn. Not only was I awkward, but I was also uncoordinated.

"Crap, my hair's caught." I let out a groan, jerking my head.

"Don't move," Dante ordered, stepping closer, making my heart pound as he trapped me between his body and the car. Could he hear my heart hammering in my chest? Because I could, and it made me sweat more.

He tugged at the hair.

"Do you have scissors? Ow. Ow!"

"No moving," he said, this time in a low tone. As if I *could* move, with him half naked and only inches away. My head bowed slightly and I froze, watching as his hands hovering over my chest, perilously close to my breasts. I could feel my nipples tighten against my shirt under the coveralls.

"These zippers are always a pain."

I held my breath as he used his long fingers to gently tug the strands out of the zipper's teeth while lowering it a fraction. It didn't take much to imagine him stripping all my clothes off, and I exhaled softly. His hips seemed dangerously close to mine too.

Don't think. Don't breathe. Don't speak.

He eased the zipper down slowly, tooth by tantalizing tooth, so as not to snag my hair further.

"You're extremely precise," I whispered.

He lifted an eyebrow. "Of course I am. That's what makes me a champion driver. And a champion unzipper. I'm especially good at the latter."

He was close enough so I could feel his breath on my forehead, and I knew I was flushing pink from embarrassment and excitement. The hard wall of his bare chest was teasingly close, and my fingers itched to reach out and caress everywhere. His muscular forearms. The hollow between his collarbone and his shoulder. His nipples, which were little peaks against the smoothness of his skin.

"There. All better." He arranged my hair behind my shoulders and zipped me up all the way to my neck, as if he wanted me fully covered for my own good. Which was probably for the best. Had he unzipped me even a little more, there's no telling what I would have done.

Embarrassed myself, probably. Gotten fired, even. God, what had come over me? I wasn't normally ruled by my hormones. I wanted to smack my own face.

Raising my head, I stared into the dark, molten pools of his eyes.

"*Tu sei bella,*" he whispered, enunciating each word and sending a wave of desire crashing through my body. I knew those particular Italian words because I'd listened to the unit on flirting in my language app.

You are beautiful.

He slowly tucked an unruly curl behind my ear and everywhere, from my toes to the top of my head, tingled.

"Th-thank you. I guess. But that seems a bit inappropriate for a driver and pit crew member. Unless you say that to all the guys too. Do you?" An awkward laugh exploded from my mouth. If my back weren't wedged between the car and his half-naked body, I would have stepped away. I wondered when he was going to move. Maybe I didn't want him to move.

He didn't budge, just stood there with that sexy half smile and those glittering dark eyes.

So I gawked at his face, rapt, as his eyes roamed mine. What was he doing? *Dear God.* Was he thinking of kissing me? It seemed like we were in the seconds before a kiss.

That's when I heard the noise. It was the unmistakable rapid-fire clicking of a camera shutter, and Dante's head whipped toward the open garage door. Mine did, too, in time to see a photographer with a press pass around his neck lower his telephoto lens and shoot us a wicked grin.

CHAPTER FIVE

SAVANNAH

Back in my hotel room, I showered, replacing the smell of oil and rubber clinging to my hair with my favorite scent: jasmine. Even in shampoo form, it reminded me of sultry Georgia nights at my childhood home in, yes, the historic city of Savannah. My mom loved the city so much that she felt her baby girl should be its namesake.

It wasn't that I was homesick, not at all. I was digging this Italian adventure. Proud of my performance in the pits. Tomorrow we'd fly to France ahead of the start of the season, and I couldn't wait for my first race. Jack had said I might still have to observe for the first several laps, but he'd consider putting me in as a tire changer, depending on how the race unfolded.

In all, a personal victory.

Except for that little episode with Dante earlier. That had been weird. But I was trying to put him and our strange encounter in the garage out of my mind. The less I thought about him, the better.

I climbed out of the shower, wrapped my hair in a towel and my body in a fluffy white robe, and flopped on the bed. It was nine at night in Europe, which meant it was three in the afternoon back home—the perfect time to call Kayla. I used my tablet to make a video call, and she picked up right away.

"Savvy," she cried.

Squealing at seeing my best friend's dazzling smile that popped against the deep terra-cotta color of her skin, I settled in for what I hoped would be a proper catch-up. Kayla and I had met on the pageant circuit as preteens—we were both beautiful tomboys with overzealous moms. Turned out that we enjoyed competition, but not the kind that revolved around beauty. After our pageant days, we'd both ended up at UGA: Kayla for prelaw and me for engineering. Despite our different backgrounds, interests, and careers, we'd remained close and had even shared an apartment our senior year of college.

"Where are you? In Monaco yet?"

"No, still in Italy. In the hotel. We leave tomorrow. See?" I turned the tablet around so she could get a peek at the sleek, modern, gray-and-white decor of my hotel room. "I've been here for three weeks. It's the closest hotel to the test track and headquarters. And you should see the race car. It's downright dreamy. And the test track. And the team headquarters. It's like heaven for gearheads." I let out a pleasurable groan.

"Ohhh, sweet. I can't wait to hear all about it! You called at the perfect time," she said, shifting on her sofa so I could get a peek at her tabby cat. "I'm so sick of studying. Even Muppet is bored with me. I'm bored with me. It's nonstop test prep."

I propped the tablet against a stack of pillows, recalling how she'd been putting in long hours to take the LSAT because she was applying to law schools. "When is the exam again?"

As she talked about her upcoming test, my shoulders relaxed even more than they had in the hot shower. Hearing her familiar voice was soothing, and I leaned back into the plush, tufted headboard.

"That sounds so hard, but I know you're going to do well," I said. "Are you able to go out at all?"

She lifted a perfectly toned shoulder, and I mildly envied her pink tank top. My days of wearing cute stuff were probably over, at least for the next several months. "I did go out to a bar with a few people from school. Oh, and guess who I saw? Your brother. We had drinks together."

The horrified look on my face made her dissolve into giggles. "Kayla. You know all about my brother. Please tell me—"

She interrupted with a wave. "Don't worry. I would never."

I clutched my chest with both hands. My brother, Alex, was one of Atlanta's most eligible bachelors. Women thought him handsome, but I considered him a giant goofball. The thought of him and Kayla hooking up was too weird for words. "Oh thank God. You nearly made my heart stop. I thought I was going to have to fly back and shake some sense into you."

"Yeah, we were at the Kimball Lounge and Alex was in top form, holding court at a big table with a bunch of guys."

I groaned. Alex's friends were mostly cringeworthy former frat boys.

"No, it wasn't all bad. He invited us to have a drink . . ." Her voice trailed off and I noticed that she scratched behind her ear, something she did when she was being coy.

"And? Do I have to fly back to Atlanta to kick *his* butt? Was he gentlemanly?" My hand balled into a fist.

She nodded. "Oh, one hundred percent. He called me his honorary little sister. But he did introduce me to a friend of his. Travis."

"Travis? That doesn't ring a bell. But Alex has a lot of friends. All of whom I'm skeptical of, to be honest." She was bursting to tell me something. "So tell me about—"

"Not much to say. Yet." She broke into a giggle, a little unusual for her. Neither Kayla nor I were gigglers, and neither of us had ever had a serious boyfriend. As far as I knew, she was a virgin, like me.

"He's taking me to that new steak house downtown. Travis seems like a good guy. He's an executive at a company here in town. Beats studying for the tenth night in a row."

Kayla's expression glittered in a way I'd never seen before. I was about to probe when she continued. "Tell me all about Italy! What's it like? Is everyone treating you okay?"

"It's gorgeous here. You should see the sunrise, and sunset. They're stunning. And the food is incredible. We even have pasta catered for lunch, and it's better than the finest restaurants in Atlanta. I've been mostly busy with human resources stuff, but the last couple of days I've been observing in the pits, and today I even changed tires during practice." I didn't even try to hide the excitement in my voice.

"Have you told your mom all this yet?" Kayla knew about the pitched battles between me and Mom in the days before I left.

"No, I'm trying to stay superficial in our conversations. The other day I hung up on her when she started in with the 'I don't know what I've done to deserve a daughter who abandoned me.' Of course, stupid me, I called her the next day, but steered our talk to the weather, her dogs, and Gram's latest shenanigans." My grandmother—Dad's mom—was in her eighties. Like my father, she fully supported my decision to join Team Eagle. "Everyone is lovely here. Seriously. They couldn't be nicer. They're treating me like one of the guys, minus any sexist locker-room banter. Honestly, almost everyone is superprofessional and it's obvious we're here to win. I couldn't be happier . . ."

"But?" Her eyes narrowed. "I noticed you said almost everyone."

I freed my hair from the towel. "There might be a problem with one of the drivers. I'm not sure."

"Aren't there only two drivers on the team?"

"One is fine. He's actually our age, German, a little arrogant but polite. It's the older, superstar driver. Dante. I'm not sure about him."

I launched into everything that had happened today, ending with the camera capturing the moment when Dante tucked a lock of hair behind my ear.

"Savannah, that's weird. He's playing games and I don't like that."

"You think? He seemed pretty pissed that a paparazzo got our photo."

"Look at you, already using the local dialect. Nice roll to that *R*, also."

"That's what he said—*Fucking paparazzo.* He shot the guy a nasty look, shouted something in Italian, and the guy ran off.

Then Dante got real cold and said good-bye in this formal way and basically stalked out of the garage. It was so odd. I don't know what to think. I couldn't find Jack or the team owner afterward, and a couple of the guys basically told me to ignore the whole incident. Apparently other teams hire photographers to spy on competitors' cars here, so it could've been that."

"Sounds like there's a real devious undercurrent there. You need to watch yourself. You don't know who hired that photographer, or why. Maybe they were spying on the car. Or maybe on Dante. Or even you. Savvy, be careful. This is way different than NASCAR, with a lot more international intrigue."

"This isn't *Scandal* or some TV show. It's motorsports. I'm sure it was just that, some guy trying to get intel on Dante's tires or the chassis." I went on for a while about why Team Eagle's chassis were different until Kayla's eyes glazed over.

"Sorry. I get carried away when we're talking mechanics."

"I know. Be careful. And try not to be alone with Dante again. I don't trust him."

"I'm not sure I trust him either," I admitted, feeling a little guilty that I'd omitted telling Kayla about how handsome he was in person. His photos online didn't capture the way he seemed to vibrate with energy. Or maybe that was my own interpretation.

Yeah, that was probably exhaustion and the excitement of being on the team. "Oh, not to change the subject or anything, but have you thought any more about Rio?"

When I'd gotten the job with Team Eagle, Kayla and I had studied the race schedule. Rio was one of the last races of the season and a place she'd always wanted to visit. It was also a circuit where our team had a full week in the city—many were only few-day stops—and I figured I'd be able to hang with her a little, at least.

"Once I take the LSAT, I'm planning on buying a ticket as my reward," she said in a singsong voice, her face lighting up.

For the next half hour, we talked about my first day on the job, her family, and what we'd do in Rio together. Visit the Christ statue, sunbathe on Ipanema Beach, and drink caipirinhas until dawn. When I hung up, my heart was full of friendship and plans, more certain than ever that I'd made the best choice by coming to Italy for this team.

CHAPTER SIX

DANTE

I strode onto the team's private jet at six in the morning, eager to get to Monte Carlo. Aside from being on the track, this was my favorite part of being a racer. Traveling to a new city every week. Always being in motion.

I'd stepped into the aisle and was headed for my preferred spot on any private plane—a plush, swiveling seat on the left side facing forward, with a desk-height table, so I could review endorsements, send emails, and sign sponsorships—when I realized someone was already occupying that very spot.

A gorgeous, redheaded someone.

What was Savannah Jenkins, pit crew member, doing on the team plane normally reserved for drivers? Max was supposed to be here, but I'd gotten an email saying that he'd gone on a sponsor's jet—a fact that left an aftertaste of annoyance.

Savannah raised her head and spotted me.

"Good morning," she said, beaming. Oh, she was probably one of those sunny morning people.

Then, possibly sensing my confusion as I was standing frozen in the aisle, staring from behind my mirrored aviator sunglasses, she stammered, "M-Mr. Bronson asked me to fly with y'all over to France. I think there was room because Max flew with Vodafone."

"Pit crew members usually take the team bus from Italy to Monaco." I didn't bother to hide the annoyance in my voice. I cleared my throat and she blinked several times, her green eyes sending little zings of lust through my body.

"Well, I guess it's only us today. Won't be a long flight, but maybe you can tell me about what it's like to drive the street circuit. I was reading up on your last Monaco race, in fact." She pointed at her phone.

When it was clear that I wasn't sitting, she looked back up and blinked again. "Oh! Am I in your seat?"

"I prefer to sit in the same place every flight. I like to sit facing forward. Don't like to look back."

A flash of annoyance crossed her face, but she must have realized that since she was the most junior member of the team and I was the star driver, she'd have to capitulate. She scrambled to gather her belongings, sliding a purse, a magazine, a phone, and some girly makeup stuff across the table, finally taking the seat opposite me.

"This okay?" she asked. Then she pointed to another seat behind ours, one without a table. "Or do you want me to sit over there? I chose this because I like spreading out."

"It's fine, I guess," I replied in a clipped voice, declining to explain how I had certain superstitions and rituals before a race. Many of them, in fact.

"I was going to ride with the rest of the team on the bus, but Mr. Bronson texted me this morning and told me to show up here instead. He said he wanted to talk to me—to us—together."

This set off alarm bells in my head. Why would Bronson want to fly with us? I was about to ask Savannah but decided to keep my mouth shut. Didn't want her to know I had no clue what was happening either. So instead, I clammed up and watched her put all of the stuff on the table into her enormous gray canvas purse. I kept my sunglasses on, so it wasn't obvious I was checking her out.

She was beautiful. Not in a conventional way, not with all that flaming hair and a smattering of freckles across her nose and cheeks. Savannah was pale, almost ethereal, and had the brightest, most vulnerable-looking green eyes I'd ever seen. Every few seconds, she'd peek at me hesitantly, then a cute smile would spread on her face.

Every time she stared like that, my insides softened. Well, except my dick. That was decidedly un-soft.

Spreading my legs so as to get comfortable, I swiveled in my chair so I could look out the window onto the tarmac. From the way she'd reacted to me in the garage the previous day, I knew it wouldn't take long to get her horizontal, with those legs wrapped around my waist and her tongue in my mouth.

While I wasn't entirely serious about seducing her to get her off the team, the plan certainly had its appeal. I'd practically sensed her body quaking when I touched her hair yesterday. Quite delicious.

I smirked in her direction and she responded with a sweet

smile. Dammit. That innocent look of hers was disarming. No, I wasn't prepared to be charmed by her, or to be so attracted to her.

Didn't anticipate that all I'd want to do was to press my mouth to hers. Run my hands through her hair. And now that she was dressed in something other than fire-retardant coveralls, I wanted to tear off her clothes and explore every inch of her body with my hands. Today she was wearing a simple white Eagle Racing T-shirt over a pair of tight jeans. She also wore black canvas sneakers (Converse), making her look positively endearing.

Her body was perfect, with full breasts, a little waist, and deliciously wide hips. There was nothing better than a woman with curves, and I wondered if her freckles decorated other parts of her skin. I pondered this for a bit, imagining kissing each beauty mark slowly as I made my way down her naked body to the juncture of her thighs.

This flirtation went on for several minutes, until the plane's flight attendant interrupted my fantasy.

"Your Pellegrino, sir," she said, setting the bottle of sparkling water and a glass in front of me.

"Grazie. And my teammate, maybe she would like something?" I gestured to Savannah.

"Oh, thank you," she said. "I'd love a Coke. With ice. Lots of ice."

The attendant walked away, and I smirked. "You're so American."

Savvy tilted her head. "Why do you say that?"

"Only Americans like ice."

"I'm from Georgia, home of Coca-Cola. There's nothing better than an ice-cold Coke. You're missing out, Italian boy."

I scowled. Did she call me "Italian boy"? What was with this informality? I'd have to have a talk with her about this. And yet, visions of ice cubes and what I could do with them and her body danced through my head.

I'd seduced plenty of women over the years, but never had I been so instantly interested—or instantly annoyed—by one. Here I was, about to enter my twelfth season in racing, eager for a seventh championship, and I had to focus. Not fantasize about some redheaded American girl. One who might be the worst possible woman for me of all, given our team circumstances. There was only one option: I needed to sleep with her. Purge her from my system and hopefully get her the hell off the team.

Speaking of the team, what must they think about Savannah? I needed to discreetly ask around, or talk with Jack—who was on the bus. The fact that she was on a private jet with me probably rankled more than a few of the guys.

The flight attendant returned with the Coke and she sipped it daintily, keeping her eyes on her phone. Probably trying to play it cool. We sat in comfortable silence, me looking from her to the window, and back to her again, and her glancing at me, then back at her phone.

Looking again in Savannah's direction, I saw her tap and swipe on her phone. For a second, her eyes widened, then she blinked at me. This time, there was no sweet smile. She swallowed and looked back at her phone. God, how I wanted to kiss her.

I'd almost come close yesterday in the garage, when I helped her with the zipper. Maybe it was a good thing the photographer had interrupted us, although that had pissed me off. Damn spies. Savannah's cheeks were tinged with a deep pink flush, which was impossibly sexy. She'd surely look like that after a wild romp.

Maybe in Monte Carlo, after the race, I'd see if she wanted to have dinner with me. Pre-race was out of the question, because I didn't drink or have sex in the days prior to competition.

Post-race, however, was fair game. I enjoyed a few simple formalities and flirtations before bedding a woman. I might be a womanizer, but I wasn't a brute.

I imagined us talking and drinking wine on the hotel terrace, with its sweeping views of Monaco's harbor. Wait. What was I thinking? She was a pit crew member. My pit crew member. I couldn't be seen in public with her.

No, I wanted her in my bed. For a couple of nights, max. There could be no formalities with this one. Only raw, hot sex as a reward for winning the first race of the season. I again smiled at her and she returned a wan, tight-lipped expression in return.

"Where is Bronson, anyway?" I asked.

She stammered, and when she finally spoke, her voice didn't have any of the earlier sassy confidence. "I saw him earlier. He's in a conference room at the back of the plane with Tanya and a few assistants."

She pointed to the rear of the jet, which was concealed by a sliding partition.

My phone buzzed in my pocket but I ignored it, preferring the dirty movies racing through my mind, all starring the lovely girl across from me. The flight attendant came by and instructed us to buckle our seat belts and turn off our phones. The jet sped down the runway, and I watched Savannah look out the window. She crossed her arms over her chest and took a deep breath.

For some reason, she seemed nervous and wasn't returning my flirtation. She also hadn't touched her Coke. Surely she wasn't afraid of flying?

Once we'd cleared ten thousand feet, I heard the partition in the back slide open.

"Good morning, kids," boomed a rich Texas accent.

It was Bronson. He dropped his sturdy self on the leather sofa across from us. Savannah and I both swiveled our seats to face him.

"How are you both doing this fine Wednesday?" he asked.

"Stupendous," I said.

"Fine, sir," she piped up. Why did she sound so shaken?

"That's real good, you two. It's a great morning and I can't wait for the race. Savannah, thanks for flying with us instead of going to Monaco with the rest of the team. I'm sure you both know why I asked you here," Bronson said.

"Actually, I don't." I looked to Savannah and saw her worrying her bottom lip between her teeth. "What's going on?"

"You didn't see the photo?" Bronson asked. "I texted it to you. I can tell Savannah's seen it, from that shocked look on her face."

"What photo?"

She slid her phone across the table to me.

There, in full color, was a picture of me gently tucking Savannah's hair behind her ear. I was shirtless and we were standing closer than any driver and pit crew member have ever stood in the history of motorsports. It looked like a still from a movie. An X-rated one.

I swore out loud, then switched to a string of Italian profanities. "Where was this published?"

Bronson rattled off a list of websites and newspapers. He ran a hand through his thick ash brown hair. "More like, where *wasn't* it published?"

CHAPTER SEVEN

SAVANNAH

I couldn't form words, much less sentences, and knew a scarlet flush of humiliation had crept onto my cheeks. Blushing was the downside to being a redhead. I sat frozen, my mouth agape. Oh, this was bad. A disaster. Surely I'd be fired.

Bronson slipped on a pair of reading glasses and read aloud as he tapped his phone. "Here are some of the headlines: 'Fiery Redhead Snags Racing Star's Heart,' 'Beauty Queen Turned Pit Crew Girl Turns Driver into Shirtless Boy Toy,' 'Jenkins Auto Heiress Puts the *Racy* in Racing.'"

Oh God. It was worse than I thought. I groaned and shut my eyes as nausea bubbled in my stomach. I'd been employed less than a month and I'd already screwed up. I'd brought shame to the team and humiliated myself because of a man.

How had I let this happen? Since leaving pageantry, I'd tried so hard not to rely on my looks or my femininity to get ahead. And I'd been successful at that, working hard to prove I was competent. Now I'd screwed that up big-time, shattering my carefully crafted, no-nonsense image.

From what I'd seen on my phone, all the papers had that same photo of Dante looking at me as if he wanted to consume me. By the hungry look on my own face, it seemed as though I was seconds away from ripping my coveralls off. Seemed? No, that was exactly what had been in my mind the moment the photo was snapped.

Classy. Real classy. More like epic in its awfulness. I'd call a taxi the minute we landed and make my way to the nearest airport so I could fly back to America.

I opened my eyes. There was no explaining this away. My attraction to Dante was evident, and there was only one possible option at this point. I needed to own up to my horrible mistake, pack my bags discreetly, and leave the team once we landed in France.

God, my parents would be so ashamed. Mom would somehow turn this into an *I-told-you-so* moment. Or worse. It would be evidence that I wasn't ready for a career in this world.

Maybe she'd been right after all. Still, I had to do the honorable thing.

Tears threatened to fall, but I wasn't going to let my emotions get the better of me. "Sir, I apologize. This is wholly inappropriate. Shameful, even. I'd like to offer my resignation from the team. It's the right thing to do."

Bronson took off his reading glasses and looked at me with a stern expression. Then he beamed. "That won't be necessary, Savannah. In fact, your leaving the team is the last thing I want."

"Excuse me?" Dante asked. "I feel like Savannah's doing the right thing by offering to resign. I don't know how we can work together. I think accepting her resignation is the proper thing to do."

"What?" My voice was louder than I'd anticipated. "You're throwing *me* under the bus when it was you who acted all seductive in the first place?"

Dante did a *what-can-you-do?* shrug. "It was a little uncomfortable, to be honest. As if she was coming on to me. She asked me to help with her hair—" "

After you stripped down to practically nude and played with *my* hair," I interrupted. "Also, back up. Are you accusing me of sexual harassment?"

He snorted, which made him look like a sleek thoroughbred. "Sexual harassment, well, those are your words, not mine. But that's a pretty apt description, I'd say. It was hot and I took my shirt off. You obviously couldn't control yourself around me."

"What? You nearly kissed me! You fondled my hair."

He pressed a hand to his chest. "Me? Kiss a pit crew member? Fondle? Never! You're an insubordinate little thing, you know that?"

At that moment, the flight attendant emerged from behind a curtain at the front of the plane. Her presence startled me, and I looked at her, then at Bronson, alarmed. He waved her away and I turned back to Dante.

"So much for working together as a team," I spat back. Unreal. I folded my arms tightly across my chest. He smirked. Probably thought he looked sexy, and he did. Which annoyed me even more. "Like I'd want to seduce my driver."

"Kids," Bronson said, chuckling. "Stop. I don't care if you two went at it like bunnies on the hood of the race car. But since this photo is in the press, it gave me an idea. An opportunity. A strategy of sorts. To make this work, I'll need something from you both."

Dante and I stopped glaring at each other to gape at Bronson, who leaned forward.

"Let me explain. We're having a real bear of a time getting out from under this technical theft scandal. The press is all over the team because of it."

Dante flopped back in his seat with a long groan.

"What scandal? What are you talking about?" I unbuckled my seat belt. "Is this about Max and the technical info? I read something about that the other day in *Autosport* magazine."

"Max, that little shit," Dante grumbled, shaking his head.

His reaction surprised me, because from everything I'd read, the two drivers got along famously.

"That's correct. Basically, we need to divert media attention away from Max and this team," Bronson explained. "I don't want this chassis crap to appear in the press over and over. It's ludicrous to think we're using insider information. I don't want team morale to suffer, and I don't want the sport's regulating board to launch an investigation. Not during this first race week in Monte Carlo, and not at all."

Dante raised his eyebrows. "What does this have to do with Savannah and me?" he asked in an icy voice. The way he said my name was as if he'd suddenly discovered poop on his shoe.

"Here's my plan, and I think it's a brilliant one. You and

Savannah will pretend you're in a relationship. It'll create a media frenzy. Imagine," he said, sweeping his hand in the air as if scanning a theater marquee. "'Racing Star Falls in Love with Pit Crew Girl.' The PR will be incredible."

My jaw dropped. What? *Pit crew girl?*

"Oh, come on!" Dante roared and waved his hands in the air in a wild gesture. "That's ridiculous. Like I'd ever date *her.*"

"You should be so lucky," I shot back. "Jerk."

"Like I'd ever want the likes of you." He uttered the words as if the concept of dating me was the most absurd thing he'd ever heard.

"Arrogant clown." Turning to Bronson, I demanded, "Is this a joke?"

"Nope." Bronson shook his head. "I've talked it over with our publicist, Tanya. We can probably keep the reporters occupied with this fake story for a while. Maybe for the entire season, if need be."

"The entire season?" Dante asked. "That's several months."

Bronson shrugged. "Admittedly, it might cramp your style with other women. I'm sure you'll manage, though. So be discreet."

He expected Dante to sleep with other women and pretend to be my boyfriend?

"What about all those things you said the other day—how proud you were of hiring the first woman pit crew member in Formula World? How can you believe that when all you want is for me to be arm candy to this dude?" I waved my hand in Dante's direction.

"This *dude* is the top driver in the world," Dante retorted.

"Whatever."

"This is women's empowerment, Savannah," Bronson said.

"What?" I shook my head.

Bronson's eyes were so glittery that I almost thought he believed his own crap. When I didn't immediately agree, he continued. "You can work in the pits and have a relationship with the star driver. Isn't that every girl's dream? A career and a rich man?"

I made a half-gagging, half-snorting sound. "No, not even a little."

To his credit, Dante made similar noises, probably because Bronson's words were so absurd. Or the thought of pretending to be with me was that awful.

Holy crap. The seriousness of the situation dawned on me. Not only was this lunatic of a team owner trying to entice me into a charade of a relationship under the guise of feminism, but also Dante clearly hated me and loathed my mere presence.

"How do you know I won't go to the reporters and tell them about this little plan?" I challenged, figuring at this point, I had nothing to lose by showing my scrappy side. "That would be even worse for the team than any espionage allegation."

Bronson smirked. "Read your employment contract. Nondisclosure clause. You can't talk about anything to anyone outside the team. Can't even talk to your family about what goes on. I'll sue you and your rich father for everything you have if you do."

There was no way I could get my father involved in this. Not only would he be terribly disappointed in me, but it would also be a scandal for *his* company. I thought of Mom and my CEO brother, who were both so image-conscious. "And if we refuse?"

Bronson lifted his shoulders again and smiled cynically. "I can get another tire changer. And another driver."

My eyes went to Dante, and I watched his mouth drop open.

His hands, which rested on the seat next to his muscular thighs, balled into fists.

"I'll let you two talk it over in private, but I trust you'll come to the right decision. I'm headed back into the conference area to do some work with my assistants, but you two get comfy." Bronson stood, then paused, his head ping-ponging between me and Dante. "You actually make a gorgeous couple."

He strode out of the cabin, giving us a little wave before he opened the small door to the back of the plane and disappeared. I snorted.

"That asshole," Dante hissed.

"At least we agree on one thing." I sank back into the plush leather seat and stared out the window. What had I gotten myself into with this team? I wanted to weep in frustration, but I wouldn't. I didn't cry in public, ever. Or in private, really. And especially not in front of Dante, that *loser*. Yes, I was calling the world champion a *loser* in my mind. I might tell him to his face, too, in about five seconds. No way could I go along with this. I sighed audibly, but the noise sounded more like it came from a strangled ferret.

Eagle had been my "in," my ticket to a career in world motorsports. And my father was sponsoring the team. I'd have to call him and Mom to explain the photo. As my mind spun, I rested my forehead against the cool oval window of the plane.

If I did say yes to this stupid plan, I might be able to leverage the situation. Maybe I could turn this into an opportunity to learn more about the sport, then jump to another, more scrupulous team next season. Pretending to be Dante's love interest would be a matter of a few public appearances, nothing more.

Right?

And after all, I was a good actress. I'd pretended I was happy during years of beauty pageants, when I was anything but. That couldn't be any more difficult than acting the part of a sports star's girlfriend.

Life is about putting on a happy face and acting the part, my mother always said.

I hated when my mother was right. And it dawned on me: *there* was the advantage to this fake relationship. By pretending to be Dante's girlfriend for a season, my mother might stop hounding me about returning to Atlanta. She'd likely be thrilled.

Then my fake relationship with Dante would eventually end, and Mom would leave me alone to grieve the breakup, buying me even more time. She'd micromanaged my life all through my pageant career, and my quitting had left years of hurt feelings in its wake. She'd talked me into staying in Georgia for college. I suspected she'd wanted me to do what she couldn't—have a fabulous, glamorous career in Atlanta. She'd married young, too young, and I often felt she'd regretted it. Instead of admitting that sad fact, though, she'd clung tighter to me, all while trying to knock me down.

Her parting words to me—*you'll never succeed in a man's world*—had become my inspiration. I had to prove her wrong by any means possible.

Success was the best revenge.

I lifted my warm forehead from the window. Dante was across the table and had swiveled his body in my direction. His eyes were filled with a disquieting fierceness. This would be so much easier if he wasn't incredibly handsome.

"We're going to do it," he said in a steely tone.

In that instant, because of his insistence, I changed my mind.

What had I been thinking? If I went through with this stupid proposal, I'd be the laughingstock of the team. Of all of motorsports. No damned way. I wanted respect, not a reputation for sleeping my way to the top. It was already bad enough that I was Dale Jenkins's daughter.

I wouldn't get respect for hitching my wagon to this arrogant man.

"No. We're not. It's nuts. I'm going to refuse and we'll see what happens. I'm going to call his bluff."

His nostrils flared. It would have made me giggle if the situation wasn't so serious.

"Look, Savannah," he said, his smooth voice taking on a distinct edge. "I'm not one to, how do you say in your language, sugar things."

He paused and I frowned, not immediately understanding his phrasing. "Sugarcoat," I finally said.

"Yes. That. I am not happy you are part of this team. But we're going to have to work together on this. It's my career on the line here."

I pressed both hands to my chest, as if he had tried to mortally wound me. "Really? Why are you unhappy? What have I done to you?"

Once again, the gray curtain at the front of the plane whisked open and the flight attendant came charging over.

"Signore? Another Pellegrino?" she asked. "And signora, a Coke for you?"

He shook his head and smiled. I held up my hand, wondering if she'd overheard everything and if she'd sell our info to the tabloids. No one could be trusted.

"Thanks a bunch, but not now," I replied.

She retreated, and Dante and I exhaled in tandem.

He shoved his hair back from his forehead, a fascinating motion because the planes of his masculine hand looked so stark against the thick, black strands. "It's not what you have done to me. It's what you could potentially do to me, and to you, and to the team. But that's no matter now. We're being forced together."

With wide eyes, I spoke in a fake, honeyed cadence reserved for debutante balls and sorority soirees. "Such anger. Goodness. You must have been really damaged by a woman to have these strong feelings. I'm so sorry. Maybe you should explore your feelings a bit with a professional. It's not healthy to hold negativity inside."

"I can honestly say no woman has *ever* damaged me."

I took a long, fortifying inhale. I was used to inappropriate sexual banter because I'd majored in engineering and had been around guys for years. I could easily give as much as I could take. Yes, I had privilege because of my family's wealth. But I tried to work hard to prove myself.

Open hostility or the questioning of my abilities because of my gender, well, that was foreign territory. Dante was not only rude but also insufferable.

"Maybe you need to explain—or *mansplain* to me. After all, I only have an engineering degree. Please. Clue me in. What harm am I causing? At this point, I don't want to be here. You're the last man I want to be around. But I'm offended you think I'm bad for the team. And in case you didn't realize, it's also my career on the line too."

His dark brows drew together into a savage scowl. I'd never seen a man look so sexy while scowling, and the thought made the corners of my lips lift.

"What? You think this is funny?" he hissed, his eyes growing darker. "This is my championship you're playing with. My life. It's in your tiny, girly hands every time you change my tire. Don't forget that, Savvy. This isn't a glorified internship for me, as it is for you, a rich daddy's girl from America."

He said my name with such animosity that I reared back. Dante's jaw was set in a rigid clench and he straightened his shoulders. How could I think a caveman like this was sexy? I needed to unpack my feelings about this later, but for now, I was ready for combat.

"I don't think you're in the best position to evaluate my employment and motorsports connections, Mr. Annunziata. If I recall, you started with nothing, as the underdog. I'm also the underdog, as a woman. I'd hoped you'd have a little more sympathy for my situation and would want to help me succeed. You're not the only one with something to prove here, my dude."

I licked my lips and noticed his eyes flicker for an instant toward my mouth. Instead of staring at his handsome face, I focused on the view outside the window. We were plowing through thick, fluffy white clouds.

"I'm going to ignore your insubordination to your driver because of the circumstances. We're going to have to work together and go along with Bronson's stupid idea. But here's how I feel. Women don't have any place on a team unless they're in a revealing outfit and holding an umbrella over my head while I do interviews."

As I laughed, I studied his smooth olive skin, his arrestingly graceful yet powerful neck, and his earlobe. It looked so soft and downy that I desired to take it in between my lips and tug. I hated myself for thinking about that right now.

Where had that thought come from?

"Bless your heart," I said in a soft voice, playing up my Southern accent.

Dante's eyes narrowed. "Are you mocking me?"

"Perhaps, Mr. Annunziata."

Surely an Italian wouldn't know Southerners used the phrase as a caustic comeback, a polite way of saying, *You're an idiot.*

I rose from my chair to saunter up and down the minuscule aisle. Might as well make him sweat a little as I made up my mind. *Ass clown.* "

You don't need to call me that," he grumbled. "Dante is acceptable. Mr. Annunziata makes me sound old."

I sank onto the long sofa flanking one wall of the plane. Unbuckling his seat belt, Dante stood and crossed the aisle to sit next to me. He was close, too close, and I could smell his lime-spice cologne.

"Please?" His tone was different now. Soft and silky. He grabbed my wrist. "Look. I might not want you on my crew, but I acknowledge that I need you now. For my survival. For the championship. Don't you want to be part of a winning team?"

I swallowed, ignoring how his words—*I need you*—made my heart crash against my ribs. And unknowingly, he'd tapped into the one thing I loved: competition. If I had a chance to win, anywhere, I'd do everything I could to make it happen. Video games with my brother, soccer in elementary school, pageants. I loved to win.

Faking a relationship with the world's richest athlete might be going a little too far.

"Of course I want to win. That's why I'm here, doofus. But I sense that Bronson is manipulating us, and I hate feeling that way."

"Did you just call me a doofus?" A look of pure confusion crossed his gorgeous face.

"Yes."

"I'll ignore that too. Why do you want to win? Why's it so important?"

"I want to prove to the world that a woman can do this job. That's what I mean—it's my career too. But why should I go along with this? It's humiliating. Aren't you shocked by Bronson's proposal? Don't you think it's slippery and scheming?"

"Perhaps. But I'm not shocked at all."

A part of me wanted to wrench my wrist out of his grip, but he worked his hand into mine, intertwining our fingers. Desire whispered through me. I'd never felt such an intense touch from a man. He squeezed gently and I swore my blood heated up as it coursed through my body.

"You're getting a little cozy with my hand there, buddy."

He squeezed my fingers and his voice took on a conspiratorial, chummy tone. "Shush. We're getting to know each other. Anyway, listen. Teams lie to the press all the time. There's all sorts of tricks and half truths flying around." Dante went on to mention the name of a famous retired driver, adding that he was gay.

"I thought he was engaged to that Hollywood starlet, the one in the action movies."

Dante shook his head and squeezed my hand again. "Nope. A total publicity stunt. I felt terrible for him, that he thought he had to do that."

Wow. Apparently there was a lot I didn't know about the inner workings of the sport, and how it was packaged to the world. I stared into Dante's deep, dark eyes and was shocked to see he wore a serious, pleading look.

"Why is this so important to *you*?" I asked. "If you walk away today, you're still a six-time world champion."

"This is my last year in racing. This is my final chance for another championship. A world record. After this, well, I'm not entirely sure what I'm going to do with my life. Maybe I'll have to grow up."

"Heaven forbid," I shot back.

I tried to ignore the warmth of his body. He was wearing shorts and his muscular thigh pressed against my jean-clad leg. I looked down at our tangled hands and a rush of sheer need went through me. I imagined how our naked bodies would look when pressed together. The fantasy made me unsteady and I focused on my sneakers for a second.

"Okay, look, I get it," Dante said. "You want to show the world that women are equal. And I'll admit, it's a worthy goal of yours, wanting to be the first woman in the pits. Even though I don't personally approve. So let's do it. Let's prove this together and win. I'll help you. I swear to God, I'll help you become the best tire changer in the sport."

I raised my head. "You'd do that for me?"

"If you promise to help me win. And pretending to be my girl-friend, taking the heat off Max and his stupid scandal, might be the best way you can do that."

"Why should I help *you*, though? Especially when you don't even want me on the team?"

"I'm going to have to put my biases about you and about girls in motorsports aside. I recognize my shortcomings, and I will keep my word about boosting your career. Look, I have the chance to be among the greats. This is my last opportunity. Do you know how much it means to me? I once made a promise to someone important to me that I'd try to reach this milestone. I'm so close, Savannah. I'm willing to put everything aside and practically sell my soul to the devil for a seventh championship."

This was all about him. Selfish jerk. Still, the way he said my name made me melt. And I understood a competitive spirit. My brows knit together and a pang of jealousy went through me at the thought that someone was so important to him that he would pretend to be in a relationship with a total stranger to fulfill his promise to them.

"Who? Who did you make the promise to?"

"My sister. Right before she died." He shook his head vigorously, knowing what I was going to ask even before I did. "I don't want to get into it right now."

Now it was my turn to squeeze his hand. This entire plan was insane, but his expression of fierce determination told me that perhaps I would get something out of it as well. Setting aside my anger over Bronson's blackmail might be for the best. "Okay. We both have the same goal: to win. I'll help you if you return the favor for me. Let's do it, let's be a team. Let's pretend we're together."

The corners of his mouth turned up.

"Thank you." He paused and stroked the back of my hand with his thumb. "You know, this actually could be fun on many levels. I'll be able to teach you so much, Savannah."

My pulse kicked and surged. Could he detect how fast my heart was beating simply by touching me? His hand let go of mine and went to my hair. Taking a strand, he wound a curl slowly around his finger—which was exactly what he was doing to my insides: making them coil. The only thing I could do was bite my lip because I was frozen in place, unsure about what would happen next.

As much as I despised him, I also wondered what it would be like to press my lips to his.

"Maybe a hug, or a kiss, to seal the deal?" Dante asked in a low, velvety voice.

Whoa. The exact thing I wanted was obviously the wrong thing to do. Especially on the team's plane. Kissing this arrogant jackass, who obviously hated me and merely wanted to use me? No way. Even though his lips looked so soft and kissable. No damned way.

"Disgusting. Don't even think about it. Get that right out of your head, that we're going to fool around because we're pretending to be involved. This isn't a friends-with-benefits situation because we are not friends." I wriggled away from him and launched off the sofa, wanting to keep my distance. "Go tell Bronson I'm on board. Do it quickly, before I change my mind."

His laughter rang in my ears as he rose and walked to the back of the plane, opening the door to the room where Bronson had slithered.

Plucking a magazine out of my bag to distract myself, I realized with dismay that I'd neglected to worry about something else when considering the bizarre proposition: I'd covered the bases by thinking of my career, my reputation in the motorsports world, and my mother . . .

Now I had to go along with this whole ridiculous deal, if only to spite Mom. An added bonus, I suppose, was the fact that I'd annoy and grate on Dante for several months.

But how could I—someone with almost no experience with men—be in such close proximity to Dante and not succumb to his charm?

CHAPTER EIGHT

SAVANNAH

The next three days were a whirlwind. We set up at the track on day one, essentially building a garage from scratch. The following day was devoted to practice, when Dante and Max tested the cars on the track. Unlike most of the Formula World races, Monaco's was a street circuit, with drivers racing through the historic, beautiful neighborhoods at 180 miles per hour. Although that seemed incredibly fast, it wasn't the fastest track in the sport, because the twists, turns, and famous Monaco tunnel meant drivers had to approach the race with finesse, not speed.

It was the first race of the season, and most experts agreed that it was the most challenging. There was little room for error because there were few places where the drivers could run off the track and quickly get back to the asphalt.

If you crashed, you crashed, and you were out. A win here was not a typical victory; it often gave the drivers a psychological edge for the rest of the season.

For the pit crew, it was one of the easier races because it was a one-stop race—meaning that the drivers only roared into the pits for a single tire change.

Jack had emphasized that I'd mostly be observing while in Monaco. I wasn't sure if that plan had shifted, given the situation with Dante, but I didn't want to push. More than anything, I wanted to fade into the background and blend in with the racks of tires. Every time someone looked at me for more than a second, I worried they were thinking about me and Dante.

Fortunately, no one on the team brought up the photos, although I did see a few knowing smirks and eyebrow waggles on the guys' faces as we set up. Each time that happened, my cheeks grew hot and I turned away in humiliation. In the garage, Giorgio sidled up and asked me about the private jet.

"Was it swanky? Did you get champagne on takeoff?" he probed.

"No, I had Coke with a lot of ice. Usually I get, like, two cubes here in Europe, but the flight attendant was more generous."

He grimaced. What was it about Italians and ice? Jeez. I hoped that would end the conversation, since the last thing I wanted was my colleagues accusing me of getting special treatment because I was (allegedly) sleeping with the star driver.

But when I walked into the garage on practice day and over-heard two other tire changers murmuring my name—then clamming up when they spotted me—I realized that it was too late. People were talking. So I held my head high and focused on the task at hand, which was taking inventory of all the tools in the garage. Not exactly the high-octane assignment I craved, but it allowed me to keep busy.

At least until Tanya pulled me aside into a small, makeshift conference room in the team garage about an hour before Dante and Max were to begin their practice sessions.

"Okay, so we've come up with a strategy," she said, tucking her straight, dirty-blond hair behind one ear.

"For what, exactly?" I didn't like the sound of this.

"For you and Dante, of course." She tapped on a tablet and it flickered to life. "We're not making any statements about your relationship until after the race. You've already signed the non-disclosure about talking with the media unless it's authorized by us, so don't respond to any reporters. Have you had any calls, texts, or visits to your hotel room?"

"I did notice a random guy at the hotel last night near the elevator on my floor. He seemed to be hanging around for no reason. I took my mace out of my purse as I walked to my door. When I got inside, I collapsed with exhaustion and didn't hear anything else."

In fact, I'd missed a call from my parents. They'd somehow rung at one in the morning, probably forgetting about the time change. I made a mental note to call them later.

She shot me a tight smile. "You'll get used to the rhythm of race week. But yeah, setup day is always exhausting. And so is practice, since everyone's feeling out the track. Oh, and that guy outside your room might have been a pap."

"Pap?"

"Paparazzi."

"Of course."

"Ignore them. The hotel's supposed to provide security but the paps are clever and persistent. They're going to want another salacious photo of you and Dante. But," she swiped on her tablet, "we're not scheduled to give them that until Montreal."

"What?" I straightened my spine. "Scheduled? How salacious?"

"You're to visit a nightclub together after the Montreal race, and that's when we will tip off one of the tabloids," she said coolly. When she saw me gape at her, she giggled a little.

"I don't find this funny," I said in a dour tone.

"You'll come to think of it as a game. Anyway, here in Monaco, we're going to play it pretty straight. We've got one interview scheduled with the two of you, and there's a post-race party. Even that's up in the air because if Dante loses, he won't want to go. When he loses, he likes to stay inside the hotel."

I scrunched up my face.

"If he wins, we'll have to attend a party together?"

"Not exactly. You'll be spotted talking together. Think of this as a striptease for the media. We don't want to give them everything right away."

"I don't want to give them anything at all," I muttered. "Isn't this disingenuous?"

"You'll come to realize this is a fun diversion from all the high-stakes competition." She laughed. "Trust me, I've been around Formula World for ten years, and this is my third team. You're in a great position. By the end of this season, you're going to be the most famous tire changer in the sport and a hot commodity. Think of it that way."

"I suppose."

"Keep doing what you're doing. Work hard, put your head

down, don't talk about Dante to anyone. Tonight there are some scheduled parties, and Dante will attend alone."

"I don't know who will be happier about that. Me or him."

She flashed me a warning stare. "Go back to the hotel when you're finished here, order room service, and catch up on your sleep. I know it sucks, since we're here in Monaco and you probably want to explore. Keeping you out of the spotlight is essential right now, to preserve the mystery of what's really happening between you two. So don't worry about a thing. We'll take care of the details."

That was what worried me. How much would Tanya and Bronson take care of, and how could it end well for me? They seemed exceedingly shrewd. Questions swirled in my mind as I observed Max's and Dante's practice sessions.

Both men drove flawlessly, and when Dante returned, I was thankful that he ignored me when he walked into the garage. I guessed that Tanya had gotten to him too.

For the rest of the day and the one after that, I did whatever Jack and the other team leaders asked. I arranged wrenches, helped with inventory, sat in on strategy sessions. I took notes as Jack discussed suspension settings, picked tires, and decided on optimal fueling levels. Each decision could mean winning or losing, and in the most dramatic terms, life or death for the driver.

During qualifying, the drivers had more flawless laps around the track. Dante was the more confident driver, I noted while watching his laps on the monitors at the team control center. His experience with handling the car—and his knowledge of the Monaco street circuit—was evident.

Max, however, was a risk taker. He took too many chances when hugging curves, and I saw Jack's body tense as he watched Max drive.

"Come on, mate," Jack whispered at the monitor. He pointed and leaned toward me. "See how sharp he's taking that turn? The newer drivers like Max get too close to the barriers."

"Whereas older drivers like Dante know how to drive without getting close. They have more finesse," I replied. "Dante knows when to let off the brake."

"Exactly. He knows he can ultimately be faster if he slows in certain spots and doesn't lose control."

Exchanges like that kept me going. It was why I was truly here, to learn the nuances of the sport.

By the end of qualifying, we found out the good news: Dante had been fastest, so he was in the pole position for the race. Max came in third. The team was ecstatic, and the mechanics clamored to hug the two men. I hung back, watching Dante. His expression was one of pure happiness, and his eyes met mine.

I gave a little wave, probably looking stupid. "Great job out there, dude," I called out.

"Er, thank you, Savannah," he said in a stilted voice. His wave was almost sheepish. He didn't make a move to come hug me, and I wasn't going to fling myself at him, so I turned and pretended to inspect a rack of tires.

That's when I realized: this situation might be as awkward for him as it was for me.

◊

Later that night, after a delicious room service dinner of linguini with clams and a decadent flourless chocolate cake, I sat on my balcony and watched the pink-orange hue of the sunset over the stunning Monaco harbor. The city was abuzz with yacht parties, hotel soirees, busy nightclubs, and packed bars, with people from around the globe here to watch the race and rub elbows with the rich and famous. Money and privilege practically laced the very air I breathed. It was a little heady even for me, someone who had grown up in a fairly wealthy family.

But if I wanted luxury, I'd have come as a tourist, or stayed home. Even though I was bone tired, I felt like I'd learned a lot today, and a feeling of satisfaction had replaced most of the shame I'd had about the Dante situation.

If the rest of the season was like this, with only allusions and rumors, things would be peachy. The press could speculate all they wanted, and I'd be able to work and spend time alone in my off-hours.

As much as I would have loved to see the city, I was content. Growing up as the youngest in a family of extreme extroverts made me—an introvert—cherish any time alone to recharge. This was perfect for now, and I felt the tension of the day seep out of my body.

My phone buzzed. *MOM*, the display read. Moaning aloud, I steeled myself and answered.

"Hey," I said in a fake, singsong voice. God only knew what she was going to say. She might talk about her latest shopping trip or say something snarky about my life choices.

"Savannah Marie Jenkins, what is going on with you?" my mother screeched in her most dramatic Southern accent. It was two in the afternoon back home, which meant Mom would've just returned from lunch at the Wright Square Café, where she'd have had her usual chicken salad and sweet tea. The memory of that meal made my stomach rumble.

"Nothing. Nothing's going on with me. I'm kinda tired."

"Couldn't you have called to tell me your news?"

Oh boy. This was going to be a doozy of a call.

"What news? I'm sitting on my balcony, looking at the gorgeous sunset over Monaco. Want me to send you a photo? It's incredible."

"I do not want a photo. I've been to Monaco and I know what it looks like. Your father and I went there on our honeymoon. Are you alone? Or is that man with you? One of the ladies from the country club forwarded me an article from a London tabloid, and I was shocked. You were canoodling with an Italian man. It was almost obscene. I didn't raise you to be a tramp, young lady."

Oh great, now I was a tramp.

"Canoodling?" I ground out. "Definitely not."

"The two of you looked like you knew each other in the Biblical sense." I groaned. "Mom—"

"Couldn't you have told me what was going on? I had to hear about it from Phyllis Peden and a newspaper that you're dating that foreign driver."

I let out a strangled wail. Probably I should've guessed the news would reach the United States, but I'd secretly hoped it was confined to the European press. "Does Daddy know?"

"Of course he knows. It's all we've been talking about. We tried to call you last night. But I guess you were busy at one in the morning." Her tone was pointed, and I knew what she was getting at. "Savannah Marie, nothing good happens with a man at one in the morning."

"I wouldn't know because I was asleep. It was a long day yesterday. The team set up the garage. I crashed early. *Alone*. In my own bed."

There was silence on the other end.

"Mom? You there?"

"I'm disappointed that you didn't tell us first. I don't like the sound of this, you being a new team member and all. I told you this wouldn't be easy for you. I don't think you understand the implications. Dating the driver will make everything more complex."

No kidding. "Mom, there's nothing to tell."

"The world's press is saying that you're dating the driver, so I know there's a lot to tell. I saw the photo. He is quite handsome, I have to admit. Does he speak English? When can we meet him?"

"Of course he speaks English." I snorted. "I don't know when you'll meet him. Maybe never. No, definitely never. Please don't believe what's in the papers."

"That was quite quick, how you two met and, ah, connected. I've never known you to be so smitten with a man. Remember when I thought you were a lesbian?"

I lowered the phone and counted to ten in an effort to gain composure. When it felt safe, I raised the cell to my ear. "Do you believe everything you read? Dante and I are friends. We aren't a thing. Listen, I can't get into it now and I don't want to talk about it. Is Daddy there?"

"No, he's out with your brother at a charity golf tournament."

At least I didn't have to explain this to Dad. Not yet, anyway. Eventually I'd have to say something.

I rubbed my temple, wanting to extricate myself from this conversation. I couldn't tell her that my relationship with Dante was a sham. Or could I? Would that break the nondisclosure agreement? Mom would likely blab to her friends, so I decided to keep quiet.

"Okay. I'll call you both tomorrow after the race. I've got to go."

"Why? Are you going out with him tonight? From what I've read there are a lot of parties in Monaco on race weekend. You're not going to tell me any more about Dario?"

"Dante. His name is Dante."

"What a handsome name. I'm going to do a little internet research on him tonight. I wonder if he'd enjoy visiting our vacation home on Tybee Island for our family reunion in July."

"He doesn't want to visit, Mom," I warned. "He's not invited."

"Oh, of course, in July you'll probably both be at a race halfway across the world. But if not, please let him know he's welcome. Or we could do it in the off season. I'll pull out all the stops, and we'll have a good old-fashioned seafood boil party. Maybe rent a tent. Oh, and invite the society columnist from *Southern Living* magazine."

"Mom." My voice was sharper. "He's not coming to the Tybee house, ever. We are not having a seafood boil, and we're not inviting any columnists over."

"Our house is probably a little shabby for a man as rich as him, though. It would give me an opportunity to redecorate. I suppose I could call the interior designer tomorrow. She might be able to squeeze me in."

"Mom, stop. Please. This isn't what you think. I can't say anymore, okay? We're friends and nothing more. I promise."

Friends. Yeah, right. We weren't even that.

She sputtered for a few seconds about whether he'd enjoy Southern food and if his parents might like a vacation on the Georgia coast.

"I don't even know his parents," I said through gritted teeth.

Mom was undeterred. I knew enough not to say a word, so as to avoid giving her more ammunition. When she was finished chattering, I promised to send her photos of the city and call her after tomorrow's race.

I hung up with a ball of tension lodged in my stomach. My phone pinged, this time with a text. It was Kayla. She'd included a photo of her computer screen showing the picture of me and Dante.

What's this all about? Good Lord, he's sexy AF.

I resisted the urge to hurl my phone over the balcony, in the direction of a packed mega-yacht. I could hear the strains of the bass from the DJed music from here.

Fake-dating Dante was going to be much more difficult than I'd anticipated.

CHAPTER NINE
DANTE

"Nice and easy, mate. Final lap. You've got this in the bag." Jack's voice on the in-car radio was smooth as fresh asphalt, so only I could detect its quiver of excitement.

From the first lap, I was the race leader. Others had ducked, bobbed, weaved, and swerved in an attempt to overtake me, but between the car and my driving, my performance was flawless.

Maybe it wasn't time to retire . . .

I shoved that thought aside as I covered my final 2.75 miles of the track. Because of my comfortable-enough lead, my brain registered everything I passed in split-second images, as if my entire career was flashing before my eyes.

The casino. The Hôtel de Paris. The Fairmont Monte Carlo. The most beautiful part of the track near the sea, and then my favorite stretch, the tunnel. I downshifted my car inside the tunnel and reveled in the high-pitched whir of the engine echoing off the walls.

Jack's voice crackled in the headset. "You're on track for the fastest lap, mate. Good going. Bring it home, Dante."

I emerged from the tunnel and everything came in a blur: the Miramar, the swimming pool, the curve named after Anthony Noghès, the founder of the Grand Prix, and finally, the stands.

The crowd erupted into a roar as I approached the checkered flag. The radio exploded with Jack's voice and the whoops and hollers of the team.

I'd won.

Never before had any driver won seven times at Monaco, and I took a victory lap, waving and loving every second.

$\emptyset$

Back at the pits, I jumped from my car, triumphant. I'd broken every world record at this track, and it was the best possible way to start the season. Plus, Max—that little upstart—had come in second. The best of all possible outcomes for Team Eagle.

Pulling off my helmet and gloves, then tossing them to the ground, I ran over to my team, who were clustered near the paddock, and hugged Jack tight. I high-fived an Italian mechanic and shook hands with several others. My dad was there too—he always came to the season opener, while my mother always attended my home race in Italy (plus they divvied up some other races, depending on their schedules)— and he embraced me.

"Amazing race, son," he said in Italian, his voice cracking with emotion. "I am so proud of you."

We hugged for a few long seconds until someone pulled me away and Dad faded back into the crowd. There were more shouts and cheers as I made my way through the throngs.

I stopped when I reached one particular pit crew member.

Savannah.

I'd purposefully ignored her during practice and qualifying, wanting to project a professional image to the team. To my relief, she hadn't been in the pits this race because Jack had wanted her to observe.

We hadn't spent time alone together since arriving in Monaco five days ago, because I'd sequestered myself from all distractions prior to the race. That hadn't stopped the press from speculating, though.

Now she was standing so near. Ready to congratulate me. Wide-eyed, breathless, beaming. Caught up in the excitement of the win. For some reason, all I wanted was to kiss her, transfer the adrenaline I was feeling into her body.

And why couldn't I? The world's racing press already thought we were sleeping together.

I moved toward her, clamping my hand on the back of her neck and pulling her close. My lips lingered on her cheek for a few seconds, and I trailed my mouth perilously close to her ear. I was sweaty and smelly, but I didn't care.

"Grazie. Thank you for doing a good job, *fidanzata mia*," I murmured.

My girlfriend.

I let out a genuine laugh, high from the excitement. Despite the roar of the crowd, I heard her lightly gasp, which led to a delicious twinge in my dick.

Jack and the other men on the team pulled me away, hoisting me to their shoulders. Photographers crowded close, and as they snapped away, I lost sight of Savannah. No worries. I'd catch up with her later, and maybe we'd do some celebrating of our own. Winning Monaco for the seventh time during the day and seducing a beautiful American girl after dark. Could life get any better? Tilting my head back in the sun, I laughed.

There was no better aphrodisiac than victory.

An hour later, after Max and I had drained two magnums of champagne on the podium—we sprayed it on anything that moved—and after the official press conference was held and the celebration had died down, Bronson slapped me on the back.

"Impressive, Dante. So proud of you, dude." Bronson squeezed my shoulder. "I told ESPN you'd do an exclusive interview. The reporter is an acquaintance of mine, and they wanted a one on one. You don't mind, do you?"

"Not at all. I'd love to talk about the race." Maybe Bronson wasn't such a bad guy after all, because he seemed to understand how I enjoyed attention from the press almost as much as winning races. We walked toward the paddock together.

"Great, the crew's right over here. But, uh, here's the thing. They want to talk to you and Savannah. The story's actually about her. So you need to give enough details about your, uh, relationship. But don't give too much away. Tease them a bit, y'know what I mean?"

"*Excuse me?*"

"They're doing a story about how she's a groundbreaker in motorsports. First female pit crew member and all that. She's a great publicity draw for Eagle." Bronson lowered his voice. "It's why I hired her, you know. They're going to ask you about your relationship, and I want you to reveal a few details. Not many. Maybe give her a hug for the camera."

"A hug? Now? I'm the one who just won Monaco for the seventh time. That's not good publicity?"

"Dude, I'm sure they'll ask you about that. C'mon."

I considered whether it was worth pitching a fit and refusing to do the interview. The last thing I wanted was to be ordered to touch Savannah. I'd touch her when I damn well pleased— and when she gave her explicit consent—not on command like a trained circus bear. Several paces away, she was animatedly talking to a guy reporter and camera crew. She batted her eyelashes at the reporter, and I wondered if she flirted with every man she met.

I stalked up to Savvy and stood by her side, trying to mask my annoyance. How could my historic win be overshadowed by this little American chick?

I was the star, not her.

"Brilliant, there's Dante," the TV reporter said. "Hi, and congrats. We're interviewing Savvy about her role on the team and her take on the race. If you could hold on for a few, we'd really appreciate it."

Taking a back seat to anyone, much less a rookie pit crew member, spiked my blood pressure.

"Savannah, please give us your post-race analysis. Both Dante and Max drove flawlessly, but in your opinion, what put Dante over the top?"

"Max is clearly an emerging talent. But Dante"—Savannah looked to me as if she were sizing up a new set of drapes—"he's experienced, and in situations like this, experience makes all the difference when races are won by a fraction of a second. The way he maneuvered around the corners without any excessive correcting, the way he kept steady on the throttle, that's what put him on top. Well, that and the team's choice of tires. Going with the soft compound tires at the beginning of the race, and then switching to the hard compound after the pit stop for the final third was crucial, in my opinion."

I adjusted the sunglasses on my face, hoping the shock didn't register in my expression. Savannah's assessment of the race was as spot-on as any veteran motorsports analyst's would have been.

The TV reporter turned to me. "We wanted to get your take, Mr. Annunziata. Do you agree with her post-race analysis?"

Couldn't people stop calling me that? It made me feel old.

Still irritated, I fixed my unblinking attention on Savannah, gesturing with my hand in a uniquely Italian way. After slinging my arm casually around her shoulder, I forced a smile.

Her slim frame fit so perfectly in my embrace, and I drew her a few inches closer.

"Look at her. She's a wonderful asset to Eagle." I caught a whiff of the fragrance in her hair and wondered how she smelled so fresh after hours of wearing a helmet and coveralls. Her floral scent—I think it was jasmine—lit up my brain, and I wished I could press my nose into her red curls, which tumbled haphazardly out of her ponytail.

"We had heard from some in the pit crew that you grumbled about a woman on the team. At least until you and Miss Jenkins became involved with each other. Is that true?"

"I'll admit that the concept of a girl—no, a *woman*—on the pit crew was a bit shocking at first." I ignored the rest of the question.

"But you're fine with it now?" the reporter prodded.

"As long as I'm winning, I'm fine with anything."

Savannah smiled wide. "That's what we have in common. We're both extremely competitive, and we both want to win."

I cleared my throat and the reporter turned to me with a reluctant look, as if Savannah was much more interesting than my race. "Oh, Dante, yes. What can you tell us about your relationship with Miss Jenkins? Does being on the same team make things awkward? She said everything's going smoothly."

I turned to look at Savannah, who had tilted her head to gaze into my eyes adoringly. Good God, why did she have to be such a convincing actress?

"She told you that, did she?" I murmured, folding her into my chest and kissing her temple. "Isn't she incredible?"

I tipped Savannah's chin toward my face with my finger. "Yes, I think this one's a keeper. *La mia fidanzata bella.*"

"Tell the viewers what that means in English, Dante." The reporter laughed.

"My beautiful girlfriend." I pecked a kiss onto Savannah's tiny nose and stifled a laugh when I saw the surprise on her face. "My beautiful American girl."

Impulsively, I closed my eyes and leaned forward to brush a soft kiss on her lips. Forget about a damn hug.

Let the cameras capture this.

I slid my tongue against her bottom lip. After a beat, Savannah kissed me back, and the warmth of her breath and the feel of her lips were stunning. The stark desire almost knocked me over. What was happening here? Maybe I was dehydrated from the race. That must be it. I shifted back and opened my eyes. She touched her fingers to her lips, and I turned to the journalist.

"Anything else?" I asked, smiling rakishly.

The reporter rubbed his hands together, obviously thrilled with our little display of affection. "Thanks, you two lovebirds. That'll be all. Good luck with the rest of the season."

CHAPTER TEN

SAVANNAH

A few hours after the race, right as I'd stepped out of the shower and was wrapping myself in a towel, Tanya called. She didn't even say hello.

"We need to discuss party strategy for tonight," she said briskly. "I didn't see you at the champagne celebration in the garden this afternoon."

"I was at the reception," I replied. I'd attended for approximately five minutes, long enough to gulp down a glass of champagne and make sure Bronson noted my presence. Then I'd fled upstairs to the confines of my hotel room. In truth, I was hiding from Dante after that scorching yet embarrassing kiss during our interview.

I was still unsteady, as if the world had shifted off its axis.

"You didn't respond to my email," Tanya chided.

"Sorry. I forgot, with all the excitement. I was thinking I'd show up around eight, have a drink, and leave. I'm not much of a partier."

"Hmm." Her hum was one of disapproval. "We're going to require a bit more than that. What are you wearing, anyway?"

I stifled a noise of annoyance. After years of pageants, and my mother nitpicking my wardrobe for public events, I hated when people asked what I was wearing. Even Kayla knew not to press the issue.

"I brought a black wrap dress."

The sound of her tongue clicking against the roof of her mouth echoed in the phone. "I don't think that'll quite do. This is Monaco. The party's at the most lavish venue in the city. You need something with glamor, but tasteful. Especially tonight. Surely you're familiar with an evening gown?"

"Yeah, I've worn a few." I didn't even try to hide the sarcasm in my tone.

"Great. There are boutiques on the first floor of the hotel. I suggest you explore those first. If you get a move on, you'll have plenty of time to pick out something suitable. The party starts later, around nine. Dante should be there closer to ten, because he has sponsor obligations. If you're in doubt about which dress to choose, text me a photo. And if you'd like help with your hair and makeup, give me a call—I can see if we can get someone from the salon to your room. See you later!"

She hung up and I screwed my eyes shut. I'd planned to take a nap before the party so I could recharge my batteries. Hoped I could scrub the memory of that kiss out of my brain.

"Crap," I whispered, pulling on a pair of jeans, a Team Eagle sweatshirt, and my Converse. The last thing I wanted to do was shop. I pondered this while unwrapping a chocolate truffle from a three-tiered tray. They were delicious, and housekeeping seemed to replenish them every time I left.

I ate a second truffle. That was another thing I didn't miss about beauty pageants: Having to watch what I ate. Or what I wore.

For a second, I wondered if I should don my black dress as a protest, but I didn't want to mar an otherwise perfect race week-end. If nothing else, I longed to be a good team player.

I gathered my hair into a ponytail, slung my simple black purse around my shoulder, and headed out of the room, ignoring everyone who looked like they could be a tabloid photographer.

Which is to say, everyone.

Tonight's post-race victory party, and the team's rooms, were at the iconic Hotel Metropole, a sprawling belle epoque–era building in the heart of the world's richest city.

From what I'd read in a brochure in my room, the enormous hotel was built in 1886. It was possibly the swankiest place I'd ever seen, with a lobby decorated in sumptuous gold and amber hues. Even now, as I passed through, I couldn't help but gawk at an enormous fifteenth-century tapestry on one wall, and marvel at the glass-paneled ceiling, which let in the most incredible light, as if the heavens had blessed only the Côte d'Azur.

Part of me wished Mom could see all of it, but especially the massive pink hydrangea arrangement on one table. I pondered whether I should take a photo for her, then decided against it, figuring it would make me look like a country bumpkin.

This was the famed Monaco, and I was a tire changer from Georgia. I hadn't thought to bring a ball gown, but why would I have? I hadn't expected to attend any swanky parties as part of the pit crew, but as Dante's *girlfriend*, I now had *obligations*.

After that post-race kiss, I wondered whether Dante would want different kinds of obligations. *Gah. Don't even go there.*

I wandered into a small, impossibly upscale boutique on the bottom floor of the hotel, still thinking about the kiss.

What the hell was wrong with me? It was only a smooch, and one for the cameras, at that. Dante meant nothing by it. In fact, he was probably mocking me to the team, for all I knew. I didn't trust anyone at this point.

Damn him. And damn Bronson for bamboozling us into this impossible situation.

I said hello to the pretty clerk, who looked like a supermodel with her sculpted cheekbones and hair scraped back into a severe blond bun. She asked what I was looking for, and I told her I needed a simple dress. Most everything appeared tiny and tight, and I gravitated to a rack with longer hemlines.

"I'll try this," I said, plucking a black gown that looked my size off the rack, then another nearly identical dress. "And this."

"How about something a little more interesting? It would look so beautiful with your hair," she said, pointing to a red dress. "Try it. You might be surprised. I have wonderful taste and am never wrong. What size shoe?"

Ick. It wasn't my style at all. But I was in Monaco and should try new things.

"Eight."

She made a quick calculation to a European size, then asked me to follow her to a dressing room.

Once alone inside the small space, I tugged on one of the two long, sleek black dresses. This one had a deep slit up the side, and I padded out in my bare feet to the store mirrors. The shoes looked too tall and uncomfortable.

Also, why these dressing rooms didn't contain mirrors was beyond my comprehension. I parked myself near an ornate, gold-framed mirror and scanned myself up and down.

The saleslady stood nearby, coming forward once to adjust the spaghetti straps on my shoulders.

"Not bad," I said. It had taken me years to get to this point, to be able to look in the mirror and not hate my image. While I was secure in the pits when hidden in coveralls, I was less sure when I was around the feminine accoutrements of my old life.

Not bad was the best I could do on most days.

"Simply beautiful, Miss Jenkins." I'd noticed that everyone in the hotel seemed to know my name. I wondered if that was because I was with the winning team or because the tabloids all had photos of me and Dante on their covers.

My gaze snagged on the window, catching two guys strolling through the hotel lobby, past the boutique. It was Dante and Jack. What were they doing? They must be coming to or from the pre-victory party in the garden. I squared my shoulders and looked into the mirror, pretending I hadn't seen them.

There was a knock on the window. Jack beamed and waved, and Dante did a double take.

I raised my hand in greeting and fled back into the dressing room, where I stripped off the black dress. I looked at the price tag. It was probably a safe option, since it was classily conservative and only five hundred dollars. *Only.* Although I could have easily used my father's credit cards to buy anything, I was paying my own way while traveling with Team Eagle. I'd insisted as much to my parents, wanting them to know I was capable of taking care of myself. The more I controlled my finances, the less Mom could control me.

I slipped the more expensive red dress off its hanger. It appeared far racier than the black one. I brought the dress closer, studying the sparkly material. Too flashy.

The boutique's door opened with a muted jingle and I heard the saleslady speaking to someone in cooing, flattering Italian. Apparently the clerks in Monaco spoke five or six languages. While I didn't understand much Italian yet, I noticed her tone was deferential and awestruck.

Please don't let it be Jack and Dante. Please.

Naturally, Dante's silky, deep voice wafted through the air and a squirmy feeling overtook my body. We hadn't talked in-depth at all since coming to our agreement on the plane, although I'd caught him staring at me several times during practice and qualifying. Then the interview and the kiss in front of the cameras. The world, even. Probably my family had seen that little spectacle already.

Dammit.

I'd been grateful when he'd said those nice things about me to the TV crew, although I suspected he'd done the interview begrudgingly. It did seem unfair that he had clinched such a historic victory and the reporter had focused only on me, my opinion on the race, and our "relationship."

Still, between Dante's hot-and-cold attitude and my body's own disturbing, lusty reaction to him, I was hoping to keep my distance for a little while. Like for the rest of the season. Or maybe the rest of my life.

"Mademoiselle, are you finding the red dress to your satisfaction?" the saleslady called out. "There's an eager gentleman here who would like to see it."

Lord, no.

I pulled the dress over my head and wriggled it over my hips and down my thighs, pulling and plucking at the silky fabric. It was long and almost arrestingly formfitting. It also made my breasts practically spill out and that, along with my red hair, made me wonder if the look was too glam for a pit crew member. I wanted to blend in, not conjure up the beauty queen I once was.

"Savannah . . . let's see if your selection is appropriate for a Formula World party in Monaco," came Dante's musical Italian voice. "I want to see what my girlfriend is wearing this evening."

I stepped into the pair of tall, strappy black heels, then swept the curtain aside and walked out to the mirrors with as much confidence as I could muster. Refusing to let him see how nervous I actually was, I pretended I was back in pageants, during the evening gown competition. I smiled wide and took a winding route through the store, passing Dante along the way.

He sat lazily, half sprawled on a low-slung, modern white leather sofa angled toward the mirrors. He had changed and showered since the race, and was wearing jeans and a black T-shirt that stretched tantalizingly across his broad chest. There was something so primitive about his smile and the way he looked at me. Like he'd already won *me* in a contest.

I tried to ignore my thumping heart and the tension between us that had suddenly invaded the small boutique. I stepped to the small fitting platform in front of the triple mirrors. Smoothing the tight dress over my hips while turning to one side, then the other, I saw the reflection of the saleslady, who handed Dante a glass of champagne.

"Congratulations on your win, Signore Annunziata," the clerk said. Dante expressed thanks and raised his glass. "Would you also like champagne?" the clerk asked me.

Trying to focus on the dress and not Dante's intense stare, I shook my head and the clerk discreetly walked away. For several long seconds, Dante appraised me, tilting his head this way and that while smiling. He openly stared at my ass. The dress highlighted my curves a bit too much.

"That looks beautiful on you." He made a circular motion with his index finger. "Turn around. Slowly."

Oh. He wanted me to put on a show. Well, I'd been on display for thousands as a pageant contestant. What was a little performance for one man? Still, the palms of my hands pricked with sweat.

"Fine." I turned, then stood before him as his eyes raked down my body. He ran his thumb across his bottom lip. I wondered what it would be like to lie underneath him while he pinned my arms above me and kissed me violently. My pulse raced at the thought. Why was I thinking such things? It wasn't like me.

"Savannah *mia*," he said, emphasizing the Italian word. "Your hair. Sweep it up, off your shoulders, and turn around for me again." Why was his Italian accent extra-alluring in the confines of this small, intimate shop?

"What does 'Savannah mia' mean?" Maybe I could cut through this tension by having an Italian lesson.

Dante smiled smugly as he swallowed his champagne. "It translates to 'my Savannah.' Savannah mia. *La mia fidanzata Americana*. Now turn around and let me look at you some more. I'm enjoying this very much."

I stood still. "Pig," I hissed good-naturedly.

"Come now," he chided. "Turn around for your boyfriend. He likes to look at you."

"Are you always this bossy?"

"Yes." He took another sip. "And, doesn't it take a bossy person to recognize one?"

I stifled a laugh as I gathered my hair and swept it up. Rotating slowly, painfully aware of his focused attention, I noticed my breathing turn shallow, first from the thrill of flirtation and then from the realization that he was devouring me with his eyes. It was as if my body was acting with a mind of its own, because I arched my back slightly, which made my chest and butt stick out.

I noticed my nipples poking through the thin fabric of the dress. So did Dante. I bit my lip as I held the pose for him. I swear I was liquid with need as he stared. Never had any man made me feel so wanted, or so pursued. In the rational recesses of my mind, I was aware he must treat lots of women this way.

I beamed in his direction. Couldn't help myself. He grinned ferally in response.

Dante raised his glass to his lips and drained his champagne as he continued to scrutinize me. "This one looks beautiful, but wear the black tonight. I think the red dress looks too . . ." He waved his hand.

I lowered my arms, hair spilling around my shoulders, and laughed. Despite his sexiness and our flirtation, I bristled. I wasn't used to guys telling me what to do.

"Too . . . what?"

He paused and licked his bottom lip. "Too alluring."

My face grew hot. I had the distinct feeling he was making fun of me. "Thank you. I'll take your opinion under advisement." I stepped down and swept past him to the dressing room.

Inside the privacy of the small space, I exhaled, sank onto a plush white tufted bench, and shut my eyes, trying to gather my thoughts and block out Dante's voice as he spoke to the shop clerk. A line of sweat had formed on my brow from the sheer exertion of bantering with him.

After several moments of deep breathing, I threw on my jeans, sweatshirt, and sneakers, and took both dresses to the counter. Dante was nowhere to be seen as I looked around the small store. Where was he?

"Your famous boyfriend left," the clerk said in her French accent. "He said he needed to get ready for the celebration tonight."

I pulled out my wallet and charge card. "I'll take the shoes and black dress." They were the better, more practical choices. I'd even be able to wear the ensemble in the States, maybe at a party back in Atlanta. Mom would be so proud to see me looking so elegant, and I planned on taking a selfie and sending it to both her and Kayla. That would appease them and possibly stop their incessant texts about Dante. None of which I'd responded to.

The clerk looked at me with amusement and more than a hint of admiration. She slid a small black velvet box toward me, and I shook my head in protest.

"Oh, no, I have jewelry." I'd brought some simple gold necklaces and earrings.

"Please put your credit card away, Miss Jenkins. Signore Annunziata has taken care of everything. He wants you to have both dresses, the shoes, and the gift in the box." I snatched the box off the counter and pried it open. A pair of brilliant, dangling earrings sparkled back at me.

"They're real," cooed the clerk. "Aren't they incredible?"

"What? Real . . . crystal? Swarovski?" I could barely get the words out.

The clerk laughed and laughed. "We don't sell crystal here, *chérie*. And I think Dante Annunziata knows that diamonds are the only appropriate gift for his girlfriend."

CHAPTER ELEVEN

SAVANNAH

Scanning the party, I tried to project a confidence in my expression that I didn't feel in my heart. For one thing, I was bone tired.

After buying the dress, I'd returned to my room, hoping to take a power nap before the party. But between the rush of winning the race, the kiss, and the exchange in the boutique, I tossed and turned for a half hour in the enormous hotel bed and then just had to get right back up again. Why had Dante bought the two gowns, the shoes, *and* a pair of expensive diamond earrings? The whole thing left me with an uncomfortable feeling. Nothing made sense.

Adding to my dismay: this was the swankiest, most luxurious event I'd ever attended. Normally I wasn't insecure about my looks or poise, but it was difficult not to feel a little inferior here in Monaco. It was as if the five most gorgeous people from every country in the world were at this particular party.

The soiree was on the pool deck of the Metropole. Part of me longed to hide, hole up in my amazing room, slip on the fuzzy bathrobe in the hotel closet, and flop down on the decadently puffy down comforter. Order the cheese plate from room service. Enjoy the silence after a day of roaring crowds and racing engines.

But I was at the city's hottest party with the winning team. Which was a charge, a once-in-a-lifetime experience. I was also wearing an indecently sexy scarlet dress and drinking a flute of expensive champagne. I'd chosen to reject Dante's recommendation, because the red dress fit better than the black, and because I wasn't about to obey the likes of him.

I was a team player, but not Dante's submissive plaything.

As I sipped my bubbly, I silently admired the crowd. All around me, gorgeous women in stunning designer gowns and four-inch heels glided about, speaking with ease in multiple languages. Most of the men were in tuxedos, although some of the wealthiest ones weren't as formally dressed as the women, and I noted wryly that men of power could afford to look any damned way they pleased—while women across the globe had to obey societal conventions of how they *should* look, regardless of class or race or social status.

I made small talk with some guys from the team, mostly about how lucky we'd gotten that it hadn't rained during the race. I prodded them into telling stories of previous wet races and was enthralled—and grateful they weren't asking about Dante or leering at me in the dress.

"Can I get you another?" Giorgio asked, pointing to my empty glass. He smirked. "Or perhaps you're waiting for someone?"

"No, who would I be waiting—" I stopped short. Of course. I'd be waiting for Dante, if he were my actual boyfriend.

Giorgio and the other two mechanics leaned in, as if eager for the answer. Shame made my throat feel like it was closing up.

"We'd have to be blind not to have seen the news," Giorgio said. "Of course, it's no business of ours what you and Dante do in private."

"Listen, I-I'm only here to help the team win," I stammered.

"Maybe you'll be his good luck charm. Dante has a lot of those."

"You mean, he uses women as good luck charms?" *Eww. How cringey.*

"No." Giorgio guffawed. "That's not what I meant at all. He's superstitious. He has little tokens and rituals, a favorite color. But who knows? Maybe you'll be his lucky rabbit's foot this season."

I held up my hand, not really wanting to be compared to an amputated animal appendage. "Okay, then. I need to use the ladies' room, so I'll grab another drink myself on the way back. Catch you later." I turned and walked away, feeling narrow cracks of tension in the air.

A lucky rabbit's foot. Lord have mercy.

My head throbbed. Life in Formula World seemed to revolve around politics, posturing, and a healthy dose of paranoia. I needed to toughen up if I was going to survive this season.

I resolved to make one more lap around the party, find Dante to show his adoring public that yes, he was indeed entangled with his tire changer, and then retreat to my room. The chocolate truffles came to mind, and I pasted on a smile as I wound my way through the crowd.

After freshening up in the ornate, gilded restroom, I forced myself to return to the throngs. Tanya was near a massive display of shrimp and oysters, laughing with Jack, and I sidled up to them both.

"Savannah." She gasped. "There you are. Holy wow, you look amazing. I almost didn't recognize you. Did you call for hair and makeup because, well, wow. I guess I'm not used to seeing you with lipstick and eyeliner."

I gave a little shrug, not wanting to talk about how I had mad skills in the hair and makeup department. "I clean up well. You look really beautiful too."

Tanya was wearing a midnight-blue gown that showed off her curves, and her hair was swept into a messy updo. I wasn't the only one who noticed how she'd transformed from a no-nonsense PR flack in a black suit to a glamor vixen—Jack couldn't take his eyes off her, and asked her if she'd like to visit a yacht party later.

Yikes. I noticed that he didn't include me in that invite. Were they a thing? How much more intrigue could I handle in one evening?

"Well, I'm off to grab another drink," I chirped, wandering away.

This scene was a long way from Georgia, I reminded myself, and the corners of my eyes crinkled in a silent smile. I needed to put on that happy face for a little while longer. This was only a means to an end—I was here to learn, and to win. Proving my mettle to my family, to the team, and to myself were my only goals.

Today was but one day of a long season. Team Eagle had won, but there were so many more races to come.

I reminded myself what Jack had told Dante on the team radio during the race: *pace yourself.*

But where was Dante? While I searched, I took in all the little details of the party. The event was held outside by the pool, but this wasn't any old hotel swimming hole. The deck overlooked the Mediterranean, the gardens, and the city's famed casino.

If only Mom could see me now. She'd be so proud. I'd love to tell her that I was standing a few feet from the Prince of Monaco and that British actor she loved. Oh, and there was the supermodel from those perfume ads . . . But if I discreetly pulled out my phone to call, I'd be subjected to another round of interrogation about what was happening, and assaulted with a million questions about Dante, and so I pushed the thought out of my mind.

I strolled through the crowd, searching for other team members and smiling at everyone who caught my eye. When I approached the bar, a shiver went through my body.

There was Dante, looking rakish in a tuxedo. Women surrounded him; of course they did. At some point, I'd have to thank him for his gift. But not when he was holding court with what appeared to be eager groupies. He wouldn't be sleeping alone tonight, I was certain. A twinge of envy went through me.

We caught each other's gaze, and he lifted an eyebrow and smirked. My cheeks grew hot, and I felt as if he knew exactly what was inside my mind. I edged away from the bar. Making a beeline to the farthest end of the pool, I paused near a white chaise lounge accented with a crisp blue pillow. A palm tree swayed overhead and I exhaled, grateful to have found a small, uncrowded spot not far from him.

A brochure in my room said the stunning blue-and-white-hued outdoor space had been created by a famous fashion designer, and I was left momentarily breathless when small, twinkling LED lights at the bottom of the pool flickered to life, making the aqua water look otherworldly.

"Like a galaxy of stars, isn't it?"

Steadying myself with one hand on the back of the chaise, I turned toward the familiar Italian-accented voice.

"Yes. It is." I hadn't been here but thirty seconds when he'd approached. Surprising, since he'd been chatting up that gaggle of gorgeous women. Oh, right. We were supposed to be dating. It wasn't as if he could ignore me, even if he wanted to. We had responsibilities, and surely there were reporters sprinkled amongst this crowd.

Because I didn't want to focus on how handsome his body looked in the tuxedo, I contemplated his face. A faint shadow of stubble graced his jaw. It made him look even more stunning. I recalled how the stubble had scraped against my face when he'd kissed my cheek after the race win, and my heart fluttered at the memory.

He stepped closer. Spoke low and slow in that accented voice of his.

"I've been here so much that I forgot what it's like to see this place for the first time. It is your first time in Monaco, and at the Hotel Metropole, no?"

His smile was the second thing to take my breath away that evening. He took another half step toward me, and it was as if I could feel him on every inch of my skin.

Where was this unbridled lust coming from? Even though I knew how to glam up and look sexy, I was a tomboy at heart. I didn't *do* sensual appeal if I could help it. But the way he looked at me, how he talked to me, made me feel like a femme fatale.

Like I was the sexiest woman at the party, which I knew simply wasn't true.

"Yes, this is my first time. My parents honeymooned here."

"How romantic." His smile was mischievous, and he motioned in the direction of my chest. "Your dress. You didn't take my recommendation."

I shook my head. "Outside of work, I don't follow directions well."

He laughed, and it was a genuine reaction. "I have to admit, the red looks even better tonight than it did in the shop. And it looked pretty amazing on you in the shop."

"You didn't have to buy—"

He interrupted, holding up his hand. "Think of it as a peace offering."

"What do you mean?"

"I owe you an apology. I shouldn't have been so nasty to you on the plane." He wasn't trying to hit on me. He was being nice to a teammate. Earlier, one of the mechanics had said he bought the men on the team gifts of cigars or expensive liquor after every race. Buying me stuff at the shop was his way of being kind. I exhaled in my relief, and realized that maybe I'd misjudged him. "No apology necessary. And thank you for both dresses and the shoes and the earrings." My hand went to the diamond earring in my right lobe. "That was a sweet gesture."

Slowly, he eyed my entire body as if I were his possession. I felt naked, on display, exposed. Maybe it was dark enough that he wouldn't notice I was turning a deep shade of scarlet.

"*Bellissima.*"

I licked my bottom lip nervously. From the mouth of any other man, his words might have sounded creepy or odd, but by now, I'd picked up on a tension, a thing, between us that went beyond casual flirtation.

Or was it my imagination? Maybe he was being polite and Italian because we were in public. Where we were supposed to act like boyfriend and girlfriend.

Flattering and flirting—wasn't that what Italian men did with all women? I remembered when some of my college friends had returned from a summer trip to Italy, talking about how attentive the men were there. That must have been it.

"It's a shame we don't have more downtime here," he remarked. "I'd love to show you around."

I frowned in his direction. "You wanted me off the team a few days ago. What's changed?"

"I admit that I can be a bit, how do you say, old-fashioned? I'm Italian." He shrugged. "I was raised to think men and women are not always capable of doing the same things."

"Feel free to explain yourself. I'm not sure I'm picking up what you're putting down."

He briefly looked puzzled by my colloquial phrase. "I don't think any explanation is necessary. Racing's a man's sport. Always has been. But I will admit, you seem to be eager to learn, and I was impressed by your post-race analysis today. Maybe you will change my mind over the season. I've decided to give you a chance and be your friend. Since we have to be more than friends in public."

Now I laughed, hard. He was so handsome, but the arrogance dripped from his every pore. If a man talked like this to me back in the States, I might have thrown a drink on him. Definitely I would have walked away. But Dante was my team driver. My decadently alluring superior. My fake boyfriend.

"You've decided to be my friend. Thank you, Mr. Annunziata. I'm so flattered." I batted my long, fake eyelashes.

His eyes narrowed. "Can you please stop calling me that? My lips have been on yours. I think we're a bit past those formalities, no? Anyway, I can't be much older than you."

"I'm twenty-four."

He took a sip of his drink. "Only a girl. I turned thirty-two last month."

I touched my champagne glass to his. "Happy belated birthday. How about this? I'll stop calling you 'Mr. Annunziata' if you stop calling me a girl."

There was a hint of amusement in his voice when he said, "Deal. Want to shake on it?" I extended my hand.

He softly, quickly, brushed his lips over the backs of my fingers, never taking his eyes off mine. I didn't know whether to be appalled or excited, and I wondered if anyone was watching.

"Is that how you treat all of your tire changers?"

"Only the beautiful redheaded ones who are supposed to act like they're my adoring girlfriend."

I jerked my hand out of his grasp. A lock of hair fell over my face and I licked my dry lips. Why did my body seem to hum with electricity every time he was around?

He was close, too close, all up in my personal space. With a gossamer touch, he gently swept the lock of hair away from my forehead, his fingertips lightly touching my skin. He tucked the hair behind my ear, tracing my lobe, pausing to admire the glittering earrings.

"I'd love to see you wearing these and nothing else."

"I beg your pardon," I said with a gasp. No, I hadn't signed on for this kind of treatment. Fighting both outrage and the deep sexual craving that had welled inside of me, I inhaled and tried to ignore the full impact of his attitude, his broad shoulders, and his sensual, amused mouth. I'd never felt such annoyance or desire for one man before.

"Good night, Dante. I'm afraid I'm tired after the excitement of today. Congratulations on winning the race."

I slowly turned to walk away. With a fluid, familiar motion, Dante wrapped his arm around my waist and his hot breath flooded my neck.

"Savannah mia." He held me from behind and my heart pounded. He brushed a small kiss on the sensitive spot behind my earlobe, then another, and another, sending explosions through my body. His voice was low and velvety. "We're supposed to be a couple. That's what we agreed to, no? Aren't we supposed to leave together at the end of the party? Unless you want to leave together now, for other reasons. Which I'm completely in favor of."

I squirmed around so we were standing close, face to face. I rested both hands on his chest and ran them slowly over the broad planes. He was solid, like a granite wall. Lord have mercy. My finger went to his sharp jawline and I skimmed his soft skin. His mouth parted in a surprised half smile. This was all for show, of course. Or maybe to torment him a little. It seemed that he enjoyed banter and flirtation, and maybe if I acted coy and snarky, he'd get the message.

"I'm exhausted, *sweetie.* I'm sure you can figure out some excuse to tell everyone why I'm leaving early, and then you can get back to your harem on the other side of the pool, no?"

I leaned up and kissed him full on the mouth, pausing to nibble on his bottom lip. Lord, he was a good kisser. Okay, maybe I kissed him longer than I'd initially intended. But it was seemingly impossible to stop. After about fifteen slow, teasing seconds of a lip-lock, I broke away.

"Nighty-night, Mr. Annunziata," I whispered.

Taking advantage of his shocked expression, I whirled and walked off. I tried to assume a fierce strut through the crowd while ignoring the shaky, unsettled feeling that had overtaken my body in the wake of Dante's lips on mine, his fingers on my skin, and his eyes everywhere else.

CHAPTER TWELVE

DANTE

The next morning in my hotel suite, I lounged on the balcony, ignoring the glittering view of the yachts in Monaco harbor. Instead, I fiddled with my phone, texting back the friends and acquaintances from around the globe who congratulated me on the historic race.

Instead of motorsports, however, my mind was on something else. Rather, *someone* else.

Savannah had all but run away from me at the party, so obviously affected by our flirtation. The way she'd looked at me with her button-like eyes, how her feisty demeanor had shattered when I'd kissed her hand, was so satisfying. Surely she'd left abruptly because she was playing some little hard-to-get game. Which was fine. Prolong the competition, heighten the sexual tension. And that kiss that took me by surprise. Sublime.

This was the fun part.

It was surprising, though, that she hadn't texted later and begged me to come to her room. Women never waited long to fuck once I'd expressed interest. I knew when a woman wanted me, and the way Savannah's green eyes flickered and flared, her desire for me was a given.

But why the hell did she have to be on the pit crew? Why couldn't I have met her at a post-race yacht party? Why couldn't she have been a trackside model? She was certainly gorgeous enough to be one. I jiggled my leg.

Damn Bronson for his stupid fake-relationship idea. I'd heard rumors that in his capacity as a tech CEO, he loved taunting and teasing the media. He'd once even bankrolled the lawyers of a B-list actress who'd sued a gossip website for defamation—simply because he hated the website.

Christ, Savannah was stunning in that red dress. While she looked like a sexy, fresh girl in her team coveralls, seeing her in a gown and makeup with her hair piled up was delicious. Had I not known she was a pit crew member, I'd have thought she was another knockout groupie because she appeared to fit so seamlessly into the Monaco nightlife.

Now that I'd gotten to know her a little, I realized she was even more distracting. And the last thing I wanted was a distraction. I had a championship to win.

Maybe if I could convince her to get off the team, she'd enjoy traveling with me as my lover—I'd even lift my ban on dating the same woman for longer than a few races. And maybe being a groupie would satisfy her need to be around the sport. Then Bronson would leave me alone to work my magic on the track.

Win-win-win.

I grinned wider, thinking about how I'd returned to my hotel suite last night—alone—soon after she'd stalked out of the party. It had been easy to ignore the numerous women who were more than willing to cater to my every desire.

The only woman I desired had walked away.

But that didn't stop me from fantasizing about the erotic nights I'd inevitably, eventually, share with Savannah.

"What are you happy about, son? The race? Your driving was impeccable." My father's accented voice boomed and echoed around the balcony as he slid the glass door closed behind him. He'd come to Monaco to watch the race and stayed overnight in one of the suite's four luxurious bedrooms.

"Nothing." I slouched lower in the lounge chair and tilted my head up to greet the Riviera rays instead of looking at Don Giuseppe Annunziata, as I called him sarcastically in my mind.

"Have you heard from your mother? That bitch was supposed to get back to me about one of our investments, but she won't return my calls," my father groused, rubbing his eyes. I laid back and shut my eyes, annoyed. Here I was, a Formula World champion, a multimillionaire, sitting on the balcony of a coveted hotel suite in Monaco—and yet I still had to listen to my parents' constant bickering. They'd been separated for years following my father's relentless infidelity. The two fools refused to divorce, citing anti-quated Italian laws, and still they dragged me into their arguments.

Their relationship had gotten so nasty that I'd insisted neither of them show up at the same race, which was why Dad came to

Monaco and Belgium while Mom attended Valencia and Monza. If they wanted to attend any other races, they had to figure it out themselves and not require me to mediate.

"I'd be willing to answer that question if you didn't call the woman who gave birth to me a bitch." Although women came and went in my life, I hated when men used foul names for the opposite sex. It seemed so distasteful, and having heard my father denigrate my mother for years meant I tried to be polite and upbeat when I spoke about my ex-lovers, especially in the press.

My dad snorted and mumbled something in Italian. For the millionth time, I wished my sister was still alive. Somehow Gabriella had been able to broker peace in the family, and after all these years, I hadn't yet figured out how she had managed that. After she died, I'd given myself completely to racing. Tried to ignore my parents' volatile relationship. Vowed that if I ever got married, I wouldn't treat my wife like my father treated my mother. No chance of that, though, because I wasn't the marriage type.

My dad waved his hand dismissively. "Whatever. So I didn't want to ask you before the race, and didn't have a chance last night, with the party . . ."

My father had stayed out later than I did, had gone to some yacht after the party at the hotel. The old man was incorrigible. Pathetic. Not dignified. More than anything, I didn't want to end up like him, lonely and searching for the next piece of ass while making my family's life hell.

It was better to stay single, in my book.

"What's going on between you and Dale Jenkins's daughter? Everyone was talking about you two last night. It's all over the papers in Italy. Her family's loaded, you know."

I slipped the phone into my pocket and smiled.

"Why wasn't she here when you woke up?" Leave it to my father to ask the most inappropriate question first.

"Because we haven't slept together yet. And this isn't a conversation I want to have with you. I believe that gentlemen don't talk about what goes on in the bedroom."

Dad squeezed my shoulder. "Maybe her father could give you a cushy position on the board of the Jenkins corporation. That would be a nice income stream."

I snorted. First a girl on the pit crew. Then the girl became my fake girlfriend. Now my father was trying to line up a job for me? It was understandable, I guess, since he'd grown up poor and had sacrificed everything for my first break into Formula World.

"I know you love money, Papa, but really? Don't you think I have enough already? Don't you think we have enough? The apartment in Rome and the villa at Lake Como aren't sufficient?"

"Just a thought, son. You're only thirty-two. You need to do something with the rest of your life. A nice, corporate position where you don't have to do much? Could be a smart move."

Merely the thought of being in a boardroom made me feel like a dark cloud had settled over all of Monaco. Oppressive. Trapped. No, I didn't care about Dale Jenkins's business in America. All I wanted was to win a championship and bed a redhead. I'd think about the future later.

That was when my phone buzzed with a text. Bronson.

Come to my suite, dude! We have a lot to discuss.

Interesting. The team owner was turning out to be quite the hands-on kind of guy. Maybe he'd give me a bonus for winning Monaco. Or he and Jack wanted to discuss strategy for the next race. Montreal was a vastly different climate than Monaco, and I had my own thoughts about which tire compounds we should use.

"Gotta run, Papa," I said. "Bronson wants to have a meeting. I suspect he's going to give me a bonus. Apparently he's quite generous like that to people who are loyal, from what I've read." *And God knows I've been loyal by going along with this silly Savannah scheme.*

"As well he should," my father grumbled. "You're winning. You were put on this earth to win. I hope he recognizes that."

I'd heard this refrain since I was a teen, and had tried my darndest to live up to it. I gave him a quick hug and walked out of the suite, grabbed the elevator, and traveled up one floor, then headed down the hall to the hotel's *other* penthouse suite. I knocked, and Bronson answered.

"Morning, dude." Bronson slapped me on the shoulder. My eyes landed on a familiar redhead, who was sitting on a sofa.

Savannah.

She was wearing a dark-blue tank top and short khaki shorts. She looked fresh and pretty, with no makeup. Her mouth had a hint of clear gloss, which made her lips pink and pouty. I noticed that her green eyes were extrabright. Like she was well rested. What was she doing here? A mix of panic and anger rose in my body. Was she sleeping with Bronson? Had she gone to his suite after leaving the party? Was that what this was about?

The jealousy inspired by the sight of seeing Savannah in Bronson's suite was so foreign to me that I almost didn't recognize it for what it was.

"Come on in and sit next to Savvy." Bronson gestured at the sofa.

As I sank down, I noticed her fresh, floral scent was even stronger today, as if she'd recently bathed. Probably showered here at Bronson's. The very idea put me in a sour mood.

"Hey, Dante." Her Southern accent was like slow syrup.

One of her long, bare legs was crossed over the other. Good God, those legs. Her hair was down, cascading in copper waves over her shoulders. All of the dirty fantasies I'd had about her the previous evening rushed into my mind. Especially the one about her on her knees.

"Buongiorno," I said roughly, evading her stare.

Bronson looked at us with something like predatory glee. "So kids, I brought you both here so we could talk about strategy. The media got a few great shots of the two of you after the race, but nothing of note at the party. That's all going to change in Montreal, which is why I wanted all of us to get on the same page."

Bronson waved his hand, and for the first time, I noticed there was a fourth person in the room. It was Tanya, the team's public relations manager. An American blond in her thirties, Tanya had been sleeping with Jack off and on for a couple of weeks, if I recalled right. I couldn't keep track of his women. I gave her a halfhearted, one-finger wave, still steaming about the idea of Savannah and Bronson.

"Dante, Savvy, from now on, we'll be orchestrating your every move before and after races." Tanya extracted a piece of paper from a folder and handed it to me, pointing to Savannah. "The two of you can look that over as I talk. By the time we arrive in Montreal on Wednesday morning, we will have tipped the paparazzi off, so they'll be at the airport to greet you. We want you to walk out of first class together, and hold hands in the airport."

"I still can't believe you're the ones who tip off the photographers," Savannah grumbled.

"*Cara*, you're so naive," I said. That earned me a nasty look.

Tanya continued. "Later that afternoon, we've arranged for you to tour the Notre-Dame Basilica together . . ."

As she droned on, I shifted my body close to Savannah's.

"Hold on." Savannah interrupted and raised her hand, as if we were in class, then tapped the paper. "It says here we're supposed to visit a nightclub from ten thirty until one and, quote, 'dance close and kiss.' You expect me to kiss him?"

"I won't bite," I teased.

She turned with a glare and smacked me on the leg, then twisted back to Tanya.

"We're not asking you to make out or anything."

"Oh, thanks," Savannah replied sarcastically.

"I didn't notice any hesitation from either of you when you lip-locked in front of the ESPN camera," Bronson piped up.

Savannah opened her mouth, didn't say a word, and then pressed her lips together. By the way the tops of her cheeks flared pink, I wondered if the memory of our kisses had worked its way into the corners of her brain.

CHAPTER THIRTEEN

SAVANNAH

"Did you think the tires were grippier toward the end of the race? I believe that's what put you over the top." I studied my fake boyfriend, who was sitting opposite me in the limousine. He'd won today's race in Montreal by a hair over a Praxis car.

"I did, in fact, think they gripped far better. Last season, on my other team, we used a different compound and I came in third. Everything came down to the tires. We had an excellent strategy today, but it was too close for comfort. Did you enjoy yourself?"

"I did. Although I'm hoping in the next race to do something more than observe," I said in a pointed voice. I'd spent my second race watching in the pits, and I hadn't gotten to change a single tire.

"That's up to Jack." Dante looked back to the window.

"You promised to help me. I think if you talked with Jack, he'd be more willing to put me in during a race."

"I'll consider it."

"We had a deal," I said. "I could discuss it with Bronson, you know."

"Like you'll get anywhere with him. The less contact you have with that man, the better."

"Why? You jealous?" She snorted. "He's not my type anyway."

"What is your type, Savvy?"

I narrowed my eyes at him. "Wouldn't you like to know. Why the warning about Bronson?"

"I did a bit of reading on the plane the other day."

"Funny, you don't strike me as the reading type."

"You misjudge me, cara," he teased. "Anyway. I was reading that Bronson has something of a vendetta against the media. They were pretty harsh with him when he started his tech company. He's never forgotten that, and ever since, he has played cat-and-mouse with them."

"Like how?"

"Like investing in social media companies that undermine traditional newspapers and television." He went on to talk about how one of Bronson's corporate investments led to a media company's loss of ad revenue. I couldn't quite follow what Dante was saying—he used a few Italian words for financial terms, saying he didn't know the words in English—but one thing was clear.

Bronson was playing a stupid game with the media, and Dante and I were pawns.

I tucked a strand of hair behind my ear. "I don't like what Bronson's led us into. How can you be so casual about it? You're discussing this as if you're talking about the weather."

"Savannah, I can't do anything about it now. I have no control. All I can control is my driving. All you can control is your performance in the pits."

An uncomfortable silence filled the limousine for a solid five minutes while I pondered all this.

"You don't have to come into the hospital with me," he finally said as he looked out the window.

From the other side of the limousine, I snorted. You'd have thought he'd be in a better mood after winning, but for some reason he was sulky.

Publicly, he treated me with a sensual attentiveness during the moments we were together and around other people.

Privately, he seemed bored and even annoyed. Then again, I was matching his emotions, ratcheting them up, even. Taunting him and getting a rise out of him was so satisfying, and every time he snorted or sighed or sputtered about something, I'd laugh—which would incense him even more.

For a few moments back at the hotel in Monte Carlo, it had seemed as though we'd come to an agreement, like we were in this mess together. But when we'd arrived at the Montreal airport to a scrum of photographers demanding to know more about our relationship than about his winning races, his mood had turned bleak.

The dramatic, handsome Italian was broody because his racing prowess wasn't the only thing in the spotlight, and it was somewhat understandable . . . but it was also getting on my nerves. Above all, I felt he should help me get more time in the pits with the cars. I'd more than proven myself during practice. It wasn't unusual to rotate team members in and out of the pits.

Squirming in my seat, I fussed with the hem of my dress. It

was black, short, and chosen by Tanya as something that would be perfect for our grand debut at a nightclub later in the evening. It also seemed to attract negative attention from Dante, who kept scowling at my bare legs.

"I'm going into the hospital with you. The publicist said we had to face the press together at Montreal General when you donate the check and visit the patients."

Dante grunted. "I usually do these visits alone, away from the cameras." If his jaw were any tighter, I'd have sworn he had tetanus.

"We have to get used to this. We'll be doing a lot of these charity visits together. Remember what Tanya said? The press is going to pick and probe at our relationship because it's so out of left field. We can't get caught faking it. I want this to be perfect."

"Well. Look at you."

"Well, what?" I asked in a surly tone.

"I find competitive women sexy."

I flashed him a smirk. Indeed, I was competitive, and when faced with a challenge, I had to win. I didn't think he paid close attention when I talked, but apparently I was wrong.

"We were told to make the appearance here, then go to the club on the top floor of our hotel. Together. Put on your big-boy pants. Take one for the team. I'm coming in with you." He looked at me incredulously and tapped his fingers on his chest. "Did you just tell a six-time world champion to *put on his big-boy pants*?"

Teasing him was so fun. Especially when his dark eyebrows furrowed, making him look moody and sexy all at once. "I don't think I've ever had a woman tell me that."

"Maybe it's about time." I suspected that women didn't stand up to him, ever.

The limo stopped and Dante cleared his throat. He twisted his wrist to look at his watch, his crisp linen shirt cuff inching up his arm. He glared at his Rolex, as if he was considering all the other exciting and interesting things he could be doing. Did he have to treat me with such contempt? He should be happy since he'd won the race earlier in the day and was already leading the pack in the drivers' championship points after only two races.

"Ready?" he asked, seemingly bored. "It's time for me to show you off."

"So offensive."

This was our first real public appearance together as a couple, if one didn't count the post-race congratulatory kiss and the little poolside spectacle in Monaco. He hadn't tried to touch me in days, and that confused me. While I'd once thought he actually wanted to sleep with me, I now knew otherwise. Clearly, he barely tolerated my presence. Probably thought I was an annoying kid. He sure seemed irritated tonight.

The chauffeur opened the limo door and Dante stepped out, extending his hand to me. I slipped my fingers into his wide palm and he effortlessly pulled me out of the car. Flashbulbs immediately popped, and as we'd planned, we didn't stop to chat with reporters on our way into the hospital. I ignored their shouted questions as hospital staff escorted us quickly into the building, but one echoed in my head.

"Dante, are you visiting this burn unit because of your sister's accident?"

The muscles in his chiseled jaw bunched. He gripped my hand tighter and propelled me inside, exhaling loudly once we were in the reporter-free space.

A hospital executive thanked Dante profusely as we all rode the elevator up to the third floor.

The executive, a French-Canadian man, spoke in heavily accented English. "We are always so grateful for your support, and the patients love seeing you. Monsieur Annunziata, we can't thank you enough. We've set aside a room for your visit and gathered six patients together, the ones who are recovering well."

Dante switched to French, and I strained to make out any words. My high school language classes proved useless. What did his sister have to do with his visit to a hospital burn ward? Why did he look tenser now than he did before a competitive race? Why was he still gripping my hand as if his life depended on it?

I squeezed his fingers as we stepped off the elevator and walked down a corridor. Pausing before a door, Dante turned to me. "This is a difficult sight. You don't have to come in. The cameras aren't capturing this. You're free to stay out in the hall."

His voice was so fogged with sadness that I was taken by surprise. Truth was, I was a little scared to see the burn patients, but the smells of the hospital—from the disinfectant to the food to the latex—invaded my senses. Everyone deserved visitors and I was grateful we were here.

"I'm going with you," I whispered firmly.

Dante raked in a breath. He moved his hand to my lower back and we walked inside.

There, six beds were filled with patients, some sporting various bandages and others with horrifically scarred faces and arms. Dante's hand left my back, and he strode up to the first bed. I stopped, transfixed at the change that had overtaken him, seemingly within seconds. It was as if the tension in his face had melted away and in its place, there was a boyish, gentle expression.

I wasn't sure what I'd expected. I knew he wasn't boorish or impolite, and wouldn't act arrogant in front of injured people. But standing and watching him talk and laugh with a woman who seemingly didn't have hands, only scarred nubs where hands should be, I could see the compassion radiating from him.

I stepped to his side. "Hi," I said. "I'm Dante's . . ."

"This is my girlfriend," Dante said in a soft voice, putting his hand on my arm. I beamed and stroked the woman's shoulder, as I'd seen Dante do a few moments earlier.

"I'm a huge fan of yours, and I have to say, I think this is your most beautiful girlfriend yet," the woman said in a thick French Canadian accent. I giggled, and a small smile crept across Dante's face.

He chatted easily with the woman, asking her questions about her family. Of her own accord, the woman spoke about her burns, which had happened during a house fire. I knelt and listened intently to her story.

"You've come so far, you're bound to pull through now," Dante said, his voice soothing. "The first seventy-two hours are the worst. You'll be good as new soon."

Side by side, we visited each of the people in the six beds, and it seemed that Dante was gentler with each patient. When we were through, neither of us spoke as we rode the elevator downstairs, and I reflected on how Dante's kind demeanor with the patients made me admire him. Scratch that: it made my heart feel as vast as Canada.

Somewhere inside that cynical, sarcastic Italian was a good man with pure intentions. I was sure of it. Yes, I had admired his prowess on the track since the moment I'd laid eyes on him. He was an incredible athlete. But his caring side gave him depth.

"Now, back to the vultures," Dante said in a mocking, cheerful voice. I was disappointed when he seemed to switch back into his usual snarky self. I'd have preferred to have gotten to know that other man, the kind one.

We stepped out to another barrage of flashbulbs, and Dante clamped his arm around my waist. His touch was so possessive, so commanding, and I leaned into his body as heat from his arm traveled through me.

I reminded myself that I was playing a part. Acting. After all, he was too. Although after seeing him with the burn patients, I wasn't sure of anything. The man talking in a silky voice to the press was the superstar; the man inside the hospital seemed normal and good-hearted.

Who was the real Dante? I tried to gaze at him adoringly as he talked to the reporters, which wasn't difficult. I enjoyed having an excuse to stare at him.

"As some of you know, I don't usually broadcast my visits to burn units, but you've probably heard that I visit them in each city after a race. Tonight, I wanted to bring my girlfriend here." He paused and winked at me. "She's shown an interest in the same charities that I support, which is a real credit to what a compassionate person she is."

He gave me a saucy little smile. The reporters shouted questions and I tuned everything out, overcome by the way Dante had shamelessly flirted. As if I was his girlfriend. A surge of joy made me feel hyperawake.

"I think I'm the luckiest driver. Not only do I have the best pit crew member, but I also found a wonderful girlfriend." Dante pulled me closer.

It was then that I sensed a mocking undertone to his voice

and that annoyed me, especially after witnessing his truly genuine display of emotion in the hospital. A reporter pointed her pen at us.

"Savannah, do you want Dante to cut his hair before the next race? It's become uncharacteristically long," she said with a starstruck giggle.

What kind of inane question was that? Did people really care what I thought about his hair? Seizing the chance to tease, I looked at him with big eyes. Reaching up, I ran my fingers through the dark locks that rakishly fell across his forehead.

"He's handsome either way, but I think he looks like such a bad boy with long hair, don't you?" I stood on tiptoes—even in heels I was quite a bit shorter than him—and pressed my lips to his stubble-roughened cheek.

"Time to go." He pulled me toward the limo and practically pushed me inside.

After the door was shut and once the limo ride was well underway, he glowered at me. "What was that little display of flirtation?"

I shrugged. "I'm acting, remember? Playing a part."

"You certainly seem to do it well. I guess I didn't realize that I'd been set up with someone so . . . *practiced* at being a rich man's girlfriend. Makes sense, though, you being the daughter of Dale Jenkins and all. I suppose you had lots of debutante balls to attend and such. Probably all of your past boyfriends have been the sons of CEOs."

"Yeah, right," I snorted. "I refused to have a debutante ball. I'd recently quit pageants and didn't want any of that crap."

"Look at you. A rebel," he remarked.

"I'm surprised that you're not more curious about my

life, Dante." I looked out the window as the Montreal skyline whizzed by.

Out of the corner of my eye, I saw him wave a hand dismissively in the air. "I know that you don't have a boyfriend currently. Still, what else is there to discover? You're a sheltered American girl who wants to prove herself on the worldwide stage of motorsports."

"You're insufferable. And mean. How do you know I don't have a boyfriend? How can you be so kind to those people in the hospital yet be so nasty to me?"

"Maybe those people are deserving of my compassion. And I know you're single because Bronson told me."

I *had* told Bronson all about my personal life when I'd interviewed for the job.

"Do you treat all of your girlfriends this way?"

He regarded me with a cold look. "I don't have girlfriends. I have occasional lovers. And I don't bring those women to burn units."

I tilted my head, wondering if he'd avoided using the word *girlfriend* because he never remained with one woman long enough. "Why?"

He shrugged. "I like to keep my love life separate from the rest of my life."

"I guess that's going to be difficult for you now, isn't it, since I'm your girlfriend? You're going to be forced to integrate a woman into your world. The horror."

His eyes snapped to mine, dark pools of sensuality.

"You know, *amore mio*," he said in a seductive tone that danced on the edge of sarcasm, "you're only a girl, but I'm sure you are old enough to understand that this constant sniping between us is due to sexual tension."

"As if." It wasn't a great comeback, but it was the best I could do, considering I agreed with him but didn't want to admit it.

"Bickering is so tedious," he said mildly. "Wouldn't it be better to simply spend a night together, clear the air, and be friends? I mean, if you're going to, as you say, 'play a part' and be my pretend girlfriend, let's do it right and go all the way. Then we can proceed as true friends."

All the way. If only he knew. I ignored him for the rest of the ride.

On our way back to the hotel in Montreal's historic city center, we had to run another paparazzi gauntlet, then headed to the official victory party at the attached upscale club. We first went to the DJ booth, where a famous electronic dance musician introduced Dante. Ever the triumphant victor, Dante waved and greeted the adoring crowd in several languages.

As we wound our way to the VIP area, Dante pulled me close. "Try to act like an interested girlfriend, Savannah. Don't glare at me. Pretend as though you like me, even if you're repelled."

"It's going to be a challenge," I muttered, and he clamped his arm around me. I wondered why my skin prickled whenever I was close to him. Dante was too insufferable, too flirtatious, and too complicated. And yet, why did my body's pulse, heart, and nerves seem to go haywire whenever he was around?

In the VIP area, I sipped champagne and the beat of the music was infectious and impossible to resist. I loved to dance, and tap had been my specialty in the talent portion of the pageants. I was about to tell Dante a funny story about almost falling off the stage during one such event, but I thought better of it. Instead, he looked so smolderingly sexy that I grinned saucily.

"Dance?"

"Why not?" He smirked.

We set our drinks on a nearby table and moved to the pulsing beat. I was happy to sway and shimmy. At one point, I accidentally lost my balance and teetered on my high stilettos, brushing against Dante's torso. Oops. One champagne too many. The giggle that erupted from me was genuine.

He grabbed me. Held me close. We were both breathing hard.

"You're playing with fire, Savannah mia," he said in a low voice into my ear.

CHAPTER FOURTEEN

DANTE

In the low-lit club, I watched Savannah gyrate in her little dress and studied her with naked lust. She was turning out to be more captivating and sexy by the day, and everything about her, from her hair to her eyes to her legs, was a huge distraction.

A distraction I didn't want, need, or like.

The way she seemed so interested at the burn unit tugged at something inside of me, though. Most women wouldn't want to be dragged into a room filled with burn patients. Long ago, a year after my sister died, I'd brought a lover to a burn unit in Stockholm, and she'd complained and whined for days afterward about how awful and traumatizing it was. I'd never brought another woman after that.

And yet, Savannah had asked as many questions of the patients as I had, and I'd overheard her talking to the administrator about putting him in touch with her father's corporate giving coordinator in the States. Was she trying to impress me with her fake kindness? Something told me no. She seemed a little too innocent, a tad too genuine, for that kind of deception.

But now she was practically crawling all over me, gyrating her hips like a little club girl. Teasing me. Was it on purpose? Or maybe she was taking this role as my girlfriend a little too seriously? I put my hands on her hips and swayed with her, wondering why she seemed to be so adamantly against indulging in a physical relationship while we were being forced into putting on this public charade.

What an enigmatic, puzzling woman. Stubborn too.

She slung her arms over my shoulders and swiveled her hips. Her big green eyes flashed. On one hand, yes, I'd love to enjoy her all night. Her mouth looked pink and plump, and I longed to kiss the hell out of her so that she'd stop looking at me in that challenging manner.

Savannah would probably be a wild animal in bed, what with that flaming hair and the beguiling eyes. But sleeping with her would open up so many complications, the least of which was the fact that she wanted to change my tires.

Still, if presented with the opportunity to make love to a beautiful woman, I never failed to seize it. Sure, I always made it clear to women that I wasn't interested in anything serious, but with Savannah, that was a given. She was acting. And so was I. And it seemed as though she barely liked me to begin with, so why not indulge in a night of hot sex and be done with it?

Maybe we could eventually clear the air and be friends. I hadn't been joking back in the limo.

I pulled her close and grabbed a fistful of her long hair.

"Do you see that group of men standing on the other side of the VIP area, beyond the velvet rope?" I asked into her ear, slowly spinning her by the hips so she could see them over my shoulder.

With a breathy noise against my earlobe—a sound that made my dick jump to attention—she said yes.

"Those are the paparazzi. They're waiting for us to kiss. They want the money shot."

"Ah. I see. What are we going to do about that?" If only she knew how her accent drove me crazy.

"I'm going to kiss you. I simply wanted to tell you so you don't act surprised and don't look like a lamb in the headlights." I worked my fingers deeper into her thick hair and fantasized about pulling it while in bed.

"A deer."

"What?" I asked, still distracted by her hair and drowning in my dirty thoughts.

"The phrase is 'deer in the headlights.'" Any annoyance I'd felt at being corrected dissolved with the sound of her soft laughter.

"Okay. Deer. Good to know. Anyway. I'm going to kiss you very, very slowly. And then I'm going to kiss you a little harder, and explore your bottom lip with my tongue. I might bite you gently. Will that be okay?"

She stiffened. "Yes. That all sounds . . . okay." Her voice was barely audible.

"Savannah, act as though this kiss is the most important thing in the world. Act like you need this kiss to survive."

She inhaled sharply. She tilted her head up so her lips rested on my neck. Her fingers, warm to the touch, clasped the back of my head. I could practically feel the testosterone surging through me.

"Are you ready for the kiss, cara?"

She lifted her head to look at me. Her glossy pink lips parted and I cupped her jaw. She was so, so beautiful. Gone was the snarky attitude, and in its place was a willing, searching desire in her eyes. I pressed a butterfly-soft kiss against her lips, trying to control my true urge, which was to capture her mouth in a hard, hot assault.

The instant our lips met was electric, and I realized that I'd never indulged in such a pure, emotional kiss with any woman. The feeling both confused and excited me, and while my mind told me to stop and assess the situation with the cold calculation I used on the track, my body urged me to keep on kissing her.

With an aching softness, she returned my kiss. She crushed her breasts against my chest and I inhaled her sugary scent. I wanted to lick her everywhere.

I kissed her harder at the thought, and my mouth turned hungry. I explored her with my tongue and nipped at her bottom lip, like I'd promised. Fuck, she tasted so sweet, and I wanted much more than a kiss. This intensity between us was unexpected and disarming, and my confused and needy feelings were reflected in her green irises.

"Oh, wow," she breathed.

I stroked her soft cheeks with my thumbs and continued to study her face. I still hadn't fully caught my breath. "'Oh, wow,' what?"

The caveman in me wanted to drag her back to my hotel room and fuck her. But my mind cautioned against it, and suggested I get us another drink, put distance between my raging erection and her enticing body.

"Maybe we should have another kiss in case they didn't get the photo at the right angle," she whispered. My heart surged like it did when I was trying to pass a competitor on the track. What was this woman doing to me?

"*Perfetto.* I think that's a good idea."

◊

SAVANNAH

When he dipped his head again so his lips could meet mine, I couldn't help but moan. Despite being a virgin, I'd kissed more than a few guys. But never, ever had any kiss been like this. Our kiss the other day at the track, in front of the cameras, had been playful and silly. The kiss at the pool was flirty and fun, with a sensual tinge.

But this kiss?

He was positively *killing* me with this one. It was all slow and seductive, with little bites and languid swipes of his tongue. It was deep and made my insides coil in a desperate way.

Part of me couldn't believe that I wanted more physical contact with this maddening Italian. Another part simply didn't care about anything but seeing how far I'd allow myself to go with him. All I wanted was to keep kissing him, to drift away on the feel of his mouth. I imagined kissing Dante was similar to how I'd feel being pulled out to sea by a riptide: overwhelmed, helpless, and resigned to being swept away into an abyss.

For the first time in my life I *desired* a man. *Needed* one. Waves of yearning crashed over my body and heat pooled between my legs. My torso was glued to his, and I moved my hips to match. That was when I felt his hard length pressed against my stomach, and with that, I slipped all of my fingers into his soft hair, pulling him closer.

God, he felt insanely good. Was this what I'd been missing?

I felt his hands travel down my back and cup my butt, and when he hauled me toward him and ground my pelvis into his erection, I stilled. What was I doing? I was a pit crew member, he was my driver, and there we were in public, making out in the VIP area of a nightclub.

So inappropriate.

A kiss for the paparazzi was one thing; putting on an X-rated show was entirely another. This had to stop. Now. I could only imagine what my mother would say when she watched this.

My eyes snapped open and I pulled away.

"We need to go," I said curtly. All I wanted was to return downstairs to my hotel room, alone, and think about why my body and emotions were so out of control. I was used to keeping myself on a tight leash, and Dante had caused my defenses, my feelings, and my carefully constructed walls to crumble.

He unfurled a lazy, sexy smile. He appraised me with lusty, half-closed eyes, and his Italian accent was more pronounced when he said, "Cara, it's the best idea you've had since we've met. Your hotel room or mine?"

When he grabbed my hand and led me out of the club, my heart thumped with terror. I realized that Dante assumed I wanted to spend the night with him.

0

DANTE

In the elevator, I stood behind Savannah. The small space was crowded with people, so her entire sexy backside was pressed against my front, her sugary scent washing over me. She smelled like macaroons or cake or something. Her body fit against mine perfectly. I didn't even bother trying to conceal my erection, and I caressed the curve of her waist and tried to catch her eye in the reflective metal of the elevator door. I trailed my lips against the scallop of her ear, and yet she didn't react.

I swallowed hard, my mouth moist. I licked my lips. My abdominal muscles clenched and I consciously relaxed them. As I willed tension out of my body, an ache remained.

A throbbing ache in my dick.

Patience was not my strong suit once I was this turned on, and I needed to get Savannah to a bed. Or a wall or a floor. Whatever, wherever. What were all of these people doing on the elevator at this hour? And why wouldn't she meet my gaze? Why wouldn't she smile when I touched my lips to her temple? She fiddled with her small, sparkly purse and kept her head bowed. Finally, the elevator stopped and the door slid open. It was our floor, where the whole team was staying.

Savannah burst out of the elevator, not waiting for me. It was then I realized that maybe she didn't want to spend the night with me. Didn't want what I thought she did. Didn't want what I did. *È impossibile*. Women never rejected me. Maybe she was nervous about going to bed with someone so famous. She couldn't possibly be having second thoughts.

But clearly she was, because she was in front of her door, and not following me to mine. Leaning against a wall, I watched as Savannah fumbled in her purse.

"I don't know where the key . . . wait. Finally," she muttered.

"Savannah."

She looked up. There was such a frightened expression on her beautiful face. I bit my lip. As hard as I was, as much as I wanted her, a little voice inside warned me to back off. At least for tonight.

Patience would be rewarded. Right?

I reached out and swept a lock of hair off her forehead and

trailed a finger down her soft cheek. My heart jackhammering, words tumbled out of my mouth. I barely recognized myself.

"Savannah mia, I'm all of a sudden so tired. That sometimes happens to me right after races. I'm sorry, I'm afraid I won't be—"

"That's actually fine," she interrupted. "I completely understand. I'm exhausted too. You had a great race today. You must be ready to collapse. Sweet dreams!"

A sharp pain sliced through my chest when I realized she was relieved. I pressed my lips together firmly. Most women went out of their way to spend time with me. And Savannah seemed so eager and willing when I was kissing her. We had shared a kiss that was so amazing that it was practically transcendent. Then she'd suggested we leave. What had changed in the span of minutes?

"Have a good night, Savannah." I dipped my head and planted a chaste kiss on her mouth. Although need and lust raged in my veins, I broke away. I studied her for a few seconds, watching her slowly trace her bottom lip with a delicate finger, as if I had bruised her with tenderness.

"'Night." Her voice was wobbly.

It was only after the lock on her door snicked that another emotion surged through me: confusion.

A woman had never treated me like this, and moreover, my interest in Savannah was even greater now than it had been when I'd met her, if the pounding of my heart was any indication.

CHAPTER FIFTEEN

SAVANNAH

It was like I was back at home polishing the silver before a family dinner, only I was in a garage in Spain, and instead of silverware, I was polishing wrenches and lug nuts and tools. It had been a long day of practice at the Valencia track ahead of the race on Sunday, and the crew was wrapping up.

It seemed that instead of allowing me to do some of the other, routine tasks with the team—engine changes, gearbox rebuilds, brake overhauls—they'd put me on cleaning duty. As I scrubbed and spit-shined a long wrench, I wondered why I'd been assigned to clean the last two days. Was it because I was the only woman, or was I somehow being punished for my status as Dante's "girlfriend"?

It was difficult to believe that it had only been five days since the Montreal race. Five days since we'd gone public with our relationship. Five days since that kiss.

Since then, we'd barely said a word to each other. We hadn't sat near each other on the chartered jet from Canada to Spain, and once we'd checked into the hotel, we'd gone our separate ways. He had endless sponsor obligations and pre-race physical therapy (according to the schedule), and I had team meetings with the rest of the crew. Probably it was for the best that we were apart, because I didn't want to be tempted by another kiss of his.

I'd been distracted enough as it was, unable to stop thinking about how it felt when his lips had touched mine. The moment played on repeat every time I closed my eyes.

Setting the wrench next to a line of other gleaming steel tools, I inspected my fingers. My hands had become rough from all the chemicals and rubbing. Sure, it was grunt work, mindless, but I loved it. And sure, I was starting at the bottom, but so what? Every day was a new learning experience, and that was why I was here. Hopefully I wouldn't be cleaning the entire season, though, and with any luck, I'd rotate into a tire-changing role in the pits.

"Savvy, hey, come help us with this fuel hose," Giorgio called out. "We need an extra hand."

I set down the wrench and took my place beside two pit crew members. Peering at the snakelike hose wrapped in silver foil, I leaned forward.

"What's up?"

One of the other guys held up a rubber seal. "We're changing this. Savvy, you've got small fingers. Slip this over—"

"Stop. Absolutely not. She's not to touch the fuel hose."

The three of us looked up. It was Dante. What was he doing here? He was supposed to be in a meeting with corporate sponsors right about now. I caught his eye and he looked incensed.

I took the seal in my hand and ignored him. "What do you need me to do, Giorgio?"

"Snugly fit it on the end of that hose—yes, like that. Then tighten that little screw," he said.

"Easy peasy." When finished, I straightened my posture and saw that Dante was still there, hands on his hips. His dark eyes had a wild, flashing expression, something between furious and fearful.

"Savannah, I must speak with you so I can clarify my request. In the office," he growled, stalking off.

"I'll be there as soon as I'm done," I said, as respectfully as I could manage.

The other crew members looked at me helplessly and shrugged. By now, everyone knew we were "dating," and had started to make little snide remarks. God, this was embarrassing. Like being the teacher's pet and getting detention. Only the teacher was a sinfully sexy world-famous athlete, one that I'd been dreaming about ever since that scorching kiss in Montreal.

"Guess you'd better go see what your boyfriend wants," one of the men said with a snicker.

The *last* thing I wanted was for the guys on the team to think I was getting favorable treatment because I was with Dante. Maybe this whole charade wouldn't get me any closer to working on the car during the race after all.

With a heavy feeling in my chest, I put the finishing touches on the last few tools I had to clean, and then stomped out of the garage.

0

DANTE

I sank into the office chair, uncapped a black Sharpie marker, and while waiting for Savannah, tried to concentrate on signing a stack of race programs for our VIP fans. My signature came out as an angry slash, reflecting my mood.

It drove me crazy how she questioned me at every turn. If I'd made the same request of another pit crew member, they'd have complied without a peep. But she felt entitled, it seemed. This fake relationship was setting all the wrong examples for my crew. I made a mental note to talk to Bronson about it, about how this was impacting the team.

The door was flung open and I looked up.

There she was in the doorway, all flaming red hair and hard green eyes. This office, attached to the garage, was a small space. Although Savannah was a petite woman, her attitude seemed to fill the room, which both irked and excited me.

"Shut the door, please."

She did, but still stood defiantly in place. "I don't appreciate being called out in front of the rest of the team. Can you at least try to treat me fairly?"

I capped the pen and placed it atop the signed stack of programs. "I do not want you touching the fuel lines."

"Why?" She tossed her ponytail and snorted in that way that made her look like an adorable pony.

Her insouciant tone made me flare with anger. First she didn't want to sleep with me, now she was disobeying my orders in my own garage. I stood up and leaned forward, resting my hands on the desk. "No explanation needed. And I'm the driver, so it's my order."

She took two steps to the desk and leaned toward me, her hands inches from mine. "No, I think it's Jack's order, since he's the chief engineer who hands out the assignments."

"Why are you in the garage at all right now? Why aren't you back in your hotel room, resting up for tomorrow's practice?"

She laughed. She actually laughed at me. The nerve of her. She stepped back and undid her ponytail.

"You are so adorable when you're angry, you know that, Dante?"

"Are you poking fun?" I could actually feel my blood heat up as it coursed through my veins. Most women, hell, most *people* wouldn't treat me like this. How was I going to survive months of this attitude? And why couldn't I stop looking at her lips and remembering our kiss in Montreal? That had been a rotten idea. Thank God I hadn't slept with her.

I still wanted to sleep with her.

"Of course I'm poking fun, silly. It's six o'clock. I'm twenty-four, not ninety, so I don't need to go to bed yet. I'm also part of this team and I need to help. Suck it up, buttercup. I'm trying to prove myself so I can actually work a race. Something you promised to help me with. Remember, we're a team?"

Involuntarily, my hands balled into fists. "As long as we're together, I want you to do as little work around fuel lines as possible. You've proven yourself a good tire changer during practice, and I've recommended that Jack put you in the pits for an upcoming race. Otherwise, all I want you doing is cleaning."

Her mouth dropped open. "It was you who told Jack to make me clean and polish the tools! Unreal."

I shrugged and couldn't help but smile. "I don't have any say about your presence on the team, and I can't control our fake relationship, but I can pull some strings to make sure you're safe on the track."

Narrowing her eyes, she came around to my side of the desk. We faced each other and the air positively crackled with tension. "You don't get it, do you? I want to be a full member of this team. I don't want to be window dressing. I want to learn while I'm here. It's the least that I can do while pretending to be your, your . . ."

It was as if the word was stuck in her throat.

"My lover?" Maybe I could distract her with my seductive powers for the rest of the season and she'd follow my commands on the track and in the garage. I didn't normally screw women in the couple of days leading up to a race, but for her, I might consider deviating from that particular superstition.

She rolled her eyes. "Stop it."

"You seemed to entertain the idea in Montreal. Why should we deny each other's needs? I want to make my girlfriend happy." I reached for her hair—God, her red mane drove me crazy, especially when it was swept up in a ponytail, like it was right now—and she backed away.

"You don't get it because you're a Neanderthal. I'm a woman, and I have goals. Someday I'm going to run my father's company, and someday I'm going to sponsor my own race team. An all-female team." She jabbed at the air with her index finger and glared. "And you know what? I don't want your help. Don't put in a word with Jack. Don't mention me at all. I want to earn my spot, even if it means polishing wrenches and doing inventory all season."

"You are so naive, cara."

"You are so anti-woman."

I scowled as a little pang of hurt thumped in my chest. "I am not. I love women."

"When they're objects, not when they're equals."

"That's simply not true. My sister was my equal and she was

in the pits . . ." I turned away. Christ. I hadn't meant to mention Gabriella, but it had slipped out.

"She was?" Savannah's voice turned soft.

"Yes."

"Why don't you want other women on the track if your sister was there? I don't get it."

I whirled and grabbed her upper arm. "My sister was working for my first racing team and changing a fuel hose when it ignited. She was severely burned and died three days later in hospital."

Savannah gasped and tried to struggle out of my grip, but I wouldn't let her. No, this difficult little wildcat was going to *listen*. "So, cara mia," I spat, "that's why I don't want you in the pits, and I especially don't want you near fuel hoses or fuel. I don't want a repeat of my sister's death. With any woman. But especially not you."

With that, I pulled her close and did exactly what I wanted, which was to crush my mouth onto hers. I kissed her, hard.

"Will this make you listen to me? Will it?" I gave her another punishing kiss, and noted with satisfaction that she kissed me back with ferocity, even slipping her hot tongue into my mouth. My dick responded accordingly. When we broke apart, she glared at me.

"Going to your hotel room?" I raised an eyebrow.

"Yes, so I can get some rest, like you suggested."

"Want company?" I called out, teasing.

She spun, her red hair whipping over her dark coveralls. With a grin, she extended the middle finger of her right hand. It was a genuine, playful smile. Instead of making me angry, I laughed harder than I had in weeks.

CHAPTER SIXTEEN

SAVANNAH

Race day in Valencia was just as exciting as it had been in Monte Carlo and Montreal—filled with crowds and parties and an unmistakable electric current in the air. For many spectators, races were an event, a once-in-a-lifetime weekend, and some of that thrill had rubbed off on me.

I'd gotten to the garage an hour early, at seven in the morning, to see if anyone needed an extra hand. Jack had told me I'd be observing on this race, as well—but working with the representative of the tire company, so we could decide which tires we'd need, since rain was in the forecast.

I stopped in the team canteen for an espresso. Being around all these Italians had made me fall in love with the high-octane coffee. As I stood near the Nespresso maker, a woman approached.

"Are you Savannah?" she asked in heavily accented English.

I turned to look into dark, deep-set eyes. She was smaller than I was—slim, with short silver-and-black hair. Her eyes were oddly familiar. She had to be at least sixty, but was gorgeous and elegant in a European way. She wore black pants, a black shirt, and a Team Eagle windbreaker.

"I am."

She put her hand on her chest. "It's so good to finally meet you. I knew I'd have to track you down because my son wasn't going to make the introduction."

"Your son? Oh!" This was Dante's mother?

"I'm Sofia Annunziata. I've heard so much about you. I got in early this morning on the first flight, otherwise I would have arranged for all of us to have dinner last night."

I opened and closed my mouth, unsure of what to say. It was one thing to pretend to be in a relationship with Dante for the press. It was another thing to lie to his mother. Surely she'd be able to see through this charade. My mom certainly would, if she were here.

"Let's sit and talk for a moment. If you have time, of course." She gestured to a table and chairs. Suddenly the canteen seemed incredibly bright, with its beaming fluorescent lights.

"I have a few minutes. I got here early because I'm trying to learn as much as possible. Right now the team engineer has me observing during races and changing tires during practice. I hope to be in the pits for a race in the future, though." I plunked down in the seat, realizing I was rambling. "But enough about me. Did you have a nice flight?"

She sat across from me and folded her hands in her lap. "I live in Rome now. Dante and his sister grew up outside of the city, in a small town on the Mediterranean coast. He bought me a home in Rome some years back because my sisters live there."

"How wonderful. Is your husband here too?" I looked around the empty cafeteria.

A sour expression crossed her face. "No. We aren't exactly together, and we travel separately."

I sensed there was a story about Dante's parents but didn't want to pry. "Do you love Rome?".

Her face brightened. "So much. It's the best city in the world. You'll have to come visit sometime. I'd love to show you around. I wanted to tell you, Savannah," she said, leaning in, "how impressed I am with you. I've been reading newspaper articles about you, and you seem like such a smart, ambitious woman. I'm so happy my son has finally decided to settle down with someone who shares his interests."

I bit the inside of my cheek. Deception didn't come easy to me, and Mrs. Annunziata seemed like a genuinely kind person. "He's, ah, one of a kind, Dante."

Was that the best I could do? I was supposed to be falling in love with him and all I could muster was 'He's one of a kind'?

His mother laughed. "My son can be quite hardheaded. I'm actually surprised that he's so supportive of your career, given what happened to his sister. That tragedy really altered his worldview."

"Yes, hardheaded is a good description for him . . ." My voice trailed off. Though I would admit that in the last couple of days, since he'd shared that detail about his sister, I'd tried to be a bit more charitable toward his fears about me in the pits.

"Don't pay any attention to that side of him. Dante admires people who want to succeed. I'm sure that's what he sees in you, and that's what he loves in you. It takes—how do you say it in English? Stomach? *Stomaco*, in Italian—a strong stomach, to do what you're doing."

"Guts," I offered.

"Yes, that's it. Guts. I'm sure Dante appreciates that quality in you."

I doubted whether Dante loved anything about me, except for my boobs in low-cut dresses, but I wasn't about to argue.

"Maybe *guts* isn't the right word. Maybe I'm stubborn too. Or delusional."

"No. You're not. We need young women like you in the sport. And don't let anyone, including my son, tell you otherwise. And speak of the devil."

Mrs. Annunziata stood up, and I twisted in my seat to see Dante and Jack walking toward us.

Jack was wearing a big smile and bounded over. "Buongiorno, Mamma," he shouted and wrapped his long arms around her.

"There's my second son," she said.

I climbed to my feet and met Dante's eyes. I expected him to be annoyed, for some reason, but instead he looked amused.

"Hey," I said softly.

"Having coffee with my mom?" He nudged me with his shoulder.

"Mm-hmm."

Jack and Mrs. Annunziata broke apart, and Dante leaned in to kiss her on the cheek. "Mamma, ciao." They launched into rapid-fire Italian.

Jack approached me. "I was looking for you because I have some news. You know Rolf?"

I nodded. Rolf was a young German tire changer on Dante's team.

"Well, he went out for a run early this morning and slipped on a patch of loose dirt. Sprained his wrist when he fell. Won't be able to change tires during the race. I'd like to put you in. If you think you're ready. I think you're ready, but I wanted to know how you're feeling."

I straightened my posture. "I was born ready."

◊

During a Formula World pit stop, it isn't every second that counts. It's every tenth of a second.

"One more lap," Jack warned in our headsets. Fourteen of us pit crew members went to our spots. I was assigned to the left front wheel, meaning the one closest to Dante. Three of us were assigned there—one man to my left and one to my right. I held the wheel gun in my hands and rested on my knees, legs spread to give me stability. The sound of the twenty cars on the track reverberated through the air like the buzz of a million angry bees.

"Remember, Savvy, lock your air wrench onto the wheel's center lock nut a fraction of a second before the car stops moving. You've done it during practice dozens of times. You've got this." Jack's voice soothed my nerves.

With a controlled motion, Dante's car veered into view.

In a flash, the car entered the pit. As I'd learned, I attached the gun to the wheel as it approached, and by the time it rolled to a stop a foot later, the nut was loose. The engine's low rumble vibrated through my body.

The man next to me whisked the tire away, and the man to my right—Giorgio—jammed a fresh tire in its spot. I pressed the air wrench to the nut and fixed it into place.

No sooner had I released the gun and leaned back from the car than Dante sped off in a whir of RPMs.

"Two point nine seconds," Jack said in our headsets. "Amazing work, team."

I sprang to my feet, finally able to exhale. Giorgio lifted his right hand and I slapped him a high five.

Never in my life had I done anything as exciting as in those 2.9 seconds.

◊

That night, instead of going to a nightclub with Dante, I went to a team dinner Bronson had organized. It was held in a bland banquet hall at our hotel, the atmosphere not as lavish as in Monaco or as hip as the nightclub in Montreal.

This was more like a big, raucous family meal, and I couldn't help but laugh with happiness when I walked in.

Dante was seated at the head of one long table. He'd come in first, again—his third race in a row. Between that and his mother's presence, he seemed more relaxed than I'd ever seen him.

Max, however, looked like a guilty Labrador puppy, sitting at the head of his own table, surrounded by his pit crew. He hadn't finished the race because he'd crashed on the final lap while trying to overtake another car. He'd ignored the directions of his engineer, which was a big no-no.

Jack privately told me it had been a boneheaded move—Max

had been in fifth place but lost it all in an attempt to get to fourth. Drivers rarely went against their engineer's recommendations, and it was all anyone was talking about on motorsports blogs in the hours after the race.

He kept pushing his blond hair off his forehead, and I noticed that he was drinking more champagne than usual. Bronson was sitting next to him, looking less than pleased. Oh dear. I'd heard rumors that Max and Bronson didn't see eye to eye on some things, but I tried not to listen to the gossip. I had enough of my own issues to deal with.

Steering clear of that drama, I took a seat at Dante's table, far from where he was sitting—or tried to. His mother spotted me and extended her hand.

"Savannah," she said, her voice rising above the mostly male chatter. "I saved you a seat up here."

She patted a chair next to her and smiled warmly. How could I refuse? At least it wasn't immediately next to Dante. I walked toward her, and she leaned in for a double cheek kiss.

"*Che bella*," she said to me, patting my hair. I'd washed and blow-dried it straight tonight, and it cascaded down my shoulders. I'd worn a simple black polo dress and white sneakers, hoping to look sporty and, well, not too sexy.

"Thanks," I replied, and caught Dante's eye. He was staring at me, which made me uncomfortable. I couldn't read his expression, and I wondered how he did that—his face animated and warm one moment, then an impenetrable mask the next.

I took my seat and tried to make small talk with Mrs. Annunziata. "Did you enjoy the race?" I asked her.

"It's always a little bit, how do you say, *nerve-wracking* to see my son drive. My heart's in my throat the entire time. As it must be for you."

"Yes," I murmured. And that's when it hit me. I'd been so worried about my own performance during the race that I hadn't yet thought about Dante's safety. I figured he was the driver, the professional, and he had that part under control. He appeared to never show fear.

But what if he was hurt out there? The very thought left me with an unsettled, uneasy knot in my stomach. I went to quell it with a sip of champagne, but over at Max's table, Bronson stood up and tapped his knife against his wine glass.

The room quieted.

"We wanted to thank you all for your hard work today. Dante and Jack and their crew did an incredible job," Bronson said. "I'd also like to single out Savannah, who worked her first pit stop. She was excellent, and the entire team was flawless."

He held up his glass of wine in my direction, and everyone erupted into claps and cheers. Dante's mom rubbed my back, and part of me felt like crawling under the table. Instead, I beamed at everyone.

In my peripheral vision, I saw Dante rise from his seat, come around the table, and lean in my direction. My eyes widened when he planted a big, dramatic kiss on my cheek. His spicy after-shave smelled so delicious, and I had to admit, the thought of kissing his mouth—later, in private—came to mind.

"She was amazing, wasn't she?" he called out, while running his hand down my hair. "She makes me look good."

Did he just pay me a genuine compliment in front of the entire team in an odd, backhanded way? I was so shocked that it barely registered when Bronson started talking about Max and his awful final lap. Everyone knew Max had ignored his team engineer, and no one was thrilled about this development.

"Now, there's no room for ego on this team." Bronson wagged his finger. "I need you all to remember that."

Yeah, right. It was all ego, according to what I'd seen over the past several weeks. And the biggest ego of all was in the man who kept winning races.

CHAPTER SEVENTEEN

SAVANNAH

Over the next several races across Europe, Dante and I fell into a seductive pattern. Our massive traveling race team would land in a city, and we'd scramble to set up and get everything ready for race day. He'd ignore me for most of the week during qualifying and practice, although each of us would check each other out during our various meetings and garage sessions. Occasionally we'd trade verbal jabs, much to the delight of the guys.

He'd call me a "debutante" or a "beauty pageant girl." I'd make a crack about how he micromanaged the team due to his need to be in control at all times. The barbs and sparring were slightly annoying, although neither of us took it to a mean or hurtful level, and I appreciated that.

Sometimes I'd catch him scowling at me; other times, he'd look at me with a sinfully smoldering stare and a wink. Both expressions left me confused and unmoored, and I tried my hardest to ignore him.

I was getting more assignments, though, and lately had been shadowing the computer techs when the drivers weren't on track. Dante seemed comfortable when I was behind a computer, and since I enjoyed the analytic part of racing, we'd come to an uneasy truce.

Then on Sundays, I sometimes rotated into the pits to change tires. Dante was having a phenomenal season. He usually came in first or at least placed on the podium.

In the hours after the race, we often had team commitments together. On our way to swanky parties and multimillion-dollar charity events and exclusive clubs, we'd chat amiably in the limousine while holding hands, and visit whatever burn unit was in that city. Each public appearance was carefully scripted and scheduled almost down to the second, but I couldn't help but question his motives for the hand-holding. He could've kept his hand on the small of my back, like he sometimes did. But more often, he'd reach for my fingers and clasp them tight.

The best moments came at dinnertime, when we were often on display for the paparazzi—but out of earshot, so we could talk about whatever we wanted. That's when we both loosened up and allowed ourselves to be kind and not snarky.

I loved how we laughed easily and told each other stories about our childhoods, or recounted the interesting moments of that week's race. I'd pump him for stories about past teams and ask questions about specs and tires and engines because his knowledge was vast.

Usually after a glass of wine, our legs would intertwine under the table, and later we'd hit a nightclub or party for the benefit of the press.

It was always during a post-race celebration when things got out of control. I'd taken to wearing sexier outfits each week: tinier skirts, higher heels. Only clear lip gloss, though, because I soon realized it was too much of a pain to keep applying color to my lips after Dante devoured them.

Yes, we kissed. A lot. Maybe too much, if the way my entire body felt like it was absorbing the heat of the summer sun was any indication.

"The photographers are expecting this," he said in Austria, assaulting my senses with an urgent kiss. It was as if his lips didn't leave mine all night. The flashbulbs of the cameras faded into the background, as if they were tired of photographing us.

"Dance closer to me," I whispered at a post-race party near Silverstone in the UK. "The paparazzi are ravenous tonight." He responded by twirling me around so my back pressed against his front, and raking his hands over my hips and stomach as we danced. Okay, and his hands found my breasts too. And maybe my inner thighs. Our bodies fused together and we swayed to the music lasciviously. It wasn't a dirty dance; it was downright filthy.

After the race in Hungary, he pressed me up against a wall and we kissed for what seemed like hours, and even dry humped like teenagers on a sofa in a private VIP area. The press was having a field day with this, with headlines such as "GET A ROOM."

It was as if we were playing out our erotic fantasies in public, while unable to admit what we really wanted from each other in private. We were driving each other mad with need.

It was stupid. And hot. Okay, more hot than stupid.

I was confused as to why Dante hadn't asked me to spend the night with him since Montreal. It wasn't as if we didn't have his private, luxury hotel suite at our disposal in every city we visited. But pride wouldn't allow me to throw myself at him and beg for sex. I was a virgin, and I wasn't sure if I should, or *could*, successfully pull that off.

Some boundaries had to be maintained.

I wondered if he was putting on this show for the cameras. But his labored breathing, his erections, the wild, dazed look in his eyes whenever we paused after all that kissing told me one thing. He was at least a little attracted to me. I guessed that was how guys like him were, though—they were drawn to whomever was in front of them at the moment.

But at the end of each night, he'd walk me to my hotel room and kiss me chastely as if we were on a date in post-war, 1950s America. That iron control he used to win on the track was proving to be maddening on a physical level. Or maybe he had his own boundaries.

Of course, our public kisses were all over the tabloids, which made it difficult to deny the relationship to my parents and Kayla. I'd taken to texting only, and finally told them that yes, Dante and I were "hanging out" but nothing more. Mom seemed less than pleased, Dad didn't want to discuss it—I think he disliked the idea of seeing his daughter lust so publicly after a man—and Kayla warned that I should carry a stash of condoms with me at all times.

"But we're not having sex," I protested in one text.

"Not yet, but you will soon," she predicted. "He'd be your first. And way better than that dude you hung out with senior year of college."

I groaned aloud as I read her text, thinking of Austin, a blond, blue-eyed frat boy who I'd briefly dated and made out with several years ago. He'd been big and burly, and my mother had loved him because he was the son of one of Atlanta's richest businessmen. When he'd pressured me for sex, I dumped his ass.

I replied with a barf emoji. Yeah, Dante didn't seem like the type to pressure. Probably because he didn't need to—women likely ripped off their panties the second he kissed them.

Lord knows I'd thought about doing exactly that.

By the time the Belgium race came around, I was strung tight with desire, impatient for his kisses, and desperate for something more. He had won the race and was still leading his competitors in the drivers' championship points, and I anticipated he would be in a stellar mood that evening.

Frankly, I was sick of playing the good girl. Sick of trying to squash my desires.

"I love that little white dress on you," he whispered in my ear as we walked into the club. His fingers possessively caressed my back and traveled lower. As we passed through a dark corridor, his hand located my butt and squeezed.

"I also love this," he said with a groan.

"Pervert," I replied playfully.

A thought dawned on me as I stared at him. Dante seemed like the perfect candidate for my first lover. I'd steeled myself against thinking I could have a *real* relationship with him, of course. He'd made it clear again and again during conversations that he wasn't the relationship type. And it wasn't what I wanted either. I had a career in motorsports ahead of me, and he was retiring. Also, he was arrogant and I wasn't really his type.

Still. This was perfect.

He was handsome, he was funny, he was sexy as sin. True, he could be maddening, like when he droned on about how it was dangerous for a woman to work in this sport. But I'd come to ignore his Italian bluster, like his mother had suggested.

What would be wrong with asking him outright if he'd make love to me? As my high, strappy sandals clicked on the marble floor of the club in Brussels, I turned this thought over in my mind. Losing my virginity to him would be fun *and* practical. Better than doing it with some former frat boy turned corporate lawyer back home in Georgia. The thought of that made me wince.

Once in the club, Dante kissed my neck and murmured something about my scent.

"Is this the perfume I bought you in London? It smells incredible."

Tonight he'd been particularly attentive, complimenting me and studying my every move. I felt comfortable with him and wanted an adventure. He was in top health and had told me in detail about how the doctors checked him weekly for everything from the common cold to STDs to high cholesterol. Why *not* choose him?

A bouncer ushered us into a VIP area—we were always ensconced alone or with a handful of other drivers or rich sponsors—and Dante slipped his arm around my waist.

"What have you got planned for the upcoming break?" he asked in an almost bored tone. I briefly wondered if I'd read him all wrong, if his attentiveness was all an act.

But then I saw his gaze soften as he stared at me, and the question vanished.

"I'm flying to Rome and I'm going to backpack around for a

week. I've always wanted to see the city. Maybe I'll have lunch with your mother. She gave me her number," I teased.

The team was scheduled for two weeks off between races, before Dante's home race in Italy. The first week was free for whatever we wanted, while the second was spent at the team's headquarters in northern Italy. For the free week, most team members went home to their families in Europe. My parents and grandma were somewhere on a Caribbean cruise—the last I had heard, Aruba—and I didn't feel like going back to the States for such a short time to visit my brother, who would certainly be busy with the family business.

A sour look spread onto Dante's face. "With who?"

"With myself. I'm staying in youth hostels. Alone."

"Youth hostels?" The way he said it indicated that he wasn't entirely familiar with the concept, and that he found the idea distasteful. I laughed. I thought I was sheltered because of my wealthy upbringing.

"Yeah, youth hostels. You know. Young travelers staying in dorms, hanging out, seeing the sights, going to clubs."

He lifted his hands in a confused gesture. "Why would you do that? Your family has money. The team pays you well. You could stay at a nice hotel."

I shrugged. "I want the adventure. Hang out with people my own age. Have fun, make new friends."

I entertained a brief fantasy of asking him along, but quickly banished the thought. He was a driver, which meant security, paparazzi, and complications—all things I was looking forward to leaving behind. But my jaw suddenly clenched at the thought of being away from him for an entire week.

CHAPTER EIGHTEEN

DANTE

I grumbled something in Italian and downed my drink. The idea of Savannah traipsing around my country alone didn't sit well. Surely she had plenty of friends back in the United States, women with money who could meet her in Rome. It wasn't that I was against women traveling by themselves; I just didn't think it was right for Savannah, since she was such a high-profile member of Team Eagle and had been in the press nonstop in recent days.

I pondered whether to invite her to my villa on the Amalfi Coast for a few days. It was where I always stayed before my home race. Where my sister and I had our last vacation together.

But that would be a terrible idea. For one, I needed to concentrate on the upcoming race and the rest of the season. It was halfway over, and I was so close to the championship that I could smell it. Spending a week with Savannah could easily throw me off balance. She'd already been doing a good enough job of that as the team had been traveling across Europe.

Still, I wanted her. Needed to see how turned on she could get, how much I could tempt her before she gave in and begged me to be inside her.

I'd never wanted another woman the way I wanted Savannah Jenkins. There. I admitted it, but only to myself, and only occasionally. The idea that I wouldn't see her for a week troubled me, and I pulled her close, inhaling the scent of her hair.

"Dante, I wanted to talk to you. Alone," she whispered in my ear.

Immediately, I turned to a bouncer and asked if there was a private area. The man led us to a small enclave with red walls, decorated with gold baroque accent pieces, and furnished with a wide gold chaise. It looked like something out of a vampire movie. He shut the door and she sat on the chaise, her ivory-colored dress fluttering high up her thighs. She patted the spot next to her and flashed me a come-hither look. "Dante, I—"

I locked the door, checking it to make sure it was secure. "Shh. You look so beautiful that I have to kiss you first."

"But there are no paparazzi around," she breathed as I moved toward her, unable to control myself.

"Better."

I kissed her hungrily and she responded by grasping the front of my linen shirt to pull me closer. The weight of my body pushed her back onto the lounger. Within seconds, I was on top of her, hard and heavy. I raked my hand over her breast, down her waist, and under her skirt, finally landing between her legs. My breath hitched because her panties were damp. I swore softly in Italian and she gasped.

"You're wet."

"Yes. That's what I wanted to tell you."

"That you were wet?" I almost gasped with astonishment.

"No, silly. I wanted to tell you that I can't stand this teasing anymore. It's ridiculous. Let's do this. We need a release from all this sexual tension. You were right."

Finally. She was giving herself to me. It was like winning the biggest race of my life.

She pulled my hair as I bit her neck and it thrilled me to hear her breath rasp. I affected her. It hadn't been an act. Her barriers had crumbled.

"You are so fucking gorgeous, Savannah. And tonight, you're mine."

"Yours," she whispered. "You can do whatever you want with me."

I groaned. Exactly what I wanted to hear. I dipped to kiss her again.

She undid the top button of my shirt, then another, and a third, until eventually my shirt was fully open. Slowly she ran her fingers down my chest. My breath caught and my muscles contracted when she traced the ridges of my stomach.

"You're beautiful," she blurted.

Her bottom lip quivered. I kissed down her cleavage, alternating with soft bites on her pale skin. Her skirt rucked up around her hips and one of my hands went back between her legs, to the lacy fabric of her panties. She swallowed, hard.

"Dante, *please*." She arched her back and again my hand found her breast. She pressed herself into my hand so I could capture it fully. The skin of her chest was cool under my warm fingers and I slid the fabric of her dress aside, exposing her breast. I'd never seen anything so beautiful.

"Bellissima."

I trailed my mouth down the sensitive column of her neck and toward her nipple, which had hardened into a stiff peak.

"I need to tell you something."

"What, amore mio?" I was barely listening to her now because my mouth was on her flesh. My tongue circled in a tantalizingly slow motion, until I closed my lips and sucked. Hard. I freed her other breast from the fabric and tormented it with my hand. She whimpered and squirmed, her body begging for more. I raised my head.

"You have put me under your spell, Savannah mia."

Tugging my hair gently, she tilted my head away from her chest and looked me in the eyes.

"Dante . . ." Her voice trailed off when I slipped my fingers down the front of her panties. She looked at me with big eyes and that made me even harder.

I sucked in a breath as I slowly explored her. "God, you are so wet. I never dreamed you'd be this responsive to me."

She gasped as my fingers found her sensitive spot. I teased her by using a light touch, circling her clit, dipping a finger inside her core, then repeating each motion. There would be time for rougher sex later. A flush formed on her cheeks, and I was captivated when her mouth parted, when she closed her eyes, and when she cried out.

"Like that, amore, like that," I whispered in her ear, feeling her tight muscles spasm around my fingers as she climaxed. "Let's get these off now."

With her eyes still closed, she lifted her hips so I could remove her panties. I had to slow down but was so overcome with need that I couldn't and ended up tearing the fragile white lace in the process. I shoved her dress hem higher up her hips, and when I saw what was underneath, I groaned with desire.

She was so fucking perfect. Everywhere.

My hands roamed her bare skin. "So soft. God, your skin is perfect."

Impatient, I stood because I wanted to take off my clothes, but then I had another idea. She looked so gorgeous, so swollen and wet, that I sank to my knees.

"What—?" she cried as I pulled her into a sitting position.

"I must taste you." I scooted her body so that her ass was on the edge of the sofa, bent her knees, and spread her legs. The top of her dress was pulled down, exposing her breasts, and she was still wearing her silver heels. The sight was sinfully erotic.

Lowering my head between her thighs, I was overcome with desire. Her smell, her taste, everything about her made me drunk with lust. I licked and licked, and then looked up at her hard nipples, her parted mouth, her long, messy hair, and knew it was finally time.

0

SAVANNAH

There was something animalistic about the gleam in his eye and the way he ripped my underwear to shreds. But there was also something tender—reverent, even—when he knelt before me.

Now he was down there, shirtless and between my legs, licking me as if I were the most delicious dessert on the planet. Actually, he'd said exactly that, only in Italian.

Delizioso.

And he was making me wetter than I'd ever thought possible. I squirmed and cried out as another unexpected orgasm wave crashed over me. He slid two fingers inside of me and I shattered, covering my face in my hands as I moaned. It was as if he'd cracked me wide open and I was more vulnerable with each passing minute.

"Stop!" I gasped, not knowing what else to say. The sensation he'd caused, the pulsing and throbbing, made me feel hypersensitive. I shivered when he kissed my thigh and flopped back on the chaise.

He stood to unbuckle his belt. I straightened to sitting, in slight disbelief that I could muster even that.

"I don't think I've ever been this hard, *tesoro*."

I stared up at him and a burst of a memory entered my mind, of when I was small and stared into the eyes of a lion at the zoo. I'd been captivated by the potential of danger. But back then, the lion was safely behind a thick glass partition. Tonight, the predator in front of me had given me two orgasms and was ready to pounce again. I kicked off my heels and let them fall haphazardly to the floor. My skin felt hot under his stare.

God, I wanted him. I'd waited for this moment, wanted the right time and the right man. As I stared at his muscular chest and the angles of his face, I was certain of one thing.

This was an excellent decision.

"Are you on the pill?" he asked casually, stripping off his pants and underwear. I shook my head.

Wordlessly, he took a condom out of his wallet, pressed it into my hand and knelt on the chaise. "Are you sure you want to do this?"

"God, yes, Dante." I trailed my fingers down his hard chest, lingering at his belly button. "But . . ."

"But what?"

I studied his face in the dim light, debating whether to tell him. I wanted anything and everything he could teach me, present to me, give me. This was an experience I deserved, with a man that was physical perfection. All I wanted was pleasure. A demanding throb between my legs remained after my last orgasm, and I suspected that once he touched me again, I'd have another. The sensation was so different than when I touched myself.

My eyes traveled down, down, down to his erection, and I gasped.

Was he bigger than a normal guy? I had no idea. He looked huge. Would he hurt me?

"What?" His smile was wide. Of course he'd be proud of his hard-on.

"Nothing." With shaking hands, I fumbled with the condom wrapper and failed to tear it. He gently took it from me and opened it, and I marveled while watching him sheath himself. It was achingly sexy to see him touch himself.

He bent to kiss me and gently pushed my body backward, nudging my legs wide apart.

"I've thought about this for weeks. Since I met you, amore mio," he whispered. "Wait, let's take this off."

He slipped my dress over my head and I was bare to him. Naked and vulnerable. I was glad the private lounge was dimly lit.

"Fuck, you're stunning. Like a goddess. My people would have carved statues of you thousands of years ago. They would have worshipped you. Like I'm about to."

If only he wouldn't comment on my looks, because I was feeling especially vulnerable. I wanted to lose myself in the sensation of him, not think about how I appeared to his eyes. I wrapped my arms and legs around him, drawing him close. Skin against skin. I could have easily stayed like this all night, feeling his body next to mine.

That's when I felt the tip of his erection between my legs and, unable to control myself, shifted my hips so that I took him in.

I gasped, loud, at the sharp sensation.

So did he.

"Savannah, you're so tight. How can you be so wet and tight? Please relax, amore."

He buried his face in my neck and thrust slowly in and out as I clawed at his back. I'd never experienced anything like this. It was a need and a fullness and something sublime. Something that made me ache and, inexplicably, made me feel complete. My hands wound through his dark hair as he moved deeper into me. I couldn't let go of him if I tried. He was sweating, and I was gasping. I didn't care.

"Faster," I begged, not even knowing why I demanded that. It was as if pure instinct was taking over. "Harder."

With a growl into my neck, Dante complied, and I felt utterly consumed when he bit the flesh of my shoulder. My nipples raked against his smooth chest and I was aware of his powerful thighs in between mine, moving and flexing. I hooked my heels into the small of his back, realizing that the higher my legs were, the deeper he'd be.

I wanted him deep.

This was what it was like to be possessed. Fully and wholly owned by a man. It felt *amazing*. So this was what I'd been missing . . .

I moved my hips just so, and he assaulted my mouth with a hard kiss. I broke away because it was too intense. Everything was too much.

"Dante, I'm . . ." I trailed off. Words were impossible to form.

"Yes, amore, I am too. I'm going to come." He cursed in Italian, gripped my hair with a powerful hand, and let out a loud groan. I felt him get momentarily bigger inside of me and he shuddered violently.

Then he stilled, and I did the only thing that seemed right after losing one's virginity: I clasped him close and stroked his hair and back tenderly, pressing my lips into his cheek.

CHAPTER NINETEEN

DANTE

Savannah's mouth was turned up at the corners in a sly little grin. Yes, that had been excellent. She'd been stunningly beautiful when she'd orgasmed, and I couldn't get her face or her little breathy gasps out of my mind. At first I'd thought my dick was splitting her in two, and I was worried I'd hurt her. Then how she begged . . . *Christ*. The sexiest time I'd had in years.

We'd surely continue back at the hotel. I threw on my shirt, then reached out to stroke her hair.

She laughed out loud while wriggling back into her dress. "I guess I chose well for my first time, huh?"

I tilted my head, confused. "So, I'm sorry, I don't understand. Wait. You . . . ?"

The joyful look on her face vanished, replaced by a dazed, horrified stare. Confusion flooded my mind. Could it be?

"You were a . . ." I couldn't push the word out.

"A virgin? Yeah. I tried to tell you, but you started to touch me and I lost all thought and, well, crap." She hung her head. "Sorry."

My gaze dropped to the sofa. The gold fabric was stain-free. "You didn't bleed."

She blinked slowly three times. "Most women don't during their first time."

I swore in Italian. "Oh. Uh, did I hurt you? Are you okay? How do you feel?"

"Physically hurt? Not really. Maybe for a second it pinched a little. Emotionally? I'm a little embarrassed. I kind of lost control. Maybe it was the champagne. But it was good, right?"

I watched her bend and pick her torn underwear off the floor and stuff the scraps into her purse. I'd torn the panties of a virgin. Dear God. This was beyond comprehension. What was I, a wild animal?

"Your silence says everything," she added in a bitter voice.

"Why are you even asking that? You shouldn't be embarrassed. My God. I'm the one to blame for taking your virginity in a club, for God's sake. How vulgar." I swore again in Italian and paced the little room. Of course she was a virgin. Looking back, there were signs. Like how skittish she seemed when I'd first touched her, how she'd avoided any talk of past boyfriends, how she was evasive when I joked about sex.

How she was deliciously, impossibly *tight*.

I whirled to look at her and blinked. "Why didn't you tell me before tonight?"

She snorted. "It's not something that comes up in casual dinner conversation. Oh, great race today, Dante. How about that rain on the track? Oh, by the way, I've never been fucked."

"You don't need to be crass." A little twinge of offense sparked in my heart. Is that what she'd thought of our time together? A fuck?

"It isn't like it's a big deal."

I scowled. "It *is* a big deal, Savannah."

"So you wouldn't have been with me had you known I was a virgin?" she asked, her voice frosty. She rose to standing, pulled her hair back, and tied it with a ponytail holder that she'd dug out of her handbag.

"Well, I-I . . ." I stammered. My sexy American minx was a virgin. After she had teased me and danced with me and kissed me so erotically for weeks. After her nipple had puckered into a hard peak between my lips. After I'd discovered she was drenched between her legs from only a passionate kiss.

My mouth dropped open. I was rarely a man without words. The sex had been incredible, and I'd chided myself for not lasting as long as I usually did because I was so consumed by her body and her sexy moans. Any control I had around Savannah had evaporated.

And now, this. The famous race car driver reduced to his base, animal instincts. By a virgin. I'd acted like an animal.

"I wanted you to be my first," she said matter-of-factly. The curious look that I had noticed in her wide eyes finally registered: she was young and innocent. *Dio*, what had I done?

My lovers were always experienced, even when I was younger. I preferred women as jaded as me. There were fewer complications that way, because everyone knew the rules. I was many things when it came to women, but I was not lacking in refinement. If I'd known I was going to be her first, I would have wanted it to be memorable. Pleasurable. Perfect. I would have savored her.

Or I wouldn't have touched her at all.

"I would have never done this had I known, not here," I said in a hoarse voice.

"Fine. Well, at least one of us doesn't have regrets."

I watched as Savannah shuddered in a breath. She looked almost in tears and that tugged at something deep inside me. "Wait—" I said, trying to grab her arm.

She didn't wait. Instead, she swept out of the room and slammed the door. By the time I'd buckled my belt and run back into the club, Savannah was gone.

◊

SAVANNAH

My cheeks were grubby with tears as I stumbled barefoot along the cobblestones of Brussels, my heels in my hands.

I hated crying. Hadn't cried in years. And here I was, in public, humiliating myself.

Of course Dante didn't want to screw a virgin. Served me right for throwing myself at him. Why would he want an inexperienced, needy girl when he could have worldly, gorgeous models that knew exactly what to do in bed? He probably regretted being with me because my performance had been so poor.

I looked over my shoulder, hoping Dante was following. Of course, he wasn't. The team hotel was only a block away and I tried to gather my thoughts as I picked my way down the street, trying not to stub my toes or stumble.

Flinging open the door to the hotel, I ran smack into a broad chest. I looked up. It was Max Becker, the team's other driver.

"Savvy." His tawny eyes glittered. "You okay?"

I murmured something and tried to step around him. He pulled me further into the lobby.

"Let me guess. Dante? He can be a real piece of work with the girls."

I remained silent and chewed on the inside of my cheek. I knew there was a rivalry between the two men on the track, and although I was incensed at Dante at the moment for rejecting me, I maintained a sense of loyalty to him for all sorts of reasons. He was my driver.

But the fact that Max knew of Dante's reputation didn't sit well with my already bruised emotional state either.

I tried to pull away from him, but he gripped my arm. The lobby of the hotel suddenly seemed very bright, and I wondered if I looked different somehow, now that I'd lost my virginity.

"He's never been good with women," Max drawled. "I knew it wasn't going to last when I heard you two were dating. I hope it's not a disaster for the team. Why don't we go have a drink together and talk it out?"

A prickling sensation on my neck made me try to shake myself free from Max. Someone was behind me. I turned my head and found myself staring into dark, angry eyes.

"The only disaster for the team will be when I break your damned hand because you're touching my girlfriend. Then you won't be able to drive for the rest of the season," Dante growled.

"Dante, please. Don't cause a scene," I hissed. Max released me from his grip and Dante grabbed my hand. *Mortifying.* I snorted in protest to both men and tried to huff off, but Dante kept my hand clamped in his.

"A lovers' spat. How quaint," Max purred. The sound of his laughter followed us through the lobby, and I wondered if the scene was being captured by any paparazzi. That was the only way the night could get worse.

By the time we got into the elevator, my shoulders drooped in defeat. Everything I'd come to Europe for—a job, motorsports, adventure—had turned into an emotionally messy slog. I suspected I had mascara streaking down my face, and I touched my fingertips to my cheeks, then inspected my fingers. Yep. Mascara.

"Max is too young and impulsive. Is that the kind of thing you like?"

"You're crazy if you thought I was going anywhere with Max."

"Whatever. This gives me another reason to dislike him."

"Why did you call me your girlfriend?"

He didn't answer. Instead he side-eyed me and shook his head. The elevator bell pinged and he got out. "Give me your key," Dante demanded.

"Why?"

"Don't argue with me, *per favore*. God, you're stubborn."

"You're impossible." I was too tired to fight and dug in my purse, handing him the plastic key card.

"Room number?"

"Eight seventeen."

He stomped down the hall. Jerk. I was the one who should be upset, after he'd all but admitted that he regretted having sex. Humiliation burned my cheeks when I thought of how close I'd felt to him in the club. I thought we were genuinely friends, with the added bonus of being attracted to one another. Obviously, I'd not only been wrong, but I'd chosen the worst possible man for my first time. I was utterly embarrassed.

With a precise flick, he jammed the card into the lock and opened the door. I followed him inside and watched him stride over to the windows and pull the drapes closed with a fury.

"Thanks for opening my door. I couldn't have done it without you." Sarcasm was always my defense mechanism when shame or anger took over, and it bubbled up now that we were alone.

Dante whirled and grabbed my upper arms with both hands. His dark eyes were molten, passionate. "Savannah, has it ever occurred to you that I do things for you like open doors and rescue you from predatory German drivers and discourage you from being a pit crew member because I want to protect you? Because, I don't know, I *like* you?"

"No, I hadn't thought of that," I tossed back. "If you liked me, if you were my friend, you wouldn't want me to leave the pit crew. You would want me to have a career and be happy."

He opened his mouth to speak, but I wasn't about to let him get a word in. Not after he was so repulsed by sleeping with me.

"And I don't need protecting. And you shouldn't care about taking my virginity in a club. It was what I wanted. My virginity was *mine* to give. You had no say in the matter."

"I would have had to think long and hard about taking your virginity. You should have given *me* the choice."

I snorted. "I thought most guys would be ecstatic to deflower a virgin. I had to pick the one who wasn't."

"I don't want you falling in love with me. Not under these circumstances, as my tire changer. I don't want complications."

"You're so full of yourself. God. Don't you think I can have sex and not fall in love?"

"That goes to show how naive you are, Savannah mia. All women fall in love with their first lover."

I made a little *pfft* sound and looked down at his hands, which were still clutching my bare arms. I was trying not to think about how I wasn't wearing panties, and how close his muscular body was to mine. Or how soft his lips looked, or how delicious he smelled.

Or how close we were to the bed.

"Wrong. Because I certainly wouldn't want to fall for the likes of you."

He squeezed my arms, shaking me a little, his passionate expression turning to fury. "Dio. You are impossible."

He released me and walked away, muttering something harsh sounding in his language.

"I don't understand anything you say in Italian," I shouted.

"Good," he spat, slamming the door.

CHAPTER TWENTY

SAVANNAH

The banging on my hotel door ripped me out of a deep sleep the next morning. I groaned and rubbed the sandpaper out of my eyes. Then the memory of being with Dante came rushing back. How could I have been so stupid? My earlier speech about my virginity being mine to give? That had been true.

All I could recall was the anger and the other, less evident emotion in his eyes. Disgust? Was that it? I felt ill recalling the entire episode. He hadn't been the best candidate after all, and regret had kept me awake well into the night.

All I wanted to do was put the down pillow over my head and hide, at least until checkout. Then I'd grab a cab to the station, where I planned to take an overnight Eurostar train to Rome. I didn't want to see anyone I knew over the next week. And definitely didn't want to answer the damned door.

"Come back later for housekeeping."

"Savannah, open up," came the American voice.

Damn. *Bronson.* The second-to-last person I wanted to see. I clambered out of bed and checked my face in the mirror hanging on the wall. My eyes were red and puffy, and my lips were too. All because of that stupid Italian.

"It's urgent," Bronson called out.

What would be urgent at this time of the morning? I scrubbed at my face with my hands, hoping to erase the memory of last night with Dante . . .

Oh crap. What if there had been a camera in the private room at the club? My heart began to pound. All I needed now was a sex tape scandal. *Perfect.*

Wearing a pink T-shirt with a cartoon kitten on the front and matching pink pajama bottoms, I flung open the door.

"Morning, sunshine." Bronson extended a cup of coffee in my direction. Behind him were a glowering Dante and an impassive Tanya.

Accepting the coffee, I ignored Dante and stepped aside to let everyone in.

As he passed me, Dante leaned in to kiss me hello on both cheeks, and I stiffened and bobbed to avoid his lips. There was no need to put on a show for Bronson and Tanya. I shot him a cross look and realized there were dark circles under his eyes. He must not have slept well either.

Probably he was so appalled by our time together that he'd been unable to rest.

Bronson and Tanya settled on the hotel room's small gold

loveseat. Dante sat on the edge of the unmade bed and inspected his nails. He was wearing faded jeans and a black T-shirt, and he looked so solid, so masculine. I remained standing, sipping the coffee. It was black, which I hated, so I went to the minibar.

"Thanks for the wake-up call." I thwacked three packs of sugar against the palm of my hand, ripped open the tops, and dumped them all into the cup.

"It is eight o'clock, but I guess you would need to sleep in after the late nights you've been sharing," Tanya said breezily. I grimaced.

"Anyway," Tanya continued, "we're here to update you on the publicity efforts. We had a little glitch last night when you stormed out of the club. But only one photographer caught that, so I think we're safe. We can always float a rumor that the two of you had a spat. The press eats up lovers' quarrels."

She frowned at Bronson, who rubbed his hands together like an evil villain. He stopped when he noticed my sour expression, and Tanya plowed on.

"Here's the great news: our internal polling shows that you're a hit. Fans are wild about the Dante-Savannah love match."

This made me snort. "I'm glad someone is."

I noticed how Dante pressed his lips together and scrutinized the carpet.

"Is that all?" Dante asked. Of course, he couldn't wait to leave. He couldn't even stand being in the same room as me. A fresh wave of shame bubbled up, and I set my coffee on a side table.

On the plus side, it didn't appear that there was a sex tape. Not yet, at least.

"Well . . ." Bronson said. "No. Max really caused a rift during the race by ignoring his engineer's directions in Valencia. And the FIA is starting an investigation into the alleged theft of technical information. We'd hoped they wouldn't, but the inquest has started. Not good."

"We have a new plan for you two," Tanya said brightly. "We think it will blow every other bit of news out of the water."

Something about the woman's perky voice irritated me. In an instant, I decided to go into full-on bitch mode due to the early hour, the lack of sugar in the coffee, and Dante's eyes, which had lingered for a second too long on my legs. I tossed my hair and channeled my best beauty pageant diva voice.

"Wait. Don't tell me. You want me and the Italian stallion"—I jerked my thumb at Dante—"to pretend we're married so we can take the heat off Max. That's the only way this could get better, right?"

"Close!" Bronson said, beaming.

A jolt of fear went through my body.

Oh, holy hell.

◊

DANTE

"We want you two to pretend to be engaged," Tanya said. She stated this as if it were the most reasonable request in the world.

"What?" groaned Savannah. "No. That's too much." I closed my eyes and inhaled. Savannah was angry with me, and I couldn't blame her. I'd acted so ungentlemanly toward her. A brute. And now *this*. I wished I'd never gotten involved with these machinations, or this team.

"Why can't you fire Max? Sever his contract. You have plenty of quality drivers in development," I said.

"Because at his core, Max is an excellent driver, and you know it," Bronson said. "He's young, he's brash, and he's arrogant. Surely you recall being the same ten years ago?"

Dammit, why did he have to bring up Max's age? But he had a point.

It was exactly what I didn't want to discuss, not after the miserable night I'd had, tossing and turning and worrying. And I still didn't understand why Savannah's angry eyes bothered me so much.

Savannah shot Tanya a questioning scowl as she flipped her long hair over her shoulder. It was mussed, and a twinge in my groin reminded me of how I'd hoped to wake up next to her, naked and ready for the next round. That was what I *wished* had happened. Instead, I'd lost control in a club and taken her like an animal.

Shameful.

I tried to casually glance at Savannah's legs, then couldn't help but check out her breasts, which were encased in a ridiculous, tight T-shirt emblazoned with a cat. She narrowed her eyes at me, and I was mesmerized when I noticed her nipples tighten almost instantly. Now glaring, she folded her arms tightly across her chest.

I smiled at her, and her lip curled upward into a brief sneer.

"It's too much. Being around him is impossible," Savannah snapped.

"Is it, though? Really?" Bronson said. "You two seem to get along fine. Well, except for last night, but that was a little misunderstanding, wasn't it?"

She exhaled sharply and raised her chin.

Bronson went on. "We thought you two could fly to Rome today, pick out a ring, and spend the week at Dante's villa. Make some public appearances there on the Amalfi Coast. You were going to visit Italy anyway. I'm sure Dante would love to take you sightseeing."

My teeth hurt from clenching my jaw. Spending an entire week under the same roof as Savannah? We would either kill each other or . . . Or?

My jaw loosened. The *or* was so very appealing.

It could be a chance to prove I was a decent man. My chance to get to know her. My chance to bed her properly, for days. Teach her, even, the art of good sex. Not that she needed any help in that department.

I shrugged, trying not to show how eager I was. Sure, it meant I'd have to pretend to be engaged for a while, but it seemed like a worthwhile tradeoff.

"The thought of spending another minute with me disgusts you, doesn't it?" Savannah spat.

"I always go to my villa alone, right before the Monza race," I explained, trying to put up a bit of a fight so Savannah wouldn't think I was *too* interested. "It's a sacred week for me."

"Dante, dude, I'm sure Savannah will give you all the privacy you need. Go out to dinner a couple of times, sail around on your yacht for a morning, make sure the press captures you having fun. Pretend you're in love. How difficult can it be? We'll be in touch about where you should go and what you should do, because we'll be tipping off our favorite paparazzi, of course."

Savannah's hands clenched into fists. "I had plans for this week."

"No worries," Bronson said. "You'll be getting a bonus in your next paycheck as compensation. Let us know if we need to reimburse you for any travel you've already booked."

Bronson looked at his watch. "Dante, we have that sponsor meeting in fifteen. The team plane leaves for Rome at noon, and we've already arranged an afternoon appointment with a jeweler. Pack up, Savannah. Tanya will stay behind to help you select something nice to wear for your engagement announcement today."

◊

SAVANNAH

Dante and Bronson walked out, and the door shut with a muted *snick*.

I slapped my hand to my forehead. "Crap," I said aloud.

"What?" Tanya asked.

"If I'm really doing this, announcing our engagement, I need to tell my family. And my best friend. I can't let them find out like this. I've avoided their questions about Dante over the last several races. But engagement is a whole other level in my culture. They're going to think something's up if I don't tell them, and I'll never live it down for the rest of my life. This could reverberate for decades. You don't even know how bad it could get."

She scowled. "I'd rather not tell them beforehand. What if they leak the news?"

"I need to. You don't understand. My mother will never forgive me. And what if reporters find her first and ambush her with the news? Please. Let me call them, okay? And my best friend definitely won't speak to any reporter."

She inhaled and checked her watch. "You have a half hour. Don't give them many details and don't tell them it's a publicity stunt. I'm going to grab a coffee, and I'll return soon so we can go over your wardrobe."

Tanya snatched her laptop bag and swept out. I fell back on the bed and took five deep breaths. Things had been going smoothly—until I decided to have sex with Dante.

I rolled over and grabbed my phone off the nightstand. It was two in the morning in Atlanta, and who knew what time in Aruba, where my parents were on vacation. I dialed Dad's number and immediately got his voicemail.

Then I dialed Mom. Same thing. They were either asleep or gambling in the ship's casino.

"Hey, everything's going really well here, but I wanted to call you before you saw something in a tabloid." I hesitated, then spoke without a pause between my words. "Dante and I are getting engaged! Just wanted you and Daddy to know. I'll explain more later. Call me. Love you, bye."

I heaved an exhale. Not how I'd envisioned telling my parents I was engaged, but whatever. It would have to do. We could hash it out later.

Already mentally exhausted, I opted for a text to Kayla. It was impossible to muster anything more.

Hey, I know you're asleep. Give me a call when you get a chance.

I added a ring emoji and pressed Send before I lost courage. Then I lay on the bed, eyes closed, trying to take one deep breath after another.

The phone rang. Crap. I couldn't avoid my best friend; she'd call and call until I picked up.

"Hello?"

"What's this with the ring emoji?" Kayla's tone was heavy with accusation.

I sat up. "Why are you up so late? Isn't it two in the morning?"

"I just got home from a date with Travis."

"Oh." I paused. "Is he there?"

"No. We're taking it slow. Get this. I think he's the one, Savvy. I can feel it in my bones. I looked at him tonight and knew he's the man I'm going to marry. We haven't even kissed, and I know he's it."

A breath caught in my throat. Her voice positively gushed with emotion, and I couldn't help but envy her happiness. This was how relationships were supposed to unfold. "Wow, that's really beautiful." My throat thickened and I swallowed twice.

"What's your news?"

"Dante and I are getting engaged." I said this slowly, almost like a robot.

"What?" Her tone was laced with confusion. "But, how? I thought you two were hanging out after races and maybe kissing a little, and that the tabloids were wrong about you being together as a couple. That's what you said in your last email."

"Nope, we're actually in love." I put the phone on speaker, untying and picking at the ribbon on the waistband of my pajama shorts.

"Why don't you sound more excited? Savannah, what's going on? Are you being held hostage or something? You never even wanted to get married. I don't understand."

For the second time in twenty-four hours, I burst into tears. Then I told my best friend everything, even though I wasn't supposed to.

0

Onboard the team's private jet, I folded my arms across my chest, not bothering to hide my sullen mood. Tanya had asked me to wear a multicolored maxi-dress that made me feel like a peacock. It was a silky, sensuous material and cut too low. As I flung myself into the rear seat of the plane, I mentally calculated how much time I had left before the racing season ended. Thankfully, no one on the team sat next to me.

I was in a special kind of hell. For the next few months, no less. Months of pretending to be Dante's girlfriend—no, *fiancé.* Months of forced contact with a man who didn't want me because I'd insisted on an awkward hookup at a club. Months of humiliation from a guy who made all of the pleasure centers in my brain light up whenever I looked at him.

Although I felt marginally better after explaining my situation to Kayla, I was back to doubting myself and whether I could keep up this charade.

Leaning forward to grab a magazine out of my bag, I accidentally caught Dante's eye. He was in the front, chatting with Bronson. I quickly looked away and tried to become engrossed in reading. Dante had avoided talking to me in the limousine on the way to the airport, probably because he was mortified that he had tried to screw someone so goofy.

After a few minutes, I felt a looming presence standing over me.

"Hi. Can we talk?" Dante's voice was soft.

I shrugged and shut the magazine, all while avoiding his gaze.

"Can we please talk in private, in the back room, Savannah?"

"Whatever you want." I followed him to the plane's rear

conference area. Once he'd shut the door, I plopped onto a sofa and stared out a window at the clouds zooming past. The flight from Brussels to Rome wasn't long. Hopefully he wouldn't want to chat for the entire journey.

"Savannah mia," he murmured, easing next to me. Why did my insides melt whenever he said my name in his sexy Italian accent? I wasn't wearing a bra because the dress plunged low on my back, and my nipples tightened against the fabric. I should've brought a sweater with me.

"I like your dress. You look so beautiful today."

"Thanks," I mumbled. He was trying to let me down gently. Compliment me first—that was probably a tactic for guys like him. This had all been an intricate plot to get me to fall for him, then to toy with my emotions.

"Come closer to me." He reached his arm around me and hoisted my body toward his.

"You're in my personal space," I said defensively.

"I know. I'm a fan of your personal space."

I pretended to brush an invisible crumb off the seat cushion, knowing my cheeks were bright pink by now. I didn't want to see the pity in his eyes.

Feeling his fingers on my chin, I let him gently turn my head to face him. "I need to apologize. I didn't handle last night well. I—"

I interrupted. "There's no need to apologize. I won't bother you again, and definitely won't throw myself at you like I did last night. Let's pretend it never happened. I'll stay out of your way, other than our official obligations."

"You're impossible. Would you listen to me?" His voice was louder than necessary.

"Shh," I shot back. "I don't want everyone on the team to know our business."

"The team already thinks we're sleeping together. Don't worry about it. Listen to me," he whispered fiercely.

He pulled me closer, wrapping his muscular arms around me. God, he felt so *good*. Why did he have to torture me like this?

His lips were so close to my ear that the space between my thighs warmed from his tone. "I've wanted you for weeks. I've wanted you since I first saw you. I was shocked when I found out you were a virgin and felt terrible that your first time was in a club lounge. I would have wanted to do it somewhere nicer. You deserve better. I didn't want to take your virginity in such a crass way. That's all."

He sounded awfully sincere. So his hesitation was about some misguided chivalry? Part of me was happy to know that he was attracted to me. Another part was annoyed. What I did with my body was my business. If I wanted to lose my virginity in a club, that was my prerogative.

"What I did with my virginity wasn't your decision," I whispered, making little quote marks with my hands when I said the word *decision*. "It's not a precious jewel or a gift. It's a fact. *Was* a fact. It's not a big deal. I'm the same person I was before. I had my reasons for why I waited, and I had my reasons for why I wanted to do it with you last night."

He kissed my cheek and released me from his embrace. My resolve and annoyance began to thaw. A little. Maybe he was being genuine.

"I'm glad you chose me. Honored. But it is a big deal. For me, at least. I wouldn't have done it that way. I'm not going to have a one-off with you in a club. It's not how I rock."

I tilted my head. It was so cute how he occasionally messed up certain English phrases. "Roll. It's not how you roll."

"Rock. Roll. Whatever."

"Slept with a lot of virgins, have you?"

"Actually, no. Never." He paused. "What I wanted to tell you is that I was hoping I could make it up to you at my villa. I'd like a do-over of our first time. Let me show you how sex is supposed to be. We should savor it. Enjoy it. We're spending the week together, so why not have fun?" He lifted a dark eyebrow.

I cleared my throat and a searing heat washed over my body. He swept a lock of hair away from my cheek.

"You're going to love Amalfi, tesoro."

He brushed his lips over mine and that was all it took to break down my defenses. I practically purred into his mouth. I wanted to kiss him fully and deeply, and looked at him with lazy, half-lidded eyes. That was what he did to me, made me feel drugged. His tongue darted out to lick his full bottom lip, and I put my hand on his thigh. He was wearing shorts, and I skimmed my hand over his skin, my fingers darting underneath the fabric.

"Don't." His voice sounded shaky.

"Don't what?"

"Look at me like that. All sexy. And don't put your hand anywhere higher on my leg. It makes me want to pull you onto my lap and ravish you. I've told you before, you're playing with fire, Savannah. My self-restraint only goes so far. It got me in trouble last night and could get me in trouble again, right now."

"You're a gentleman, you know that?" I squeezed his leg.

"I am, for about two more minutes. Take your hand off my leg or I'm going to have my way with you right here. I won't make love to you nicely. I'll fuck you hard. My patience is wearing thin, and there's no lock on the door. I'm an animal, and I'm trying to act domesticated around you. But that only lasts for so long."

Removing my hand, I shivered at the thought of him hiking my dress up and taking me. His dirty talk was so crazy sexy. I leaned into his embrace and allowed my eyes to flutter shut, pressing my nose into his neck. He wanted me. He might not like me, but that was okay. Sometimes I didn't like him either. We often annoyed each other. But that also fueled our dangerous attraction.

And why not indulge that attraction as much as possible? I could think of no plausible reason *not* to.

He took a deep breath, as if trying to steady himself. "Now, let's go out and sit with the rest of the team. I think it's for our own good."

"You're right," I agreed, because if we were alone much longer I was going to climb him like a tree. I returned to my seat in the main cabin, and he sat near Bronson. I overheard them talking about the upcoming race. Then he returned and sat next to me. We exchanged little sheepish grins and I felt my skin heat up.

We didn't talk for a half hour. Meanwhile, I couldn't get one thought out of my head: by the end of the day, I'd be engaged and in Dante's bed.

My thoughts were interrupted by Jack, who came over to where Dante and I were sitting.

"Mind if I steal her away for a few minutes, mate?" he asked Dante, who was staring out the window. "I wanted to talk with Savvy about the next race."

He twisted in his seat. "No, not at all. I'll go chat with Tanya. I need to ask her about some meet and greets for the next race anyway."

We shuffled seats, with me sitting in the spot near the window and him moving into the aisle. Jack sat where I had just been.

"Listen, Savannah," he started. "I know you're going to be facing a lot with the news of your, er, engagement to Dante."

"You know about this?" I asked, incredulous. How many people on the team knew about this sham of a relationship? It was getting so complicated.

"I'm the only one who does, outside of Bronson, Tanya, and you and Dante of course."

"Oh," I said slowly.

"Anyway, I wanted to say that if you need to pull back on your responsibilities in the garage or the pits, we can make that happen."

I gaped at him. "What? Why would I want to do that?"

"You might be overwhelmed with the press. Bronson wanted me to make it clear to you that you can take all the time you need."

Jerks. All of them. Clearly they thought I was unable to do a proper job because my feeble girl mind would be inundated with fake-relationship stuff. I fixed a steely gaze on Jack. "Do you think I'm doing a good job as a tire changer?"

"Actually, yes, I do. I think you're fabulous. You have as much knowledge of cars as people who have been on the team for five years. And you really have a feel for the tires. You've impressed everyone on the team, even though I know it's been difficult because of your personal relationship with the driver."

I reached for my magazine while fury bubbled inside me. "Good. That's all we need to discuss. I want to keep doing the job I was hired to do, regardless of my relationship status."

"The scrutiny on you will be intense," he countered.

These men really thought I couldn't handle it all. Well, I'd show them. "I don't care. I'm here to be a pit crew member, not window dressing. And make sure Bronson knows that too. I can do two things at once. Tell him that women are excellent at multitasking. It's been proven in research studies. I can handle it all. Got it?"

The corners of Jack's mouth lifted. "Got it loud and clear, mate."

I opened my magazine, signaling that I was finished with this ridiculous conversation. Jack squeezed my shoulder and wandered away. A few minutes later, I heard him and Dante telling Tanya about a race in England. I tried to ignore them and focused on my magazine for the rest of the flight.

The moment we landed, I turned on my phone. My parents had left six voicemails, and Mom had followed up with a barrage of texts. I scrolled through the increasingly alarmed messages with the guilty realization that I'd have to call them immediately.

When the jet stopped at the gate but before we exited, I corralled Dante, Bronson, and Tanya.

"My parents are flipping out," I said. The three of them stared at me as if I were speaking an alien language. "About the engagement. I left them a message with the news, but they're demanding more details. I need to call them now and explain. Especially if you don't want my father to start asking lots of questions about this team."

That snapped Bronson to attention. "Of course. Of course! Use the conference room back there."

I walked, zombielike, into the conference room at the rear of the jet, where Dante and I had been previously. I could have sworn his aftershave scent still hung in the air, which made my heart skip a little.

With a deep breath, I dialed Mom's number as I scanned the light-gray-on-dark-gray decor of this part of the jet. It rang and rang and I hung up, suddenly gleeful that they hadn't answered. But my happiness was short-lived because as I was putting the phone in my purse, it buzzed, this time with a video call. I winced and tapped the screen. This was serious—Mom never wanted to video call.

Their faces popped up, and I could tell they were on the deck of their cruise ship.

"Munchkin," Daddy said.

"Savannah." Mom slid her sunglasses down her nose. "What the heck is going on?"

My parents leaned into the camera in tandem, as if getting closer might elicit a quicker answer from me.

"Dante and I are getting engaged," I said firmly, pasting on a smile for good measure.

Mom narrowed her eyes, which were rimmed in a smoky gray. She wore one of her white linen caftans and a chunky gold necklace. I could practically smell the Chanel No. 5 coming out of the phone, and that made me miss her something fierce.

"I don't like the sudden nature of this," she replied, pursing her lips. "Something seems off. I wish you would've given me a heads-up that your relationship was this serious. Last I knew, you were friends and didn't want him coming to our house on Tybee."

Good Lord. Now I was feeling guilty for letting Mom down— over a totally fake engagement.

Daddy broke out in a smile and pulled her close. "Aww, hell, honey. You and I met and were married in, what, a month?"

She elbowed Dad, who somehow was taking this far better than I'd imagined. "Hush. That was the eighties and a totally different time. Kids are more cautious now. At least I thought they were. Savannah is acting like she was raised by wolves. Don't you think Dante should've asked you for her hand in marriage?"

Tears were on the horizon, I could sense it.

"Mom, I'm not property. Dante doesn't need to ask Dad for anything." Why was I even attempting to have a logical conversation about this?

Mercifully, Dad thwarted her drama by chortling, and the sound of his laugh made me crack a smile. His ruddy face, his big nose, his green eyes that were like mine—all of it made me homesick and I wished I could hug him.

I took a deep breath. "Look, I'll explain more later but I really need to go. We just landed in Rome. I'm still on the jet, in fact."

"My world traveler. My little girl," Dad boomed. "One day a tire changer, the next day, fiancé to one of the world's richest athletes. Of course he'd fall for you. How could he not? I'm sure he was charmed by your knowledge of engines. But don't you forget about your goals, you hear?"

Hearing him say that made a lump of sadness fill my throat and I tried to change the subject. "Are you guys on the cruise ship?"

"Yes," Dad said. "We're leaving Aruba."

"Where is Dante?" Mom demanded. "This is very odd, if you ask me. I need to know about his wedding plans. Italy or the United States?"

"He's . . . somewhere," I said feebly. I peered out the small window and studied the baggage handlers taking suitcases off another private jet.

Just then, the door swung open to reveal Dante. "Did I hear my name?"

I waved him away but Mom started to squawk. "Let me see him. This is a curious situation, especially since you were so anti-marriage until now. Introduce us, Savannah Marie."

"Mom," I warned, although she wasn't uttering anything but the truth.

Dante plopped down on the sofa next to me.

"Uh, this is the man of the hour," I stammered.

His expression was so sincere that I could've sworn he was a different person. "Ciao!"

"Oh my God, he is even more handsome than I'd imagined. Do. You. Understand. English?" Mom yelled. "Do. You. Love. My. Baby. Girl? What. Are. Your. Intentions?"

The entire cruise ship now knew our business. Awesome. I covered my eyes with my hand. "I'm sorry," I murmured to Dante.

He let out an easy laugh. "I can speak English pretty well, but I'm learning more from your daughter every day. She's a great teacher."

"Oh, sweetie, you're too kind," I said in a syrupy voice. Dante slung his arm around me.

"You're so adorable, Savvy," he replied.

All right. Enough of this ridiculousness. We didn't need to put on *this* much of a show for my parents. "Okay, you've now seen him in the flesh. We've got to run," I said breezily.

"Dante." My father's voice was a touch stern.

"Yes, sir?" It was the first time I'd heard Dante sound so . . . accommodating.

"You take care of my little girl, you hear? I think I'm going to have to come visit the two of you for a race and spend some time with you, man to man. I've been studying the schedule and was thinking about Italy. That's the next race." Dad turned to Mom. "You know how I love Italian food. I think we can make a flight after we get back from the cruise."

"That's an excellent race to see, sir. I'd love to spend time with you and show you the track. It's my home race, of course. Very special."

Dad said something about the technical racing challenges of the Monza circuit, and I held up my hand to halt the conversation. Both Dad and Dante were able to talk about racing for hours. I could, too, but prolonging this conversation would be torture.

"Okay, we need to go. The flight crew is about to kick us off since we're here at the gate. Talk soon, bye!" I waved maniacally at the screen, clicked my phone off, and threw it in my bag.

"That wasn't so bad, was it?" Dante asked in a mild tone.

My parents and Dante in the same place in three weeks? Having to fib and put on a show for my skeptical mother, who would use the situation to exert more psychological control over me? Risking a bromance between Dad and Dante?

Not so bad?

It was worse than I could have imagined.

CHAPTER TWENTY-ONE

DANTE

The media circus was in full swing as we walked from the car to the front door of Angeletti, a luxurious jewelry store along one of Rome's most fashionable streets. We'd stopped here specifically for this, so the cameras could capture us picking out an engagement ring.

Bronson was with us, probably because he wanted to soak up the publicity. The bastard grinned as he scanned the frenzy of reporters, completely ignoring Savannah's obvious discomfort.

I was used to a crush of media, but from the way her eyes widened and how she chewed on her bottom lip, I could tell she was overwhelmed. I slipped my arm around her waist and drew her into me.

"It's okay. I've got you," I murmured in her ear. "Don't answer any questions and don't make eye contact with the reporters. Keep smiling, at least until we get inside."

The shop owner held the door open for our entourage, then locked it behind us. That didn't stop the media from pressing their faces and cameras against the glass.

Savannah exhaled and looked around the store. "Wow, that was something out there."

Bronson rubbed his hands together and she shot him a withering look. I could tell that her patience was wearing thin with him, and to avoid any confrontation in public, I steered her to a glass case.

"Look at these, amore mio," I said, pointing to a dozen enormous, glittering rocks. "What do you think?"

She narrowed her eyes and the owner hustled to remove a velvet tray. "They're quite . . . large."

"The bigger the better," the owner said in accented English. "Don't all women love diamonds?"

Savannah scowled and turned to me. "How am I going to do my job while wearing this?" she whispered. I hadn't thought of that.

"You can leave it in the hotel safe when we're racing," I suggested.

Bronson materialized next to us, laughing. "Exactly, Dante. You're so diligent, Savannah. Of course you can't wear it in the garage."

I shot Bronson a pointed look and he retreated to the corner to check his phone. His presence was beyond annoying, and I felt like he was intruding on an intimate moment.

Savannah pointed at one of the stones. The owner explained that it was a two-carat, emerald-cut diamond. She tried it on.

"It fits perfectly," I observed.

She was so adorable when she looked at me, wide-eyed, and said seriously, "This is really pretty."

I studied her beautiful face. That was when I stole a kiss from those impossibly plump lips.

"The ring is yours." Good God, it was almost as if we were shopping for a real ring. What the hell was happening here?

"We'll take it," I said to the owner.

I tucked her hair behind her ear before we walked to the store's exit. My fingers itched to cup her ass in that silky dress. She was my fiancé, at least in the eyes of the world. Surely the salesclerks would later tell reporters about my behavior.

I grabbed a handful of her and groaned, pulling her closer, ostensibly so I could whisper in her ear. "Make sure you flash the diamond, cara."

"You're distracting me."

I grinned against her ear. "What was it that you said to me the other day? Suck it up, buttercup?"

Flashbulbs blinded us as we stepped outside, the bright snaps colliding with the equally bright Roman sunshine. Savannah smiled like the *Mona Lisa* and stayed close, allowing me to propel her into the limo.

What was she thinking? Did she not want me to grab her? Was she dreaming of the day she would be engaged for real? Or was she thinking about what was about to happen tonight, when we were alone in my villa?

"You did good, tesoro," I said later as we boarded the jet and took off from Rome for the private airstrip near the Amalfi Coast.

She quirked her mouth into a half smile, staring at the ring.

"What? You don't like it?"

"It's so, I don't know. Big." She shrugged. "Probably not what I would choose if I were really getting engaged."

"Thought about that a lot, have you? Having a princess wedding and all?" For some reason, the wistful look on her face made me feel . . . things.

"Actually, no. I've had enough days as a princess to last me a lifetime."

"*Che?*" I tilted my head and questioned her in Italian. She was starting to understand the basics of my language, and I'd been impressed that she'd picked up so much from me and the other Italians on the team in such a short time.

She drew in a sharp breath. "The pageants. When I competed."

"Ohh, right. Of course. Now that I've gotten to know you, you don't seem like the pageant type. You're more, I don't know. Down to earth?"

She shrugged. "My mom pushed me into it when I was little. Said I'd stand out because of my red hair. I used to dress up like a princess almost every weekend. Big hair, nails, gowns. From the time I was five.

"It's probably why I was never set on a fairy-tale wedding. Or a wedding at all. I don't think I'll even get married, ever."

"Oh, you're too young to say that. But you being a beauty queen, that explains a lot."

"It does?"

"Now I know why you're able to turn on that brilliant smile whenever you're around a camera. And how you're so poised in public. And why you can't hide all that beauty under the greasy coveralls. It all makes sense now. Why'd you stop? Didn't you want to become Miss America?"

She snorted and stared out the window of the plane. "Hell no. It's a long story."

Now I was interested in her mysterious answer. "We've got time. All week, in fact. I can't wait to hear about it." I leaned in and kissed her soft cheek.

She flashed me a wary look. "Maybe later. Dante, have you ever thought about getting married?"

It was my turn to shrug. "I don't have any good role models for marriage. My parents' marriage was—*is*—a disaster. But let's not dwell on that." I drummed my fingers on the armrest. "And your parents? How do they get along? They seemed pretty happy on that call a few hours ago."

"Yep. They actually have a great marriage, even though they're opposites. My mom's high-strung and a control freak, and my dad's more laid back. Together, they're perfect. Everything my mom does is perfect, in fact."

I wondered why Savannah looked so sad when she said that, and didn't want to pry further. So I took her hand when she turned her head back to the window and we flew the rest of the way in silence.

CHAPTER TWENTY-TWO

SAVANNAH

The Villa del Sole was breathtaking.

From its heavy wooden double doors that allowed a shaft of sunshine into the stark white entranceway to the sitting rooms with high, ornate baroque ceilings to the triple decks of the terraces that overlooked the glittering Mediterranean Sea, everything about the place was stunning. I poked my head out of one window and took in the day's fading golden sunshine. The air smelled like sun-kissed lemons, likely from the citrus grove Dante said was nearby.

He had apparently bought this place after his first winning season. At least that's what I'd read in one ESPN profile. Yes, I'd done some internet sleuthing to see what I was in for. Thankfully, when we'd arrived, Dante had set my bags in a bedroom that was obviously not his. He'd mentioned he had some business calls to make and that he was retiring to his own room for a bit.

During the couple of hours I had to myself, I'd napped, bathed, and donned a simple cotton tank dress, happy to be out of the slinky outfit and away from the media that had plagued us in Rome and on our way to the villa. All the interest in our engagement—the shouted questions, the crush of cameras, the near-instantaneous trending on Twitter—had left my head spinning. I knew Dante was popular, and recognized that people were interested in my ground-breaking place on a team. But I'd never get used to the fact that strangers cared so much about our private lives.

It was exhausting and soul sucking in ways I was only beginning to grasp. No wonder Dante was so aloof in public sometimes. Still, he'd been a gentleman during the Rome visit, keeping his arm around me at all times, as if he wanted to protect me. I'd appreciated that.

Eager to see the view from the terrace, I opened the doors in my bedroom. The view induced a spontaneous gasp of happiness.

Bright violet flowers in terra-cotta pots graced the stone-and-tile terrace, and below, the sloping mountainside was filled with lemon trees. In the distance, I could see the impossible blue of the sea. I was surrounded by intense, heady beauty, and walked to the balcony rail to inhale the fragrant air. I took a couple of deep, cleansing breaths.

Admittedly, this was way better than a hostel.

I was still wearing the diamond on my hand. The brilliant stone caught the waning sunlight and the sparkle made me unsteady.

Twisting the ring slowly, I realized my feelings for Dante—for my *fake fiancé*—could become messy and complicated. Or maybe it was lust that was surging through my body, a byproduct of the fragrant, romantic air. That had to be it. I'd never fall for a guy like him in real life, and being here in this picture-perfect place seemed to heighten the feeling that I was living in some alternate, gilt-edged reality.

"Do you like it?" came a voice from behind.

I turned. Dante padded toward me, barefoot and dressed in a simple white linen shirt and loose tan linen pants. He appeared more relaxed than during the hectic, silly engagement farce in Rome. His dark hair was damp and slightly disheveled, as if he'd recently gotten out of the shower. In his hands were two glasses of red wine.

He handed me one.

"I'm getting used to it. It sure is a beautiful ring." I wiggled my diamond-studded hand so it caught the light again.

"No, silly. The villa. The view."

"Oh! The villa! Yes, I love it. I've never seen anything so amazing. I thought I grew up with history and luxury in Savannah, but this . . . it's stunning."

"It was built in the eighteenth century," Dante said, launching into an explanation of the villa's history. "I didn't grow up with money or luxury, so this was one of the original things I purchased when I signed my first big contract."

"I know, I read the interview you did last week. You mentioned this house."

He studied me and smirked. "Been reading up on me?"

I shrugged and smiled coyly in response. "Oh, by the way?"

"Yes?"

"Thanks for being so kind back there in Rome. I was thinking about how wild it was, and you didn't lose your composure. You also made me feel protected, and that was really sweet."

He didn't say anything at first, just nodded and sipped his wine. "You get used to it after a while." We didn't talk for a few minutes, which should've felt awkward but somehow didn't.

"Tomorrow, we'll go down there," he said, leaning closer so we were shoulder to shoulder and pointing at a small marina on the turquoise water. "See those yachts? I have a surprise for you in the morning."

"You're a man of many surprises," I said, semi-sarcastically, taking a gulp of my wine.

"Mm-hmm," he hummed.

We drank in companionable silence for a few more minutes. Then he gently touched my back and caressed my spine, a move so casually intimate it was as if he'd done it for years.

Tenderly, he wrapped his fingers around my ponytail and stroked the length of my hair. He tugged ever so gently, and the motion was enough to make my skin prickle. I turned my face toward his shoulder. He smelled like fresh, spicy soap.

He set his wine glass down on a nearby table, then took mine and did the same.

"Is it time for dinner?" I asked.

He returned to my side and studied my face with that sexy, amused expression of his. "Are you hungry? I know I am."

Before I could answer, he cupped his hands lightly around my jaw, tilting my head upward and seizing my lips in an exquisite, open-mouthed kiss. The kiss, and the late-day sunshine making everything look soft and sensual, left me weak in the knees. Wanting more. Wanting it all. To my surprise, I was willing to beg for his touch, his mouth, his body. Oh dear. I was in deep trouble.

"Don't stop." I was aware my voice was breathy, needy.

"You don't want dinner first?" he murmured, a gleam in his eye.

I shook my head. "It can wait."

Taking me by the hand, he led me through the bedroom where my things were, then out into a stark white hallway and through a high-arched wooden door. The room was sparsely decorated, the focal point the tall French doors with the stunning view of the sea. They were open, and a light breeze washed into the room. The red terra-cotta tile floor was cold on my bare feet, and I shivered as he steered me to the low bed, which was decorated in a simple white coverlet flecked with gold trim.

It was so romantic that my heart hurt. As someone who was never into mushy romance, this was a bit of a shock. I wouldn't have wanted to be anywhere on earth but here, with him.

"Is this your room?"

"Yes."

"Interesting." I pretended to study the brass headboard and footboard, which looked old and elegant. My fingers trailed along the cool metal.

"You sound surprised. Not what you would expect for me?"

I shook my head. "No. I imagined you as a modern, gray/ black/white kind of guy. Also, why did you put my things in another room if we were going to end up in here?"

Dante sat on the edge of the large bed. "I wanted to make sure you had a place where you could be alone if you wanted."

For all of his macho bluster, there was a respectful man in

there somewhere. And the fact that he'd been so considerate of my needs, my personal space . . . well, that made me melt.

I stood in between his legs, and he looked up at me, tracing my bare arms with soft fingers. I dipped my head in an attempt to kiss him, and he wrapped both arms around my waist, pulling me onto his lap. We fit together perfectly.

"Are we doing this?"

"Doing what?" I loved his laugh, especially when he was relaxed.

"You know." I waved my hand in the air, in the direction of the pillow on the bed. "This."

He pressed a slow kiss to my neck. Then another. And a third. Desire with a twinge of anticipatory fear surged through my veins, and I shivered. Somehow this seemed so much more serious than what we'd done the night before in the club.

So much more intimate.

"I would very much like to do this." His hand went to my ponytail and pulled the band away. He played with my hair, alternately stroking and pulling handfuls, and tingles shot through my body. It felt decadent, what he was doing with my hair. I sucked in a sharp breath.

"What do *you* desire, Savannah? Tell me."

He trailed his mouth up my neck and over my jaw, the sensation so light that I closed my eyes and hoped for more. "I want . . ." My voice faded because I was distracted by the way he was skimming his mouth so close to mine.

"You need to know, I'm only going to do what you want," he murmured. "Nothing more. Nothing less."

"What I want is . . ." I managed to get these few words out. "You."

◊

DANTE

If there was one thing that I loved, it was an enthusiastic woman. As much as I liked to flirt and play games, I needed clear consent and passion in bed.

Savannah's desire was obvious from the way she tilted her head to mine, seeking a kiss. Crystal clear in how she slowly ground herself against my erection. Evident in the way she brushed her lips over mine and begged.

I loved every second.

"Another," she whispered sweetly. "Will you give me another kiss?"

How could I deny her? I was equally as impatient, but had presence of mind enough to slow down and make the moment perfect. For her. I kissed her, slow and deep.

Her soft cotton dress was short, and I skimmed my hand under the hem and ran my fingers up her smooth thigh. She rested her head on my shoulder and we stayed like that for a little while, with my fingers exploring her smooth skin. When I retreated to her knee she squirmed closer, and when I moved up her leg, she let out a sensual little groan.

It took all of my willpower not to throw her on the bed and bury myself inside her because she was so beautiful. But I'd promised myself, and more importantly her, that this time would be better. Longer. Perfect. And it would be a delicious torture, slowly undressing Savannah. Already her breath had quickened and her cheeks were flushed with excitement.

"Please?" she begged. "I want more."

"With pleasure." I lightly bit her shoulder, ready to do anything she asked.

But when she lifted a slender hand to stroke my face, to gracefully brush her thumb over my bottom lip, I knew I was in trouble. Women didn't usually touch me with such intimacy, such caring. The women I normally bedded knew the game. They slept with me for bragging rights, for the fun of it, a wild weekend of crazy sex.

This was different. *Savannah* was different. She had no expectations, and that made what we were about to do so much more erotic. And fraught with emotion too.

"Stand up," I murmured in her ear.

When she did, I gathered the hem of her dress in my fingers and pulled it up, above her hips. She tugged it the rest of the way off, and I swore softly in Italian when I found out she wasn't wearing a bra. Her nipples were taut and dusky, and my mouth watered at the thought of taking them between my lips.

I leaned forward to kiss the soft, pale skin of her stomach, near the lace top of her pink underwear. She gasped as I ran my tongue above the fabric. I looked up and was astonished to watch her hook the sides of her panties in her thumbs, then slowly ease them down.

Now it was my turn to groan as I stroked the curve of her waist and hips, taking in the thatch of red curls between her legs. I ached with overwhelming, rock-solid need, wanted to feel her, be inside her. But I had to take my time, dammit.

"This is why I wanted to do this here, while the sun was setting, instead of in a dark club." I skimmed my thumb over the wet seam of her sex with my fingertip. "You're too beautiful to hide in the dark."

I explored her slowly with my fingers, with far more of a gentle touch than I was used to. She was getting wetter by the second. She shifted her legs apart and I leaned forward, grasping at her hips. I gently guided one of her legs to a bent position so her foot was flat on the mattress. So she was more exposed to me.

"You are so . . ." I said in English as I reveled in the sight of her nakedness, then followed up with the Italian word for beautiful.

When my tongue made contact with her sensitive spot, she grasped the back of my head and pressed herself into my mouth. Unlike when I'd devoured her in the club, now I took my time, savoring every drop of her juices. God, she was delicious. I felt her leg muscles trembling, and I looked up. With a single, sweeping motion, I lifted her and placed her in the middle of the bed.

"Unbutton my shirt. Slowly. Take your time." I leaned over her and saw her hands quaking as she undressed me. Then she slid my shirt over my shoulders and arms, allowing it to drop to the floor.

"Now my pants." I sat up on my knees and she sat up too. I'd intended to wait to touch her more, but I couldn't help but cup her breasts in both hands.

She eased my hands off her and grasped my wrists while trailing her lips softly down my throat, over my collarbone, down my chest, and lower, pausing to nibble and kiss my stomach while on all fours.

Then she untied the drawstring of my linen pants. She slipped them over my hips and looked a little surprised when she realized I wasn't wearing underwear. This was now perfect, us naked, with nowhere to be and days to explore each other.

While on all fours, she stared between my legs, wide-eyed as if transfixed, and I'd never felt so powerful. Not even after winning the biggest championship in motorsports six times. The look on Savannah's face made me feel virile, hypermasculine.

"Before me, had you ever seen a man's—"

She cut me off. "No."

"Come here. Sit up."

She did. I took her hand in mine. Wrapping her fingers around my hard length, I moved her hand up and down, then closed my eyes and groaned while I tilted back my head. Her touch was incredible.

When I opened my eyes, I studied her face. Her expression was one of carnal need, curiosity, and vulnerability. Dio, the combination was stunning.

"Will you lie on your back? So I can explore you?" I asked, mussing her hair.

She shook her head. "No, I want to explore *you*. Lie down."

"Such an eager student." I eased onto the bed, enjoying the view of her sexy curves and all that wild, red hair.

She caged me with her arms and kissed down my chest, her long locks tickling my skin. She wrapped her hand around my erection and tugged gently, then paused as her bottom lip was poised to caress the sensitive part of my head.

"Tell me what to do," she murmured.

Shuddering in a breath, I managed to stammer, "Wh-whatever you want. I'll be happy if you're happy."

"Like this?" She teased me with her tongue.

"That's an excellent start. Be careful of your teeth and . . . pretend it's a gelato. Or a popsicle . . ."

She giggled, then grew serious. The feeling of her wet mouth taking me in made me groan.

"Slow, amore. Slow. Yes, like that."

Her hair fell over half of her face and she shot me a seductive look. I groaned again as she stopped to stroke. When she spoke, her Southern accent was thicker and that made me even harder.

"You can grade me when I'm done, *professore*."

I was dimly aware of my eyes rolling toward my forehead out of pure, decadent sensation. It was going to be an incredible week.

CHAPTER TWENTY-THREE

SAVANNAH

The next morning, paparazzi were everywhere as we boarded Dante's sleek, twenty-seven-foot Riva yacht at the Amalfi marina. Both of us refused to answer the reporters' shouted questions, but I couldn't help but smile when I heard one query tossed into the din.

"How was your first night as an engaged couple?"

If only they knew.

We'd spent every hour together, only leaving the bedroom when Dante made us a quick dish of pasta. Even that was a pleasant surprise—I'd expected him to have a chef, or drink only protein shakes, or command me to make something. I hadn't anticipated a delicious plate of spaghetti with fresh tomato, basil, and mozzarella. After dinner, we drank a little wine—decadently, in bed—and then we ravished each other again. And again.

Never did I imagine that a man would be capable of giving me *that* much pleasure, or that one would want to kiss and touch and lick me in all those places. I'd let him do whatever he wanted. It felt too amazing to deny myself.

Truth be told, we didn't get much sleep at all, but I felt awake. Alive. *Electric.*

Dante winked at me as he started up the motor. It was a sleek wooden 1960s-era boat, and it positively oozed European cool. As we glided away from land, he leaned over to give me a kiss, and I held onto my wide-brimmed straw hat and laughed into the wind. It was as if I was a movie star, sitting on a luxury yacht next to my Italian lover. Like Sophia Loren, but with red hair and minus the sexpot attitude.

Once we cleared the no-wake zone, he bore down on the throttle and the boat surged forward. I yelped at the sudden acceleration, then looked to him.

"You okay with this?" he shouted, deftly steering the boat.

"More than okay. I suspect you're a pretty capable driver." He accelerated again and the boat roared forward. Maybe he was trying to find out if I loved speed, and he was getting his answer, because I let out a good Southern whoop into the salt spray.

I took off my hat, stuffed it in my bag, and stood, the wind slicking back my hair, the splash from the water misting my chest as we bounced over the small waves. I was wearing only a darkblue bikini top and matching blue swim shorts. If Dante had thought he was getting a glamorous bathing beauty today, he was out of luck.

When it seemed like we were in the middle of the Mediterranean—I suspected we were a mile or so off the coast, well away from the paparazzi—he stopped and the yacht skimmed into its own wave, eventually stilling in the sea. He turned and studied me for a second, and the lust-filled look in his eyes made me bashful. I gripped the aluminum rail with sweaty hands.

"Come here."

I obeyed.

He wrapped his arms around me and claimed my mouth, kissing me with that familiar hunger. He squeezed my ass and nuzzled my neck. "You look so gorgeous. These little shorts you're wearing are driving me insane. And the way these bounced when we were going fast," he whispered, cupping my breasts. "That's why I had to stop. To kiss you. And touch you."

My breath caught. There he was, doing it again. Turning me on with only a few sexy words and a scorching kiss. Was this for real? I hoped it was. I ran my hands under his shirt, feeling the ridges and muscles of his back. His body really was something, a product of years of intense physical conditioning.

I'd been drunk with lust for him ever since our all-nighter. In fact, if he wanted to take me right here in the boat in the middle of the water, that would be fine by me.

His mouth captured mine again, and we made out long enough for me to feel flushed—and not from the Italian sun.

"This isn't our final destination today." He smoothed my hair back and turned away, leaving me bereft of his touch. The boat engine roared to life, the sound evaporating in the vast blue water.

For several long minutes we sped, and I wondered where we were headed. Soon, we arrived at another point along the coastline, and he pulled alongside a small marina.

As Dante tied up the yacht and sprang onto the dock, an old man hobbled toward us and said something in Italian. He held a small cooler in one hand.

Dante responded, laughing and speaking fast. He turned to me and helped me onto the dock. "Come. We're doing this so we can have a private day together and avoid all press."

We followed the man, who led us to an adjacent rocky beach. Then he pointed at a long kayak and set the cooler in the space between the seats.

"You sit in front," Dante pointed.

"I didn't take you for a kayak kind of guy."

He laughed. "Why?"

"Let's see, I've seen you in yachts, limos, Ferraris, private jets, and the most expensive Formula World car. That's why."

Shrugging, he handed me an oar. "I like any kind of physical activity and I usually love speed. But sometimes it's nice to slow down every once in a while, no?"

He waggled his eyebrows, and I knew he was referring to how he'd entered me this morning with a maddening, deliberate thrust.

I climbed in and he tossed his sandals in the kayak. Then he pushed the little boat into the water and got in. For such a muscular, powerful guy, he was agile. Graceful, even.

"Let's see how well the American beauty queen can row."

I turned and shot him a defiant look. "I'll have you know I've kayaked through swamps in Georgia. With alligators."

I loved his laugh.

We soon settled into a rhythm, paddling in perfect sync through the water.

"You're an impressive kayaker, Savannah Jenkins," he called

out. "Never would've guessed that a debutante could paddle like a pro."

His little jabs no longer annoyed me. I held the paddle over my head in triumph, then lowered it and sliced through the water.

It was a little more strenuous than what I was used to back home; we were in the choppier Mediterranean Sea, after all, and not a placid swamp.

"Savannah, stop rowing."

I allowed the kayak's oar to rest on the sides of the boat.

Not wanting to twist to look at him for fear of capsizing the little vessel, I sat motionless. The water was deep blue, hugged by rocky cliffs. Italy was so different from where I was from back in the States, but I was falling in love with the Amalfi Coast with every passing minute.

The boat rocked gently, and Dante put a hand on my shoulder. He dangled a red bandanna down my chest.

"What's this? Are we pretending to be pirates?"

I heard him laugh as I took the strip of fabric. "You are so weird sometimes, Savannah."

"Weird girls are good."

"I'm beginning to find that out, cara mia. Put that over your eyes and don't bother rowing. I want it to be a surprise where I'm taking you."

I'd noticed that since we'd arrived in Amalfi, his voice had taken on a kinder, softer tone. He was closer to that man I'd seen in the burn unit in Montreal.

I drank in the terrain for a few more seconds. The clear aqua water was the last thing I focused on before placing the bandanna across my eyes and tying it at the back of my head.

My hearing sharpened, and the sounds of Dante's oar skimming and splashing through the water, along with the slight wind in my face, told me he was propelling us forward. I leaned back in the little padded seat, enjoying the sun on my cheeks, the smell of salt, the awareness that he was in control.

After several blissful minutes, the sun and warmth faded. They were replaced by cool air. My skin formed goosebumps from the temperature change. The boat stopped moving and it bobbed in the water.

"Where are we?" For some reason, my voice and ensuing laugh echoed.

Dante's palm splayed across my back, and warmth flooded my body despite the cool temperature.

"Let's get this off so you can see where we are." His hands were at the back of my head, untying the bandanna. Once it was loose, I snatched it from my face and gasped.

We were in a grotto filled with the most stunning electric-blue water I'd ever seen.

When my eyes adjusted, I saw there were recessed floodlights both underwater and in the rock crevices. The illuminations made the water shimmer with an otherworldly blue hue.

Stunned, I swiveled my head cautiously.

"We're the only ones in here," I whispered, not wanting to shatter the silence.

"My family knows the people who run the tour groups into these grottoes. I called ahead and they cleared the afternoon for us. Got everything ready. The man at that dock is in charge of this place."

The water was so still, the silence so peaceful, to the point where tears pricked my eyelids. I wanted to twist and throw my arms around Dante but worried that if I did, the kayak would tip.

"Oh my God, Dante."

"Do you like it?"

He was rowing again, slowly guiding us toward a low, flat rock ledge.

I took it all in, astonished.

"Like it? No, I love it. It's magical."

◊

DANTE

She couldn't see my huge smile as I eased the boat parallel to the rock, expertly tying the kayak to an iron clamp bolted into the stone. With precise balance—thank God for my yoga training as part of my fitness routine—I stood up in the kayak and stepped onto the rock.

I held the boat steady and she gracefully stood, then joined me. She looked around and spoke in a hushed tone.

"Seriously. It's so beautiful that I think I could cry."

I wrapped an arm around her and kissed her temple. My heartbeat, normally a slow resting rate because I was such a conditioned athlete, was erratic and fast. I realized I'd actually been nervous about showing her the grotto, anxious to find out if she loved it as much as I did.

I'd had a feeling she would enjoy this, and I wanted to punch the air as if I'd won a race when I realized I was right. This was hallowed ground as far as I was concerned, and I hadn't ever shared it with anyone.

"I used to come here with Gabriella. My sister. We'd swim here as kids and later, we visited the week before the Monza race. But after she died, I've come every year, alone. This is the first time I've brought anyone."

Savannah leaned her head on my shoulder and hugged me. "Why didn't you bring any girlfriends here?"

"What can I say? I don't know. I didn't think any of them would appreciate it. Savannah, I'm ashamed to admit this, but most of the women I've been with are more interested in the bling of diamonds and the lights of nightclubs."

"Whatever happens between us, I'm glad you gave me this memory. It's like a fairy tale come to life."

Maybe this won't be the last time we come here together. I shoved the surprising thought out of my mind, because of course I was only bringing her here because we were like buddies. Friends who happened to be indulging in great sex.

I extracted the cooler from the kayak and laid out the spread of cheese, prosciutto, bread, and grapes. And a bottle of sparkling water.

We spent the next hour or so eating and talking. And while it did occur to me to try to make love to her in this secluded spot, I was enjoying our conversation too much. Which was a first for me; usually I wanted women around for one thing.

"Why did you give up pageants?" I asked, feeding her a grape. "You're gorgeous. You could have been a model."

She swirled a foot in the grotto's blue water.

"You really want to know why?"

"I do."

"Two reasons. One, my mother. She was the epitome of a pushy pageant mom. Yeah, like the ones you see on that reality TV show."

I blinked. "I'm not sure what you mean."

"She was obnoxiously competitive and was trying to mold me in her image. It caused a lot of fights, and it drove me to hang out with my dad. I was sick of her making me feel guilty for not choosing her preferred hobby. My brother was older and a semi-pro motorcyclist, so he was doing his own thing. I was expected to excel like my brother did, only in a more feminine pursuit. But I wanted to stop fighting with my mom, so I quit altogether."

"Seems reasonable. But difficult. What's the other reason?"

"It was fake." She sighed. "Too fake. For a while I thought I'd use my pageant platform to shed light on the problems of my state or the world. You know, during the interview portion of the show? But I'd answer the questions with some thoughtful, intelligent commentary about poverty or politics and the judges didn't care. Not one bit. The judges wanted pretty, compliant girls with hot bodies and big hair. I didn't want to be obedient anymore."

She held a hint of apprehension in her eyes, probably expecting me to say something flippant about her body or her looks.

"You were too smart for that," I replied. "You're not a product. You're a human being."

She tilted her head and a smile spread across her face. "I'm a little surprised, Dante Annunziata."

"Why's that?" I plucked a grape and popped it in my mouth.

"Because at times you seem like such a chauvinist. Like when I first came to the team. You didn't want me in the pits. Still don't, I can tell."

"That's different."

"How? You think I'm a human being but not one capable of being in motorsports?"

I cleared my throat. "It's not that simple, cara mia."

She let out a low growl. "It is if you allow it to be. Come on, Dante. Come into the twenty-first century. The water's warm. We feminists won't take away your manhood. Promise."

I didn't respond. For a moment, panic seized my chest, like how I'd felt when Gabriella was taken off life support in the burn unit. There wasn't anything I could have done for my sister, but a primal need to keep Savannah safe came over me and I reached for her hand.

"Tell me more about the competition and why you left."

She shrugged. "The pageant organizers didn't care about us as people. They knew that many of the girls had eating disorders. And sometimes they'd joke about it. It made me hate them. I realized that all of us were trying so hard to fit into a stereotype, an idea. It was unhealthy. We were being used to perpetuate that stereotype of femininity. I hated being used and manipulated. It was the worst feeling in the world."

I shook my head, trying to get Gabriella out of my mind.

"Do you understand?"

"I guess I do. I never thought about it that way. I thought most girls, oh, *women* liked to look feminine and be seen as pretty all the time. That they'd all want to be in a beauty pageant."

She blew out a breath and spoke slowly, as if I wasn't quite capable of understanding. "It's not that we don't want to look pretty. Some of us, most of us, want to do it on our own terms. We don't want society to tell us that we need to look a certain way. Pageants perpetuate that attitude, that all women should have big hair and big boobs and tiny hips. That we should all strive for the same look."

"But you don't look that way."

She arched an eyebrow.

"I mean, you're gorgeous but you're unique."

"I'm unique because I choose to be. Quite a difference from your other lovers, no?"

I dipped my legs in the water. Savannah had a way of going straight into the facts. I wasn't used to such direct conversations. "I dunno. I confess that I haven't ever had a long-term relationship. I've been devoted to the sport, so women are more for sating my physical needs."

"You've never been in love?"

I rubbed a hand over my head. "I don't . . . I guess . . ."

She laughed and the charming sound echoed off the grotto walls. "No need to continue. I already know the answer is no."

"I'm not ruling out a relationship in the future, though."

"No?"

"It might be nice to find someone who I could travel with after I retire, someone I could enjoy life with and share things with. I haven't met the right woman yet, I guess. I think it's going to be pretty lonely once I retire. My dad's been hounding me to align with another team as a consultant, but I don't know if I want to be around racing that closely once I'm not in the driver's seat. Having a girlfriend, or a wife, could help me settle down." I kicked my foot through the water, sending a spray into the air. "Or maybe not. I don't know. I'm always wary because of my parents' relationship."

"Yeah, I noticed that your mom and dad came to different races, alone. How long have they been divorced?"

A snort escaped my mouth. "They've lived separately for years."

"I wondered about their relationship, from something your mother said to me. Are divorces hard to get in Italy or . . ." Her face contorted in confusion.

"They're stubborn and seemingly enjoy both hating each other and making each other miserable. My father has had multiple affairs, and my mother is a bit of a martyr, and it's a big mess. I hate being in the middle."

"I'm sorry." Her voice was soft. "No wonder you're wary. And why you don't know if you want to settle down after you retire."

Even the word *retire* sent a chill through me. "One swim before we head back?" I asked, eager to change the subject.

She sprang to her feet and pointed. "How about I race you to the other side? To that rock ledge over there."

I stood. "What do I get if I win?"

She leaned over and whispered in my ear, describing a certain position we'd been in early that morning. "You know, the one where I was on top of you but turned around, instead of facing you? The one where you said you loved looking at my butt?"

Oh yes. *That one.* I felt my dick stiffen. "Sounds like a reasonable bet."

We dove into the blue water at the same time, and I powered forward, knowing there was no loser in this competition.

CHAPTER TWENTY-FOUR

SAVANNAH

The week on the Amalfi Coast with Dante might have been one of the best of my life—although I'd never tell *him* that. I didn't want to give him the satisfaction; after all, he was still an impossibly arrogant athlete. But I suspected he knew how I felt from the way I became more relaxed by the day, how I laughed more, how I'd throw my arms around him randomly and kiss him wildly.

He seemed to enjoy my silliness and humor, and I saw glimmers of goofiness from him too. Like the way he ordered three pounds of gummy bears to be delivered to the villa—then proceeded to pick out all of the pink ones for me, knowing they were my favorite.

Truth be told, everything about him was growing on me, now that he'd explained how he'd clawed his way out of a depression following his sister's death to become a top driver. He was an incredibly mentally strong individual, going on to win all those championships after suffering such a trauma.

While there were a few team obligations meant for the paparazzi during those days, we mostly spent time at the villa, acting like a real couple. I loved when he cooked his simple pasta dishes and when we'd make each other laugh so hard, while sitting on the terrace, that we'd spurt prosecco out our noses.

In between kisses, of course.

And the sex, well, that was possibly the biggest surprise. Dante was a ravenous lover, and he couldn't seem to get enough of my body. Exactly as he'd promised, he'd shown me how to please him. And taught me more than a few things about my own body's erotic desires, as well. The lessons were mutual too. By the end of the week, I'd not only learned what turned him on but figured out how to tease him to the point of madness.

"What's this?" I asked one morning in the kitchen, while standing near an open cupboard. It looked like peanut butter, only darker.

"You've never had Nutella?" He took the jar from my hands and unscrewed the lid. "It's from Italy. It's what all Italian children eat for breakfast. My mom would spread it on bread for me and my sister and serve it with cold milk."

I peered into the jar and inhaled. Nutty. Sweet. I watched him dip a long finger into the creamy substance, then wag it in front of my lips. "Try it."

Keeping my eyes on his, I licked, slowly. He groaned as I took his finger all the way in and sensually slid my mouth away. Dear God, it was like candy. Or hazelnut heroin. Addictive. I needed more.

I smacked my lips. "Holy crap, Dante! What is that? It's better than an orgasm."

He burst out laughing. "I've been upstaged by Nutella? Wait, you left some on your mouth." He licked my top lip. "Mmm."

As he devoured my mouth, I got an idea. An excellent idea. One that combined two of my favorite Italian flavors. I took the jar from his hands. Setting it on a nearby counter, I shrugged off my T-shirt and panties.

"Take off your clothes," I whispered. "What? Why—" I looked to him, then to the Nutella, and at the erection poking into the fabric of his shorts. It was impossible for me not to lick my lips like a cat watching a mouse.

"Take 'em off, dude. This Southern girl has some catching up to do on Italian cuisine." I dipped a finger into the open jar, then licked it seductively.

Grinning, he stripped quickly and I sank to my knees right there in the kitchen.

0

"Dio, Savannah Jenkins, you're going to be the death of me." I was in bed, out of breath, and drunk on his body.

It was our last afternoon in Amalfi and we'd intended to nap. But it was impossible for us to keep our hands off each other.

"This. I love all of this." He ran his hands over my red bra and matching lace panties. I was on top and biting his neck when he tugged my hair, which made me moan.

"I love the color red. Love your lingerie and your hair."

"I'll keep that in mind next time I buy panties."

"No. Really. I'm kind of superstitious about it. My cars have always had red elements. I was so glad to see this season's car was mostly red. I also wear red socks."

I laughed and sat up. "I've noticed your socks. Some of the drivers in NASCAR were that way. Some wore two different shoes, some prayed on a certain side of the car."

His hands cupped my breasts and squeezed. "I have lots of superstitions."

"Oh yeah? Like what?"

"I like even numbers, which is why I picked twelve as my race number. And I have some superstitions surrounding sex."

This got my attention. "Like what?"

"I don't have sex the month before the season starts."

"So you've only been with me this season?"

"Yep." Dante shifted underneath me and I could feel his erection. "Good. What else?"

"I don't have sex from Wednesday through Sunday on race weeks. Sunday night after the race is okay."

How was this going to work once we were back on the circuit? Could we keep away from each other? Would we have to share a room now that we were engaged?

"Oh, and something non-sex-related. I keep something that my sister gave me pinned to the inside of my suit, near my heart."

"What did she give you?"

"A medal of Saint Frances of Rome. She's the patron saint of drivers. There's a legend that an angel used to light the road before her with a lantern."

I leaned to softly kiss him. "Red socks, even numbers, saint medals. You're adorable, you know that?"

He grumbled and squeezed my butt. "I'm not in the mood right now to be adorable, cara mia."

"That's funny. Me neither."

I swiveled my hips against his erection. It felt incredible to be desired that much.

Squirming out of my bra and underwear, I took a condom from the nightstand and unrolled it—I'd gotten good at that—then sank onto him. I pinned his arms over his head and rocked, undulating my hips in a slow circle as I got my fill of him.

"Go faster," he commanded.

I shook my head.

"Please?" he groaned.

I lifted my hips up and sank down even slower. Grinding into him, I let up on his hands, reveling in the fact that his eyelids fluttered as he gave in to the pleasure. He grabbed my hips, hard, and moved me with fury.

"Touch yourself, Savannah. Like I showed you."

"You didn't show me. I already knew how to give myself an orgasm."

"Si. Okay. Fine. Let me watch you touch yourself when you're on top. Please?"

When my hand went between my legs, he ground out a phrase in Italian.

"What are you saying?" I asked. Jesus, his Italian was an aural aphrodisiac.

"I can't last long when I watch you get yourself off. That's what I said."

Dear God, Dante. "When you talk dirty it makes me come." My body tripped into a rolling orgasm, and as I cried out and tipped my head back, he growled something unintelligible.

"Dio mio, Savannah. You're too much for me." In one rolling swoop, he tossed me on my back and drove into me, hard. Again and again, and I loved how powerful he was, how out of control I made him.

"I can't be a gentleman because you're so sexy."

"What if I don't want you to be a gentleman?"

"Then you're going to get what you want," he replied in a rough voice, entering me with a savage thrust and holding my head still by gripping my neck and jaw with enough gentle force to be thrilling.

Indeed, this was sheet-gripping, toe-curling, multiple-orgasm-having sex. His thrusts and noises turned primitive and I could utter only one word.

Yes.

"Yes. Si. Si," he rasped as he came in long, pulsing spurts that I could feel through the condom. "This is for you. Because of you. Si."

He collapsed onto me and I stroked his back, trying to soothe his trembling. It was moments like this, like after he'd had an orgasm, that I was most vulnerable, like I was almost willing to tell him that I could fall for him in real life. The feeling usually passed, and sometimes made me sad. Today, melancholy took over. Post-orgasm blues, maybe? I turned my head to the window at the impossibly blue sky and even brighter Mediterranean Sea.

"Did I hurt you, tesoro?" His voice was low and musical. "I was rougher than usual."

"No. Not at all. I was thinking . . ."

"Of what?" He rolled off and lay on his side, brushing the hair out of my face with his fingers.

"It's not fair."

"What's not fair?"

I shrugged and tried to focus on his muscular chest instead of his inquisitive eyes. "That you're so incredible, sex-wise, and for the rest of my life I'll compare every other lover to you." He flashed me a haughty, hard stare and for the first time ever, I saw a tiny vein in his temple throb.

"Who says you'll have other lovers? I might keep you for myself."

The thought that he might want *more* sent my heart soaring. I wanted to jump on the mattress and do a victory dance. He wanted *me*. But wait. Surely he was teasing? That would explain why he was smirking.

I tossed off a laugh. "As if. This is only for show, remember? I'm your fake fiancé. And anyway, 'keep me'? Like I'm a possession? Pretty sexist, I think. Like I'd let you boss me around if you were my real boyfriend."

Why was that muscle in his jaw bunching? Oh, of course—it was because I'd called him out on being a Neanderthal. I raised an eyebrow at him.

"Yes, you're probably right, Savannah. We're too much alike, I think. Both too headstrong and stubborn. This is perfect the way it is, no? Something temporary? Or do you want me for longer?"

Of course he was teasing. My eyes stung, as if tears were about to erupt. I pasted on my pageant smile, the one I thought I'd buried years before.

"Pfft, of course it's temporary. We're only together for the good of the team, right?"

The question swirled in the air, like the fragrant Amalfi sea breeze coming through the windows.

He pulled me close, my heart splintering and cracking at the thought of the coming months, and how we'd eventually have to say good-bye.

CHAPTER TWENTY-FIVE

SAVANNAH

The second pit stop of the Italian Grand Prix was flawless.

"Amazing, team—simply amazing," Jack's voice gushed in our headsets. "One point nine one! Yeah!"

Incredible: *1.91 seconds*. It was possibly a world record.

I'd blinked once when I'd unscrewed the front right tire. Then again when Giorgio slipped the new wheel on the car. A third blink of my eyes, and I'd screwed the tire on with the pneumatic wheel gun, the vibration of the nitrogen in the device spinning it at ten thousand RPMs—and thrumming through my entire body.

I stepped back as Dante's car accelerated away from the team and into the pit lane. In the privacy of my helmet, I swore softly when I saw another car in front of his. A French team had pitted at the same time, refueled at the same time, and pulled out ahead of Dante. *Crap*. Would this hold him up on the track and put him behind? My heart thumped, and I could practically feel the guys near me holding their breath—just as I was.

Dante had talked about winning this home race for days, since it would be his last time on the Italian track before retiring. His mom and my parents were here watching from what the team called Mission Control—one of the team's luxury trailers.

He *had* to win.

Then I spotted a gray hose still attached to the French car in front of Dante and screamed, my voice echoing inside the helmet.

"NO!"

Someone on the other team had screwed up royally during their pit stop. The vehicle still had the fuel hose attached and it waved in the air. I watched in horror as a fine mist of fuel, almost invisible if it hadn't been for the waves of vapor, sprayed Dante and his car.

"Fuck, he's on fire!" one of my Eagle teammates yelled. Out of sheer instinct, I took a few steps at a running pace, but Giorgio grabbed my arm and held me back from the flash of flames.

"Stay back," he said.

He was right, of course. What could I do?

"What the hell is this?" Dante's voice growled on the in-helmet team radio system.

Jack, from the control booth, responded quickly in his soothing Australian brogue. "Easy, mate. Drive around it. You're going to be fine. Get onto the track as quickly as you can."

My whole body shaking, I watched as Dante maneuvered out of the pit lane, slower than he normally would. Miraculously, the flames quickly extinguished, and he expertly wove the car around his competition, which had stopped on the side of the lane with the hose still attached.

Dante zipped onto the track. Obviously, he wasn't going to let a small flash fire slow him down. Not in Italy.

"I'm not on fire, I'm fine. I'll recover," Dante said into the radio, and I gasped in a few more breaths.

"Of course you will," Jack said. "Now we've gotta make up those few seconds. Push! Push! Do you have vapor in your helmet?"

Dante's answer was garbled, but I could make out a string of Italian swear words and the next phrase, in English: "I'll be okay."

Intellectually, I knew what had happened: a fine spray of fuel had covered Dante's car and it had ignited because of the warm weather and his car's scorching exterior. While it looked terrifying, it probably hadn't caused any damage to the car. At least I hoped not.

Emotionally, I was a mess. And on top of it all, my parents were here, watching the race with Dante's mother. We hadn't been able to spend much time with them because of pre-race promo demands and my own work with the team—which was fine with me, since the less of my mother's scrutiny and drama, the better. My parents had amused themselves with wine tastings and sightseeing, and tonight we'd arranged to have dinner with my parents and Dante's mom.

No pressure there. And now, this.

The team radio crackled to life again, jarring me out of my thoughts. "He's fine, folks. He's okay," Jack repeated into the radio, probably more for his own benefit.

I heaved an exhale but couldn't stop trembling. I kept my helmet on for longer than necessary because I didn't want to risk people seeing my face, which was splotchy with anxiety. Honestly, it was a miracle I was still able to stand, my legs were so rubbery. Although I knew Formula World was a dangerous sport, I'd pushed thoughts of a possible catastrophe on the track out of my mind.

Until now.

For the next twenty laps until the end of the race, I ran through all the possible scenarios. Had fuel gotten in his eyes? Had he been burned? Was he breathing dangerous vapors that could later cause cancer? It would be like him to be stubborn and drive through his pain; I'd watched over recent weeks as he nursed an old shoulder injury, downplaying his aches through punishing physical workouts and the g-forces in the car that took practically superhuman strength to handle.

I couldn't wait for the race to end so I could see with my own eyes that he was all right.

This was the danger of a pit crew member becoming involved with a driver. While everyone on the team cared about Dante's well-being and safety, I felt like I'd been put through the spin cycle of a washer. Tremors had invaded my lips and they quivered with fear. When I pulled off my helmet, I made a show of wiping sweat off my face—but the liquid on my cheeks was tears.

When the checkered flag finally waved, I was able to relax my shoulders away from my ears. Dante rolled into the pit and I hung back, fighting the urge to fuss over him. He popped out of the car and slid off his helmet. His face was covered in sweat and his hair was drenched too. I longed to wrap myself around him.

But I couldn't.

Girlfriends didn't fuss over drivers in the pit, and crew members definitely didn't either. Fake girlfriends never did.

"What the fuck happened back there?" he roared at Jack, who

put his arm around Dante and steered him to the garage. "My eyes still sting from the fucking fuel. The vapors got into the helmet."

Oh God. A wave of fear flowed through me and caused me to freeze.

One of the engineers handed him a washcloth, and Dante scrubbed his eyes in between his bouts of wild gesturing.

I'd never seen Dante so angry. Because of the pit debacle, he'd finished fifth. At his home race. It was his worst showing of the season. Although he was still leading in the points overall, I knew how important it had been for him to win in Italy and how livid he must be.

I followed Dante and Jack and the team's other engineers at a respectful distance, then stood in a doorway as the men talked inside the garage before the final press briefing. None of them saw me, and my heart pounded as I listened. Dante's eyes were as blazing as the fire that had nearly consumed his car.

"Where was Savannah in all of this? How far was she from the fire?"

"Several yards away, mate," Jack replied. "Two garage bays."

I stepped forward. "I was with the rest of the crew. I changed your front right tire."

Dante fixed an angry gaze on me. "I know which tire you changed. I wanted to know where you were when the fire broke out. I'll deal with you later. Go stand with the rest of the crew. Or better yet, stay with my mother. She's probably worried. I'm in a meeting with my engineers and you have no place here."

What the hell?

He was dismissing me, shooing away the insignificant little woman from the important men's discussion. I glared at him, then looked to Jack for backup.

"Yes, go be with Mrs. Annunziata, and your parents," the engineer replied.

My cheeks stung as I whirled and walked out of the garage. The fire hadn't been my fault. Hadn't been Eagle's fault at all—it was a screwup on the other team. Dante had reasons to be angry, but not at me. I'd performed perfectly, and he was making me feel less-than simply because of my gender and mere presence in the pits. Wholly unacceptable.

I'd have to have a word with him later, in private. Many sharp words.

I found my parents, and Dante's mother, at the Mission Control trailer, which was outfitted with ten different TV screens showing the race broadcasts, and a few other monitors with data such as track temperature, weather, and lap times. This was where Jack and his junior engineers sat, and where the most important VIPs—such as Dante's and Max's families, and the occasional celebrity—spent the race. It was lugged to every race location in Europe, and when we flew across oceans, spare garages, control rooms, and equipment were sent months ahead of time via cargo ship, while the cars and parts were placed in the cargo holds of planes.

"There she is," boomed my father, whose expression was so joyful that it made me wish I'd been able to spend more time with him alone this weekend. He was sitting at a table with Mom and Mrs. Annunziata.

Steeling myself, I plastered on a smile and walked up to them. Being around our parents made me deeply uncomfortable. Fibbing to them about our fake relationship seemed unusually absurd, cruel even. Although we were acting like a couple and sleeping together, so it didn't seem like pretending. But knowing that our relationship would eventually end made everything so much more complicated, especially when we were around people who knew us well.

I'd successfully avoided Mom's questions over the past two days since their arrival, claiming that I had a mountain of work. Now that the race was over, I couldn't avoid her. Especially with our dinner planned for tonight—although I wondered if Dante would be in any mood to socialize.

The moms greeted me, and I kissed the side of Dad's head.

"Quite a race," I said, sliding into a seat next to Dante's mother.

"Thank goodness Dante's retiring this year. I don't know if we could handle this kind of stress." Mom fanned herself with a program. "Savannah, I'm not sure this is something you can stomach for the long term. What if he gets back into racing? This is terribly dangerous. My heart was in my throat watching him out there."

I willed her to stop, not wanting a reminder of the terrible scene on the track.

Mrs. Annunziata smiled and placed her hand on my knee. "I'll admit I was a little worried there for a few seconds, but I knew Dante would pull through. Like he always does."

"You seem so composed." I finally smiled, for the first time in hours. "I think my heart rate is starting to come down."

She let out a breath. "I take an anti-anxiety pill before watching every race. Well, *two* before the races I attend in person. I've gotten used to it over the years."

We looked at each other for a couple of long seconds, and I felt as though she was sizing me up. I thought about whether I should pump her for information on Dante and how to handle his moods, but now definitely wasn't the time. I wondered if she'd told my parents about Gabriella—and whether Mom had turned the conversation around and made it about her.

"Savannah, I was telling Mrs. Annunziata about your pageant career. And how beautiful you were," Mom piped up. She leaned toward us. "I also told her how you always fought me when I tried to put you in a white gown. You never wanted to be a bride, so that's why it's so unusual that your relationship happened *almost overnight*."

"Sometimes people fall in love," Mrs. Annunziata purred.

"That's right!" Dad chimed in. "The heart wants what the heart wants."

Did Mom somehow sense that Dante and I were pretending to be in a relationship? Or was she trying to make me look bad?

I cleared my throat and stood up. "Well, I'm glad all y'all are okay! Just wanted to check in. I have some post-race duties, so perhaps everyone should head back to the hotel to get ready for tonight. I'm going to check in with Dante once he's done with his interviews about what he wants to do for dinner, and I'll let you know in a group text."

With a quick wave, I scurried off, hoping that Mom would keep any more doubts to herself.

◊

The five of us ate dinner near the hotel, in an upscale trattoria. Because everyone in this city recognized Dante, we sat in a private dining area. He didn't want to be hounded by fans about the dismal race. The place was decorated in shades of cream and silver, with a single modern painting sporting six squiggly black lines along one wall.

"They call that art," grumbled my father, and Dante actually laughed in response. It was the first glimmer of cheer I'd seen from him in hours.

I assumed he'd lapse back into his foul mood this evening, given what happened at the race. To my surprise, he grew warm and gracious, asking my parents questions about their lives in between sumptuous pasta and seafood courses, telling stories of his early days in racing in tandem with his mom, and casually throwing his arm around me. Every so often he'd stroke the skin of my shoulder with his thumb, sending little waves of desire through me.

My emotions swirled as if we were a real couple. I was still upset with him about earlier, though, and tried to tamp down my anger over his dismissing me after the race. He had to stop doing that. But I had to pretend that we were fine, and get through dinner.

Dante was wearing a black button-down shirt and jeans, and I couldn't help but stare as he talked. He sure was the portrait of Italian, masculine perfection, and every now and then, I'd slip into a fantasy of being with him for real. Which was exactly the wrong thing to do, especially since he'd treated me so badly several hours ago. Why was this fake relationship becoming so complex?

After we stuffed ourselves with tiramisu, Dante's mother excused herself for the ladies' room. Dante and I faced my parents.

"So what time's your flight tomorrow?" I asked. "Did you say you were headed to Paris for a few days? Also, did you know that Kayla's going to meet me in Rio? I can't wait." I babbled about Kayla's law career for a few sentences, hoping to distract my mother from whatever ridiculously prying question she was poised to ask.

"Dante, I'd like to have a word with you. In private," my father said in his most stern, corporate tone. "Perhaps we can step over to the bar for a few minutes."

Oh, blergh.

"Of course, sir." Dante gracefully stood up and left his napkin on the table. On the way out, he kissed the top of my head.

I leaned into Mom. "What's that about?" I hissed.

"Your father wants to feel him out."

"About what?" I gulped my wine.

"I can't quite put my finger on it, but something's up with the two of you. It's such a short courtship, and you never wanted to marry. I find the entire thing odd. And of course, you're not helping matters by being so secretive. Honestly, Savannah, I wish you'd open up a little." Mom raised her well-plucked eyebrows and her eyes threatened to water. "I asked your father to grill Dante a little, to make sure he's serious. It's better if he asks the questions, man to man. I need to know where we stand, in terms of organizing a wedding."

Her narcissism was wearying. It was almost enough for me to say, "Of course he's serious," but I realized that would be an outright lie. Even I couldn't keep up the charade to that degree only to spite her, so I settled for another tack. "I wish you wouldn't meddle in my life. It's my relationship. Please stay out of it. This isn't about you. We'll deal with wedding preparations when the time comes."

Which would be exactly . . . never.

"I'm your mother, and I'm looking out for your best interests. Now here comes Mrs. Annunziata, so hush. Goodness, I adore her handbag. I wonder if she'll tell me where she bought it."

CHAPTER TWENTY-SIX

DANTE

We'd no sooner gotten back to the hotel than Savvy stared at me with a flinty expression.

"What?" I asked. "

Why did you send me away from the discussion today, after the race? Why do you continue to treat me as if I'm inferior?"

"You're not, and I don't treat you that way. You do a great job as a tire changer. Truly."

"Then why did you freak out and blame me for the pit fire today?"

"I didn't blame you." I collapsed into a chair. "This is why I didn't want you on the team."

We were in my suite—*our* hotel suite, actually, since it was important to keep up appearances because of the prying eyes of hotel staff, now that we were officially engaged.

It was nearly eight hours after the Italian GP had ended, and my heart rate still hadn't slowed entirely. I wasn't sure if it was because I'd come in fifth in my home race, because that asshole from the French team had nearly lit me on fire, or because Savannah had been in the pits only feet from the blaze.

Or all three.

I'd barely held it together during dinner with my mother and Savannah's parents. Mamma had a way of keeping the conversation flowing, and I'd never appreciated her more. I'd almost put my anger aside because she was so charming with Savannah and her family.

Then came that strange conversation with Mr. Jenkins at the bar. Over a glass of cognac, he'd asked me what my intentions were with his daughter.

What could I say? I was trapped.

"I care for her more than my own life, sir," I'd replied. Like I needed that question after the day I'd had.

But, in so many ways, my answer was the truth. Savannah might be my fake fiancé, but her safety was a top priority. Today's fuel incident made me furious. Not at her, though.

Now that we were back in the lavishly decorated, Baroque-themed hotel suite, anxiety clawed its way back into my brain.

"It's too dangerous for you," I ground out, for the second time. "But I'm not angry with you."

Savannah sank onto a cream-colored brocade loveseat. "I was at least five car lengths away from the fire. I don't understand why you keep talking about this. I get that you're upset about losing the race because of the other team's error. But don't pin it on me."

She swung one long, smooth leg over another. "I did my job, and I did it well."

I swore in Italian. "It's also because we had sex."

"What? Are you crazy?" She scrunched up her nose.

"We've been screwing all week. I don't usually do that. My rule, remember?"

"I don't think our bedroom activities have anything to do with the French team's incompetence. You're being old-fashioned and superstitious."

She still didn't understand. I walked to the ottoman positioned near Savannah's legs and sat. She'd been an exceptional tire changer for every race. And the French team was at fault. I caressed her bare, shapely legs and tried to modulate my voice, something that was near impossible because I was so pissed off. So secretly scared. The idea that Savannah had been anywhere near flames sent chills down my body so icy that I felt as if we were in Antarctica, not Italy.

But I couldn't tell her that. No, I'd have to try a different tack. Maybe appeal to her more feminine side.

"Amore mio." I thickened my accent because I knew she loved it. "I don't like you being around all these potential dangers. So I've been thinking about this. I actually thought about this in Amalfi."

"Thought about what?" She crossed her arms.

I leaned over and kissed one knee, then the other. Her skin smelled like a spring bouquet, and the scent was now both familiar and tantalizing to me. She'd changed into a casual T-shirt over short jean shorts, making her look like that actress from that old American TV show, the one I'd watched as a kid.

"I was thinking that I'd go to Bronson and tell him that you and I are now dating in real life. Plead with him to take you off the team. I'll bet he'd comply now. But you could travel with me to races"—I kissed her knees again—"for the rest of the season. As my mistress! Just think: You could go shopping in all of the best places around the world. Singapore. Tokyo. Abu Dhabi. I'll pay for everything."

"What? Your what? *Mistress?*" she yelped, jumping up and practically kneeing me in the mouth. "You haven't said anything to Bronson, have you?"

"No, I was thinking in Amalfi about this but since the incident in the pit today, I think it's essential that I do it soon. Maybe we can call him now. Where's my phone?"

"Are you joking?" she yelled.

I watched her pace the luxury suite barefoot. Why was she so angry? "Cara, most women would be thrilled to get an offer like this from me."

"Good Lord, Dante, I'm not like that. I don't want an offer from you. Haven't you figured that out? I could seriously strangle you right now." She stood in front of me and shot me a fierce glare as she jabbed her hands into her hips. "Why the hell would I want to go on a worldwide shopping spree on your dime? I have my own cash. A mistress? That is so freaking offensive. As I've explained to you about, oh, I don't know, a thousand times, I'm here to learn racing from the ground up. You need to stop dismissing me because of my gender. That's going to stop, right now. I want to be a pit crew member, not a groupie. I'm not going to be deterred from my job by my fake boyfriend who wants to keep me safe because I have a vagina."

"What if you'd been burned?" I shouted, waving my hands in the air. "And why are you bringing up your vagina? Your vagina has nothing to do with this. You wouldn't be a groupie. You'd be officially traveling as my girlfriend or mistress or lover. Or whatever."

"Fiancé."

"What?"

She held up her left hand, pointing to her diamond ring. "The world thinks we're engaged. We can't go back to being boyfriend and girlfriend."

"Whatever. Better. It looks more authentic." I shrugged. Maybe she was coming around to my way of thinking. "I keep thinking about what would've happened if you'd been hurt. I couldn't deal with that."

"What if *you'd* been burned? You were the one on fire," she hissed. "It's way more dangerous for you as the driver than me as a pit crew member. Don't you think a thousand scenarios went through my mind today as I watched flames surround your car?"

"But I knew what to do. I'm an experienced driver."

"I watched you drive through fire." Her voice cracked and I reared back, surprised at the sheer emotion in her tone.

"But I was fine," I grumbled.

Savannah visibly paled as she drew in a breath. "This is a dangerous sport. We both know the risks, Dante. And you're more in danger behind the wheel than I am in the pit."

"I don't want any risk to *your* life. I can handle myself. But I can't control what happens to you if I'm not around."

My words hung in the air. She stared at me and for a hopeful second, I thought she'd give in to my demands. Maybe she'd agree because I was right. Because she wanted to please me. Wouldn't that be nice? Or maybe she'd agree because she was feeling all of the messy, complicated things that I was feeling.

"Oh my God, I finally get it," she said in a soft voice, sinking into the chair. "This is about your sister."

"Don't bring her up, please." My leg jiggled of its own accord.

"You're worried you're going to lose someone like you did her. That's why you don't trust women in motorsports. It's why you don't trust me."

I pressed my lips together, unable to say anything.

"That's what's behind all this misogyny. Your sister. This isn't about me, or keeping me safe. It's actually kind of sweet, in a misguided way. But it's still sexist."

"It *is* about keeping you safe."

Her fingers found my chin and she tilted my head up to meet her gaze. "You're not going to lose me. I promise I'll be extra-careful. We've only got a handful of races left in the season."

"And next season? And the next? I'm retiring, but you . . . you don't belong in this sport." My voice trailed off.

"Sweetie, I'm going to overlook what you said because I know where you're coming from now. It's not a place of chauvinism. It's from your heart." Her Southern accent again made me melt, and she slid into my lap and straddled me, kissing my mouth with an aching softness.

"I promised your father I'd keep you safe."

She threw her head back and groaned. "Oh God, is that what the two of you talked about? Was it some outdated patriarchal crap?"

"Maybe." I wasn't going to say that her father had clapped me on the back and threatened to cut my Italian balls off if I broke his little girl's heart. After those exact words, I'd sworn on my sister's grave that I would do everything in my power to keep Savannah safe and happy.

All the more reason for her not to be part of the team.

"What else did you talk about?" she demanded. "Tell me now. I think my mom suspects we're not a real couple."

I shrugged. "We talked about guy stuff. And why did your mom keep asking if I eat something called crawfish? I don't know what that is."

"It's a thing we eat in the South. Like a lobster. But tiny."

"Sounds tasty." I stroked her hair. "Your dad told me it was obvious we were crazy about each other. My mom said the same thing."

"Hmm." She appraised me with a stern look. "Crazy about each other. Right. Or just crazy."

I ran my hands over her jean-clad ass. Why wouldn't she go along with what I wanted? It would be so much easier that way, and would fulfill my promise to her father. She wriggled on my lap. Dammit. My thoughts turned to sex. *That's* what I needed. A distraction from the events of the day.

"You look like that girl on TV with the cutoffs," I murmured, pressing my face against her right breast. "What was her name? The old show. Daisy something."

She shifted back, a look of exasperation etched on her face. "Daisy Duke."

"What?"

"First, you stereotype my gender, and now you're stereotyping my Southern roots."

"What? I loved that show as a kid when it was on in reruns in Italy. *The Dukes of Hazzard.*" I paused and frowned. "Daisy is *hot*."

Savannah tilted her head. "You're adorable when you're clueless, you know that?"

I roughly pulled her close. "We're supposed to go out later

tonight. Tanya and Jack are meeting us downstairs to go to that sponsor's cocktail party. But I guess we could tell them, tell the press, that I'm not feeling well after the race . . ."

She cupped my face in her hands and stroked my lips with her thumb. God, I wanted to possess her tonight, to be inside her. Something about the close call on the track made everything between us seem so much more urgent.

"I think this is the perfect night to stay in. Didn't we have enough excitement with our parents?" She wriggled on my erection.

As we kissed, I couldn't get the image of the flames that had surrounded my car earlier in the day out of my mind. I hugged Savannah tight.

"Please, would you think about allowing me to talk to Bronson? I would feel so much more comfortable if you weren't in the pit every race. Spend some time in the control room."

Her body stiffened and for a moment, I thought she might slap my face. "You're impossible. You haven't listened to a word I've said over the past three minutes, or the past several months."

She wrenched herself off my body and took a few steps. She spun to face me. "And I'm not your sister, so stop thinking I'll end up like her. I'm . . . I'm . . . hell, I don't know what I am to you. I'm your tire changer—that's what I am."

She stalked into the suite's main bedroom, slamming the door behind her. I followed, hoping to at least have make-up sex. I needed her touch tonight. It grounded me.

The door flung back open and she emerged, jabbing a finger in my chest.

"And I'm not going to take any chances by asking Bronson for anything. He could replace you in a second."

I captured her finger and kissed it.

"He'd never do that," I murmured. "Not as long as I'm winning."

Savannah snorted. "He's got so much money that winning doesn't mean anything to him. He's in this for fun, I think. Did I tell you what I read?"

I wrapped my arms around her and planted a kiss on her forehead. "No."

"That Bronson would call reporters himself and pretend to be a spokesman for his company. He'd get the reporters to ask all kinds of stuff, and he'd leak tidbits. Isn't that crazy?"

"Mm-hmm." I stroked her cheeks with my thumb. "What does this have to do with us?"

"Oh Lord, you are dense sometimes. You're winning the season so far and I'm not doing anything to jeopardize your championship or Eagle's ranking. Period. We are working well together as a team and that's the way it's going. To. Stay."

Dio, my little American kitten was fierce when she wanted to be. However dangerous her idea of women in motorsports was, there was no question: she was intensely loyal.

To me.

CHAPTER TWENTY-SEVEN

DANTE

Singapore was the toughest of all challenges for Formula World drivers for so many reasons.

First of all, it was a night race. Which meant all the sessions—the practices and the qualifying leading up to the main event—took place at night. So the entire team's eating and sleeping schedule shifted.

That, added to the country's intense heat and humidity, and the fact that I was now sharing a room with Savannah but not having sex because of my pre-race rules, made me edgy and horny. Two days before the race, after a late-night practice, I bullshitted with Jack in the living area of the suite I shared with Savannah.

"You want to grab a drink or a bite to eat down at the bar, mate?" Jack looked at me hopefully.

I yawned and peeked at my fake fiancé, who was sitting on the sofa reading a book. We were at a table several feet away. "Nah, I'm a little tired."

Jack guffawed softly. "You've become quite the homebody, haven't you?"

"Going to ignore that." I stood up and so did Jack, then I walked him to the door.

"See you tomorrow," he said, then winked. "Make sure you get at least a little sleep, okay? I want you fresh for the race."

"Fuck off." I shut the door and sauntered over to the mini-bar. I felt Savannah's eyes on me, and I met her gaze. As usual, the sexual tension between us crackled. I grabbed a Pellegrino. I was trying to ignore how sexy she looked in her little blue cotton shorts and a plain white T-shirt with what looked to be a cartoon sushi roll on the front. She was in striped socks that came up to her knees and her hair was in a ponytail. This whole college-girl look was driving me out of my mind.

She winked at me and I laughed. "I'm sorry, Savannah mia, I can't make love to you."

"I was actually into my novel, but now that you mention it, I wouldn't mind some sexytimes."

She could be so adorably goofy, and I'd come to love that about her. Usually women—hell, men too—were so serious and awe-struck around me. Savannah treated me like an equal. Sometimes a little too much, in my opinion. But I secretly loved it.

"Stop it, kitten. Remember what I told you earlier in the season?"

"Oh, how you don't have sex days before a race? I thought you were telling me that to tease me. You were serious?"

"I was."

"But we had sex the night before the Italian GP."

"And look how that turned out," I muttered.

"Okay, I get it. You're superstitious and want to wait until after the race. Fine." Her head dipped to her book.

I sank next to her on the sofa. "Let's do something else. Other than have sex."

She looked up, an amused smile on her face. "Okay. Like what? It's not like we can go out. It's one in the morning and you've got qualifying tomorrow. But it's only five p.m. European time. I'm all discombobulated."

"What shall we do?" I wasn't used to hanging out with women outside of clubs or bed. Women normally didn't want to hang out.

"I know!" Savvy got up and went to the television, kneeling before the sleek, modern entertainment center and opening a drawer. My eyes went immediately to her ass, her sweet, curvy ass. I studied it as she pulled out remote controls and video game controllers.

"A PlayStation," she said brightly. "Stop looking at my butt. We can play a game. Look! They have Formula World racing! Oh, and they have good steering wheels and floor pedals."

"I don't do video games."

She spun around and shot me a mock-glare. "What do you mean? You've never raced on a gaming console? I thought all drivers played video games to train." She rattled off the names of a few drivers who had said such nonsense about video games in interviews.

"Max does. All the young drivers do. They were raised with this virtual reality foolishness. I'm a purist." I sipped my sparkling water and slouched low on the sofa.

"Whatever. Don't be an old man. Let's play." She fiddled with the television and electronics and passed me a steering wheel contraption. I caressed it with my hands, as if I were in my own car. It was almost like the real thing. Huh. It had paddles to shift gears on the wheel, like my car. What a fun toy for kids.

"Oh, and here." She was on her knees in front of me, positioning a little box with floor pedals at my feet. "You know what to do with these, right?"

I made a *pfft* sound. "I've never played, but I'm sure I'll figure it out. I remember the game creator had me voice some ads and asked me lots of questions when they were making this."

"But you've never even tried it?"

"For about five minutes in front of the press. It bored me."

"Silly boy. This is fun."

She returned to the sofa with a second steering wheel and floor pedal unit.

"Wait, we're competing against each other?" I asked.

"Well, duh."

Sometimes she was so hilarious, I couldn't help but laugh. "That hardly seems fair. I'm the world champion, you know."

"You've never played. I'll kick your Roman butt."

"You've played before?"

She shot me a smirk as her thumbs whizzed over the remote. The TV flickered to life. "Totally. My brother and I played all the time. I'm a good driver. An excellent driver, in fact."

"We'll see about that." I shrugged and sat straighter.

"If you're so confident in my lack of ability, I'll pick my driver and car first."

"*Certo*. Sure."

I watched as she navigated various screens, then saw an avatar of my face highlighted. "Hey! You can't pick me!"

She looked at me sideways. "Of course I can. You allowed me to pick first. I'm picking the best driver."

"So I can't even be myself in this race?" I frowned. "How do I do this?"

"Here." She leaned over and pressed some buttons, making me feel like a guy who had grown up with sticks and rocks and camp-fires. "You can be Max."

"I don't want to be Max." My teammate's smarmy young face appeared on the screen. "Tough. This race will be the practice session." She pressed another button and the track flickered to life on the TV.

"Oh, we're racing in Spain, are we?" I murmured. "I've always done well there."

"Oh yeah? Too bad I have the best driver."

The checkered flag waved, and my heart rate spiked. She whooped as she floored her virtual race car and pulled out ahead of me on the track.

◊

SAVANNAH

"You're not such a bad driver, Dante Annunziata."

It was four in the morning and we'd been playing racing video games for hours. We'd taken a break to order a pizza from room service, and now we were stretched out together on the suite's sofa, laughing. I was having a blast with him, mostly because it was so damned fun to see him relax as we played and joked.

It dawned on me that Dante had never had the chance to be a

young man. He'd always been a racer, since he was a kid. Always been competing. Kind of like I had, only on a worldwide stage. From what I gathered, his father had pushed him, and when he kept winning, he'd pushed harder.

In that sense, we were so much alike. His father, my mother—both had inserted us into the limelight as kids. I wasn't sure if he saw the parallels between our upbringing, because he was always quick to point out our differences. Age difference, cultural differences, food preferences. But in my opinion, the reason we got along so well—like tonight—was because we were so similar.

"I thought you were going to beat me there in the beginning." He ran his hand through my hair. "You're a pretty excellent racer yourself."

"For a girl, you mean."

"I didn't mean that at all. I was surprised at how lifelike the game was. I should use it for training . . ." His voice trailed off. "Of course, there will be no more training after this year."

"Does that make you sad?" I lifted my head from his chest.

"Sad? A little. I guess I wonder about the future and what it holds. I'll have to grow up some. A lot."

"Do you not want to grow up?"

"I do, I think." He shrugged. "I don't want to be like my father, who was only focused on pleasure and women. I want more from life. Something meaningful. I need to figure out how to do that."

I put my head back down on his chest. Dante's family situation seemed far more complicated than mine.

We lay like that for long minutes, with him stroking my arm and me listening to his heartbeat. An average person's resting heart rate was around seventy beats per minute, but drivers like Dante had resting heart rates closer to forty because they were so fit. The beat in his chest was so slow that at one point, I had a flash of panic when I wondered if he was even alive. It was a miracle, really, when I finally heard the slow thump.

"Tell me what all these mean." He interrupted my thoughts by caressing the charms on the silver bracelet around my wrist.

I shifted so I was lying on my back, half on top of him. "Oh. Mom started this for me. She and my Daddy get me a charm every year. I have twenty-five charms, one for each year I've been alive, and one for good luck."

I explained each charm, starting with the ballet slipper.

"So you began ballet at four?"

"Yep. I loved it. And this one, of the lipstick, that was when I turned eight, for my first big pageant."

"Eight! My God. You were so young."

"Yep. I wanted to kick all of the little girls' butts onstage. And I did."

He laughed. "Brava. That's my girl."

Twisting my wrist, I touched another charm. "And a book, for when I entered first grade."

"What's this one?"

I held a charm of two stick-figure girls between my fingers. "This one is from my best friend, Kayla. You'll meet her in Brazil in a few weeks. And this other one is an angel. My dad got it for me the year I turned fourteen and went to high school. It was the year he took me to my first NASCAR race. I consider my dad my angel."

"You're an angel." He kissed my palm, sending a shower of sparks up my arm. "And the frog?"

"My mom got that for my twenty-fourth birthday earlier this year. She was hoping I'd find my frog prince."

"Perhaps . . . well, never mind. What's this? A fish?"

"Oh. I got it before I left for Italy. It's the only one I've bought for myself." I unclipped the little charm. "This is what's called a dolphin downspout. They're found only in Savannah. The real ones are put on the ends of drainpipes."

"Downspout?"

He sounded confused, so I continued. "Y'know, drainpipes, so the water can flow away from a building. They're considered good luck in my city. They're all over Savannah." I sat up and straddled him. "Here. I want you to have it. You need the luck the rest of the season."

"You don't have to—"

"No, I want to. I want you to have good luck at the night race, and all the races afterward." I pressed the charm into his hand.

"Thank you. I'll wear it next to my sister's charm."

That struck me as incredibly sweet. Vulnerable, even. "Epic." I leaned to kiss him as he pinched my butt.

"Now I'm going to bed, in the guest room." He caught my wrist. "Why not sleep next to me? I'll be good."

"You're the one with the no-sex-before-races rule. You might be able to control yourself tonight when we're both tired, but will you be able to resist tomorrow morning when I'm crawling all over you, half asleep, wanting you inside of me?" I pressed my mouth to his.

"Of course I wouldn't be able to resist you." He groaned. "I guess you're right. But Savannah?"

I slid off his body. Now standing, I looked down at him. He reached up and trailed his fingers on the side of my thigh. "Yes?"

"Lock your door. Because I'm already tempted."

CHAPTER TWENTY-EIGHT

SAVANNAH

Singapore was kicking our butts.

It wasn't because the competition was held at night; the track was brightly lit, so visibility wasn't a problem. It was the intense heat and humidity that was draining for nearly everyone on the team.

The drivers had an additional challenge: the track had twenty-three turns, which meant neck-snapping g-forces, intense braking, and fierce arm muscle workouts every time they climbed in the car. It was also the longest race of the season, which added to the difficulty.

Even Dante, who had raced here several times, said it was the biggest physical test he'd ever faced. He'd come in third to two of the French team's drivers during qualifying, and I knew he was miffed by that, especially after his dismal performance in Italy.

When the race began, I watched his car on the pit bay television. Dante surged ahead, parallel with one of the French cars. On the first turn, his prowess kicked in, nudging the other car out of the way while avoiding the barrier that was only inches away. Methodically, he did the same thing three laps later with the second French car, and took the lead for the next twenty-two laps. He was three seconds ahead of the second-fastest car—a reasonable amount by Formula World standards, but within striking distance. He couldn't let up on the throttle.

A fine, misting rain began to fall from the sky. It was unsurprising because of the amount of moisture already in the air.

"Let's go to the wet tires. Get in place, team." Jack's Australian accent was smooth in my headset. "Dante, I want you to pit on the next lap."

"Got it," Dante replied.

I assumed my position with the wheel gun. The high-pitched whir of Dante's engine hit my ears and he rolled into the pit. The guys and I performed our choreographed dance in 3.1 seconds. He pulled away, and my heart jumped into my throat.

Hopefully we'd been fast enough to keep Dante in the lead. Races were won or lost during the pit stops, and while ours had been fast, it wasn't a team record.

"Aaaaand he's back in first place, mates," Jack crowed into the team radio.

I let out my breath and watched the TVs, barely blinking, as he resumed the race.

He came in first, despite starting from third place. I let out an ecstatic squeal when he climbed out of the car and into my arms. Normally we just high-fived each other after races, but I didn't care who saw us today.

"That pit stop was flawless." His grin was huge. "You fucking rock, Savvy. Kiss me."

"And you're the best there ever was," I whispered in his ear. He planted a kiss on my lips in front of the cameras and the crowd and the world.

Several minutes later, he was on the podium and spraying me with so much champagne that my hair was soaked. I screamed and laughed and hopped up and down like a goof, but I didn't care. The win was so, so sweet.

There was more champagne later in the night, when we shared a bottle at the famous Amber Lounge after-party, which was packed with at least a thousand people and three of the world's hottest DJs. I barely paid attention to the music, however.

Oddly, after Dante's enthusiastic display of affection after the race, he'd turned uncharacteristically cool at the club. A switch seemed to flip in his brain, and he went from ebullient to serious. He barely kissed me, and kept his hand firmly on the small of my back. The music was too loud for any meaningful conversation, and when there was a lull in the beats, Dante had talked with Jack about his car's braking system. I'd occasionally interjected with my own opinion on hydraulic master cylinders, but kept my hands and mouth off Dante.

We returned to our suite, exhausted from the long night race and the after-party. He was dressed casually, in jeans and a just-right-tight T-shirt with the name of an energy drink sponsor on the front. He hadn't shaved in a week and the stubble on his jaw, and how it framed his perfect, bowshaped mouth, made him look raw and primal. I'd wanted to stroke his face all night, but hadn't dared because he seemed so distant.

"Maybe you shouldn't shave."

"You like the rough look, hmm?"

There. He was finally thawing. He was likely beat from the night race, which could do strange things to racers' eyes and minds.

We hadn't had sex since we'd arrived in Singapore because of his silly superstitions. But tonight, now that the race was over, he was mine. I was horny and needy and wanted his skin fused to mine. I stepped onto the balcony and took in the humid air of Southeast Asia.

"Come join me out here," I called out.

"No way. I'm taking a shower. I can't stand this humidity."

Funny, because I didn't mind it. The air sort of reminded me of Georgia in the dead of summer.

In the second bathroom, I quickly changed out of my dress and into something more comfortable. With a little bounce, I went back to the main bedroom and hopped on the bed. I wore a long T-shirt that said *I'm a Georgia Peach* on the front.

The shower in the en suite stopped, and after a few moments, Dante strode out in only a towel. His hair and skin were still damp and my breath hitched. God, he was a beautiful Roman warrior.

The look of surprise on his face made me hesitate. Oh crap. Maybe I should've worn something sexier than a T-shirt with a peach on the front. A pang of humiliation went through me.

Quickly, I rose onto my knees and not-so-gracefully pulled the T-shirt over my head. Now I was kneeling, naked. Offering myself to him. I was a terrible seductress, and the fact that he was so sensuous only magnified my ineptitude and lack of experience. Another pang rose in my gut when he stopped and stared. A confused look crossed his face.

New insecurities bloomed, ones that normally didn't cross my mind. This was all a sham. Why would he want me when he could have sophisticated actresses and models? He'd had his fill, and now was biding his time until the end of the season, when he could extricate himself from our public demands. That was why he'd been so cold.

Shame burning in my chest, I grabbed the T-shirt. I was stupid for being so forward, for seeking pleasure. All of those beautiful, intimate days in Amalfi? They were all a lie. I scooted myself off the bed, T-shirt in hand.

Dante no longer desired me. If he ever truly had.

◊

DANTE

"Where the hell do you think you're going?" I growled, ripping the T-shirt from her hands.

"Back to the other room. It's pretty clear you're not interested."

I huffed out an incredulous laugh. "What?"

I hadn't been able to indulge in her body in days, and I was practically blind with lust. I'd been surprised to see her there in the middle of the bed, looking luminous and fresh after the day we'd had. Then when she stripped naked, I was too captivated to say a word.

The woman was impossible and yet I couldn't get enough

of her. Not when I woke alone in one of the suite's two bedrooms, wishing she was near, not when I climbed into my race
car, and not when she was next to me, torturing me with her
beachy-sugary scent.

And now her beautiful, nude self was tantalizingly close
after long hours apart, and all I wanted was to feel her body
next to mine.

"Not interested? You teased me all day with those green eyes,
then tortured me all night in the club when you rubbed your hot
little ass against mine. Now you take off your clothes and offer
yourself to me in my bed, then try to leave? No, cara, you're not
going anywhere. You'll stay here for as long as I want."

She gasped as I allowed the towel to drop and flung her shirt
to the floor. "Does this look like I'm not interested?" I caged
her with my arms and legs, rubbing my nearly painful erection
on the smooth skin of her stomach. Nudging her legs apart, I
ground against her without entering. Slowly, the way she loved.
I'd learned so much about her body since our week together
in Amalfi. How she became ticklish when I trailed my tongue
up her inner thigh, how she loved it when I stroked her with a
light touch, and how she could orgasm if I circled my tongue
just so on her most sensitive spot.

Dio, what I'd learned was burned into my mind. I might
never forget until the day I died.

I didn't want to forget.

"Does this feel like I'm not interested?" My fingers explored
her wet folds.

She whimpered in response. I backed her up onto the bed.

"Hands on the headboard, Savannah mia. And don't move."
The bed had rattan slats and she reached back and clasped them.

Starting with her neck, I kissed languidly down her body, pausing to admire her beautiful breasts, cupping them together and licking one nipple, then another. I nibbled my way down her belly. When I reached the area between her legs, she squirmed and bucked her hips.

"I told you not to move." I circled her thighs with my arms so that she was immobilized. While consuming her with my mouth, I felt her quake. This made me smile against her skin.

"I love when you have an orgasm on my tongue. Taste yourself. Here."

I moved up her body and assaulted her mouth with mine, groaning as she sucked on my tongue. Breaking away, I fumbled for the condoms on the nightstand. It didn't take long to sheath myself or find my way inside her.

"Not interested," I rasped as I thrust into her, hot and hard. "This is me being not interested."

Her half-lidded eyes flew open and she inhaled sharply. "Kiss me again. Please, I want to feel your mouth and your tong—"

"Shh. I'm not going to last long tonight because I'm tired and because you feel so . . . fucking . . . tight . . . and . . . amazing." Tonight also felt raw and honest, in a way that sex with other women never had. My exhausted mind couldn't quite process it all, and I trailed my lips over her chin and brushed against her mouth.

"Dante, yes. More," she whispered, which only served to make my inner flame for her burn even hotter.

I groaned hard and exploded, my orgasm wiping my mind of all thoughts. The day's stress from the race, the pent-up desire for Savannah, everything melted away as I came. I practically blacked out from exhaustion, dehydration, and lust. Perhaps I fell asleep for a little bit. When I came to with Savannah in my arms, it hit me as hard and fast as striking a wall at two hundred miles per hour.

I love her.

I blinked into the darkness, awash in a warm, intimate glow. One that was equally surprising as it was pleasant. Sure, I'd heard about this kind of thing. I'd seen it firsthand in various men, the way they were suddenly blinded by a woman's charms. I'd read plenty of books, seen lots of movies. Never thought it could happen to me, though.

Those three words—*I love her*—sent fear straight into my chest. For the first time, I wondered if I was worthy of a woman. And I still wasn't sure if she'd even believe me if I told her I loved her, considering how we'd started our relationship. Even tonight, she somehow thought I wasn't interested in her, which left me baffled.

"Not interested" was the opposite of what I felt for her. A man who wasn't interested wouldn't cling to a woman's body like this in the moments after sex, as if she were a life preserver in a storm.

A man who wasn't interested wouldn't care if she slept in his bed all night.

And a man who wasn't interested wouldn't worry about how to keep her around after the racing season ended, long after I'd left the sport.

CHAPTER TWENTY-NINE

SAVANNAH

"I don't think I've ever seen you so excited." Dante stared at me, an amused smile dancing on his lush mouth. He leaned in for a kiss and I pecked him while keeping my eye on the door.

"She's my best friend. I haven't seen her in months. I wish I could've picked her up from the airport."

"I'm sure Jack would've let you out of the team meeting to do so."

I fidgeted with a paper napkin. We were ensconced in a back room at our hotel's bar, waiting for Kayla to arrive. "I didn't want to ask for special treatment. And it was an important meeting with the tire company after qualifying. Besides, Kayla said she had a surprise for me and didn't mind taking a private car from the airport. She also wanted to freshen up after the flight."

"At least you'll be able to spend some days after the race with her."

As I was about to tell him that I wished he could join us—he was going ahead to Mexico with the rest of the team—I spotted Kayla. She poked her head through the door and screamed when she saw me. I jumped up and ran to her, wrapping my arms around her willowy frame.

We both squealed and laughed while we hugged each other for a solid minute. She smelled exactly like I remembered—like Coco Chanel—and I pulled back to stare at her. She wore a deepblue jumpsuit with a plunging neckline and strappy gold sandals. Her hair, which used to be straight and long during her pageant days, was in a stylish, cropped Afro.

"You look amazing," I gushed.

"Yeah, two people in the lobby stopped her and asked if she was a model."

I peered over Kayla's shoulder at the deep male voice. It came from a generically good-looking guy with sandy blond hair and a boyish smile. He resembled one of those many actors named Chris that I could never tell apart.

Kayla put her hand on my arm. "Savvy, this is my surprise. I decided to bring Travis with me. Travis, this is my bestie, Savannah."

For a second, an irrational feeling of jealousy bubbled up inside me. I'd hoped to have Kayla all to myself. But then I saw how he wrapped his arm around her waist, and how she smiled with radiant glee. I clapped my hands together and laughed.

"And I want you to meet someone," I said, taking a few

steps toward Dante, who was standing a few feet away, smiling tightly with his hands in pockets. He seemed nervous for some reason. "This is my, ah, friend. Boyfriend. Fiancé, or whatever. Dante."

"I think he's more than a friend," purred Kayla. "Come here and give me a hug."

While the two of them chatted, I steered Travis over to a table and motioned for him to sit.

"So I hear you know my brother," I said.

"Alex has become a close friend. Between you and me"— Travis scooted his chair in as he spoke, and his accent was pure Atlanta, which made me yearn for home—"he wanted me to do a little spying on you while I was here. You and your new beau."

"Great." I laughed. "Tell him I have everything under control. Better yet, don't tell him anything at all." The idea of annoying my older brother gave me more joy than it should.

Dante rested his hand on my shoulder. "She's in control, all right."

Travis stood, and he and Dante stepped to the side to shake hands and talk. Kayla slid into the seat where Travis had been.

"I couldn't wait for you to meet him, and he didn't want me coming here alone." She leaned in and grabbed my hands. "We're taking the entire week to explore. He's so wonderful to travel with. You automatically know you're in love when you can travel without fighting. He was so attentive on the plane, making sure I had magazines and sodas, and even telling me to walk around so I wouldn't get blood clots."

"Well, that's romantic," I said, and we both laughed.

It sure sounded like Kayla was head over heels for him by the way she couldn't stop giggling. But a little, nagging twinge of doubt sprang up. Dante never asked me what I wanted or needed on a plane. But why would he? Kayla's relationship was real.

Mine wasn't.

Dante eased himself into the chair next to me, and Travis sat next to Kayla. A waiter came in and took our drink order—a bottle of champagne—and we settled in.

"What's it like working together?" Kayla asked Dante, her eyes shifting to me. Before her trip, I'd pleaded with her not to reveal that she knew about our fake relationship. Now, it seemed, she was intent on grilling him. I could tell by that inquisitive lawyer's gleam in her eye.

"I'll be honest. I don't like it much because I worry about her safety." He shrugged. "But what can I do? Like I said, Savannah's in control of this situation. She's her own woman, and that's what I love about her."

"Not this again," I said. "Let's change the subject."

"Savannah's always in control," Kayla shot back in a playful yet edgy tone. "Haven't you noticed that she always speaks her mind and doesn't shy away from saying her true feelings? Heck, if a barista gives her three sugars instead of two in her coffee, she demands a redo."

Dante turned to me, frowning. "You take sugar in your coffee? I thought you drank it black."

His question, while probably innocent, struck at the heart of my insecurity. The man I was fake-dating didn't even know the small details about me.

And why would he?

◊

"Hey. What should I wear tonight? Where are we going? I want to be able to tell Kayla what's happening." I stretched, trying to summon some energy.

Although I hadn't worked in the pits changing tires today, I'd spent the entire race in the sweltering garage with the rep from the tire company. We'd taken a chance and gone with the soft compound tires on my recommendation—a move that led to Dante's win, in my opinion.

I'd never seen such a crazy crowd as when he'd passed the checkered flag. And it was as if the city exploded when Dante and Max took their places on the podium. Dante had come in first, Max second, and even better, Dante was still leading in overall points.

Now we were assembled in Bronson's suite for a post-race plan with Tanya. I was used to this by now, this carefully scripted public-relations dance. It didn't much matter to me anymore where we went, which reporters we talked with, how many red carpets we walked. Still, I couldn't wait to explore the vibrant and chaotic Brazilian capital with Kayla, even for a short while. That was often the downside of all these races, all this travel. We never really got to know any one place—when we were in a city, the only important thing was winning.

Maybe someday Dante and I would return, with Kayla and Travis.

No chance of that.

All that mattered was that the team was about to win the championship. I was trying to focus on that instead of on Dante, who had become quiet and serious since Singapore. Oh, sure, he was his gregarious, confident self when we were out in public. He was charming with Kayla and Travis, and complimented me during every interview.

But in private, he'd been formal and less talkative. I assumed it had something to do with the season winding down, and his needing to decide what to do with his post-race career. I'd gently tried to probe him about his future, but my questions were met with one-word grunts, so I'd dropped the topic.

I had no place in his life now, or in the future. Our relationship served two purposes at this point: to help the team, and to sate our desires. As far as the months to come, I had my own plans to think about. My contract was up at the end of the season, and I hoped to renew it. It was essential to focus on my career and not get lost in Dante's orbit.

I sipped from a can of Coke. "Or is tonight a free evening?"

Tanya's brown bob swished against her chin as she shook her head. "There's no plan for tonight. We've gotten word from one of the top sporting newspapers in Italy that they're going to break a story tonight that says the French team is behind the technical theft scandal. They might even lose points."

Dante threw back his head and laughed. "Ah! Thank God. I would've killed Max had he been behind this. But it makes sense that the French team actually stole the specs. They've been doing shockingly well this year."

I smiled, too, because there was nothing lovelier to look at than Dante in full-on competition mode. And it was a relief that Max was finally cleared once and for all. While he was arrogant and a more risk-taking racer than Dante, he had a bright future in the sport.

"So," said Tanya, pointing a pen at me, then at Dante, "this means you two don't have to continue the farce of being engaged. Dante will be going out without you tonight to raise questions from the press, and I'll leak the news to a gossip site later this evening. On Tuesday, once we're on our way to Mexico City, we'll put out a news release saying you've broken up."

My eyes widened and my stomach felt like Tanya had kicked it with those stilettos of hers. Rationally, I'd known this was a possibility. My engagement to Dante could dissolve as quickly as it had materialized.

But I hadn't anticipated this here, or now—I'd thought we'd have had to keep up appearances until the final race of the season. Especially with my best friend and her new boyfriend staying in the same hotel, this came as a huge embarassment.

"Okay." I tried to make my tone firm and businesslike.

"Savvy, we'll need the ring back. It was a rental, you know."

"Right." I paused before taking it off my finger, because I'd gotten used to the heavy, sparkling rock. I glanced up at Dante and he was looking out the window, not at me. Figured. He didn't give a crap. I wrenched the ring off and dropped it in front of Tanya, on her clipboard.

"There."

"Where am I going tonight?" Dante asked, a hint of curiosity in his voice. My stomach roiled with a mix of anger and shame. I really *had* meant nothing to him these past several months. He was ready to drop me like a hot rock.

As Tanya explained that Dante would be attending a VIP bash at a Rio club with Jack, I sat ramrod straight. Bronson noticed my discomfort.

"Savvy, we don't really need you here for this discussion. Feel free to order room service tonight, watch a movie, and relax. I know you and Dante are still sharing a room, but it will be the last night you have to go through that. C'mon." He beckoned me to join him near the exit.

My cheeks flared hot because I was literally being shown the door. I'd served my purpose.

"Hey, I have an idea," he said, snapping his fingers. "You and your friend should go to the spa. Whatever you want, it's on me. A nice massage, maybe a pedicure. Facial. I'll get it set up for the two of you. There's a great place in this hotel, and you can even have dinner there too. They have a gorgeous terrace. How's that?"

I shrugged, feeling like I wanted to vomit. Without looking at Dante, I left the room and went to the suite. I wanted to get away as quickly as possible, preferably before he returned to our room. The last thing I wanted was an awkward conversation.

I texted Kayla on the way, trying to focus on our evening together.

Hey, we have a spa night paid for by the team! I'm going to book now for tonight—let me know what services you'd like.

Instantly, I got a reply.

Aww that sounds amazing. But Travis and I have reservations at a five-star Michelin restaurant down the street. Why don't you and Dante join us, and we can go to the spa tomorrow morning?

Dante and I wouldn't be joining anyone together ever again. It took me a few minutes to respond, and by the time I did, I was in the suite, tears pricking at my eyes.

I think he has team obligations. No worries! We'll catch up later. Have fun!

$\emptyset$

Hours later, when I was as limp as an overcooked noodle from the spa massage and facial, there was a knock at the door.

My heart leapt. *Dante*. But why would he be knocking? He still had a key, since we were sharing the suite for tonight despite the soon-to-be official "breakup."

Maybe he'd lost it. I made a beeline for the door and peered into the peephole. It was Kayla, wearing a fabulous little black dress and sparkly black heels. I swung the door open.

"Hey," I said, standing aside so she could come in. "You look gorgeous."

"I'm so sorry." She sighed.

"For what?" I shut and locked the door, and we made our way into the suite. She sat down on a sofa.

"I didn't realize that you and Dante had, ah, broken up. I saw the speculation on a racing website as Travis and I were leaving the restaurant. I should've gone to the spa with you."

I sank next to her and pulled my knees to my chest. "Yeah, that was decided by the team. It's going to be official in a couple of days. We no longer need to pretend. And no, don't worry about it. You didn't need to babysit me."

She aimed her giant brown eyes in my direction. "What does this mean? Will he be sleeping here tonight? Do you two sleep in the same bed? Have the two of you actually had sex?"

"I assume he'll be sleeping here tonight, unless he chooses somewhere else," I said pointedly. "And the other answers are usually and yes, a lot."

Kayla sucked in a breath. "Wow. This is way complicated."

"More than you know," I said miserably.

"You have real feelings for him, don't you?" My silence spoke for itself. "Oh no. You're in love," she whispered.

"Maybe." When I started to cry, she came to sit next to me and slipped her arm around me.

"Oh, sweetie. Of course you'd fall for him. He's captivating. Even I can see that, and he's *so* not my type."

A little laugh erupted between my tears. "I didn't plan to fall for him. Hell, I didn't like him when we first met. But underneath that arrogant exterior is a good man. Kind of a goofball, even. We stayed up all night in Singapore playing video games and eating pizza. It was sweet and normal. And I guess I thought we had something real."

"How do you know you don't?"

I wriggled out of her embrace to look at her. "This was all orchestrated by the team, and all he cares about is winning. Why would he want me?"

She snorted. "Why wouldn't he want you? Good Lord, Savvy."

"We're so different, from different cultures, different ages, different views on life. He's eight years older and retiring, and I'm only starting a career in motorsports. He's, he's . . ." I sputtered. "He's used to hooking up with models. Ugh, where did that even come from? Normally I'm not jealous. It's like all my flaws are coming to light because I'm into him way more than I expected. That's pathetic."

"Not pathetic at all. And you're no slouch. Had you wanted, you could've been Miss America."

I made a little gagging noise.

"Don't let his age and his fame intimidate you. The way he stared at you at dinner the other night led me to believe he has feelings for you too. He looked like he wanted to dip you in the tiramisu and eat you up. The two of you need to talk and get past this stupid fake-relationship situation. Maybe after the season ends, you can sort out if what you have is real."

A shudder went through me at the thought of telling Dante my true feelings. My mother had drummed it into me never to tell a man how you felt before he revealed his intentions. I'd tried to reject that tired advice, but here I was, afraid.

"You're right," I said, hauling in a breath. "Now tell me all about dinner, and Travis. He seems like such a good person. I'll open a bottle of wine."

For the next hour, we drank and talked, and for those sixty minutes, life felt almost normal again.

CHAPTER THIRTY

DANTE

"It's okay to look sad, mate. You broke up with your girl. But no need to look too upset. All those chicks want you. Want *us*," Jack said, and he tipped his glass in the direction of a group of women who were smiling and blowing kisses our way.

"You're incorrigible. Where's Tanya? I thought you two were hooking up."

"She's back at the hotel. We had a fight a couple weeks back and we're taking a breather. But she emailed me with the news about you and Savvy. So how 'bout it? Now that you're officially single we can resume our old habits, no?"

I winced and surveyed the crowd in the club from the VIP platform. This wasn't where I wanted to be. Rather, it wasn't *who*

I wanted to be with. I shifted my weight from foot to foot. I didn't even feel like drinking champagne tonight. Well, not with Jack.

"Not interested. Oh, and I wanted to tell you. Please make sure Savannah's in the pits for the remaining races. She's done such an excellent job that she deserves to be there. She can handle herself and her safety."

Jack scowled and waved a hand in front of my face. "Excuse me. Who are you? What have you done with Dante Annunziata? I mean, I agree with you about Savannah."

I cracked a smile.

"What the hell's going on?" Jack sipped from his glass.

"I haven't told you any of this."

"You haven't told me anything over the last few months because you've been joined at the hip, lips, and everywhere else with one redheaded pit crew girl. You sure got the seducing part down, but you didn't get her off the team."

I pushed out a breath. "Remember that photo of me and Savannah in the garage in Italy?"

Over the next half hour, I explained what happened after the photo had circulated. How Bronson had all but black-mailed me into a fake relationship with Savannah so the press would focus on that and not Max's alleged involvement in the technical information scandal.

"I knew all about it." Jack sucked on his teeth.

"You did?" I said, gaping at him.

Jack guffawed. "Tanya tells me everything."

I jiggled my knee. "Of course. Anyway, it gets complicated." I hesitated, not wanting to reveal too many intimate details about Savannah.

"Uh-oh. Why? Is she pregnant?"

"*Ovviamente*, no." My brain flashed to an image of Savannah, big with my child. To my surprise, I wasn't horrified. Quite the opposite, actually. I shoved the thought aside with a shake of my head. "But let's put it this way. I'd prefer to be with her tonight rather than your ugly mug."

I finished my champagne. My chest had felt like it was in a vise grip watching her pull off the engagement ring earlier. As if I'd actually asked her to marry me and she'd ripped it off like she didn't care. Or worse, didn't want me. I had to look away when she removed it; otherwise I was worried I'd blurt out my true feelings in front of everyone.

Leave it on, I'd wanted to say.

I'd noticed how Bronson had taken her aside during the meeting, and I'd thought about physically carrying Savannah out of the room when the team owner had leaned close to her ear. Was it possible that he'd asked Savannah out? I wouldn't put anything past Bronson, that sneaky douchebag. Savannah wouldn't say yes to him, would she? Of course not. She was smarter than that.

"Why are you hanging around here with the likes of me? Go be with her. Go have fun. Hell, settle down with her. She's a good person."

"Settling down didn't work for you." Jack had been divorced twice.

Jack shrugged. "Racing's bad for marriages. The travel, the women. But you, you're retiring. You're starting a new chapter in life. If you've found somebody you connect with, why not give it a whirl? At least the girl knows her stuff about racing. Damn, she's smart, Dante. And she seems to know how to tolerate your bullshit."

"I know. She is. And she does." Downing my drink, I clapped

Jack on the back. "As usual, you're right. I'm calling it a night, friend. Have fun tonight, and be safe."

I stalked out, followed by team security. Several photographers followed, eager to get any scraps about how I'd broken up with my fiancé. Tanya had leaked the news to Brazil's biggest tabloid, and within hours, it was at the top of every website.

"Everything okay with you and Savannah?"

"Why are you here alone?"

"Where's your grid girl?"

The questions made me scowl, and it took all of my will-power not to snarl a response—or shove a camera into one of their faces. Once ensconced in the elevator with a security detail, I blew out a breath.

The suite was quiet and dark when I let myself in.

"Savannah? Amore?" I checked the bedroom. I didn't hear her welcoming voice, or see her reading in bed as I'd hoped. Was she still at the spa? Somewhere else?

With a growl, I pushed open the door to the second bedroom.

"Hey, I'm sleeping."

"What are you doing in here?" I shut the door and lifted the duvet so I could crawl into bed and stretch out next to her. "How was your night with Kayla?"

"She went out with Travis. But she came back here for a drink after. We had some wine. It was nice."

"Look at you. You're warm. And you're almost naked." I nuzzled her neck, and her skin smelled like sleep and sugar. She was wearing one of her soft little tank top and panty combos. "You smell amazing." My hands went to her ass and my dick immediately grew hard.

"I went to the spa all night," she said, her voice sleepy. "I got an epic, intense massage."

"But why are you in the smaller bedroom?" I kissed her mouth several times, but I was already thinking of where else I wanted to place my lips on her body. "God, you smell good. Like vanilla. I want to lick you. Can I? Will you spread your legs for me and let me—"

"Dante, I'm in here because I thought you'd want privacy when you returned. In case you brought—"

I stopped caressing her. "What? Do you honestly think I'd bring someone back to the suite while you were here? What do you take me for?"

In the darkness, she lifted her shoulders into a shrug.

"Savannah." I took my hands off her. My voice was louder and harsher than I intended. "You don't get it, do you?"

"Get what? We're over, Dante. We're done. Finished. We don't need to pretend anymore. Plus, the season is ending in two races. After Mexico City and Dubai, you can get back to your life in Italy, and I can return to mine in the US."

"Ohh, Savannah mia." I wrapped her in my arms and drew her close, making soothing *shh* noises in her ear.

"You don't even know how I take my coffee," she said in an accusing tone.

"What?"

"When we were having drinks the other night with Kayla and Travis. You seemed shocked that I drink my coffee with sugar. We've had coffee dozens of times together on planes and in the team canteen. That one little thing proves you know nothing about me."

"I know lots about you."

"What's my favorite color?"

I paused. "Red?"

"That's your favorite color. Jerk."

"This is a ridiculous conversation. Come here."

She let out a strangled, impatient noise.

"Savannah Jenkins," I said sharply, hauling her body next to mine. "I know lots about you. I know how sweet your kisses are, and how to make you tremble when I touch you in certain spots. I know that you make little moaning noises in your sleep that are a more alluring sound than any thousand-horsepower racing engine. I know you more than you realize."

After a minute, she relaxed into me.

She still didn't understand the depth of my feelings, despite my actions. I had so many things to tell her, but it was too terrifying to say the words aloud. All I could do was cup her face and kiss her sweetly, then love her in my own wordless way.

CHAPTER THIRTY-ONE

SAVANNAH

This was for the best, sleeping in my own hotel room.

Sure, it wasn't the luxurious suites of the past several races, but the room in Mexico City was comfortably upscale, with a giant whirlpool tub. And I didn't feel like going to a club anyway. Not tonight. I was exhausted from the entire week, which had started on a Monday in Rio with Kayla and Travis. The three of us had toured the city at breakneck speed, trying to pack every possible tourist trap into a sixteen-hour period.

After that, I'd flown to Mexico City, immersed myself in qualifying and practice, and now here I was, at the end of a long, sweltering race day. I'd also stuffed myself with a delicious buffet meal, along with the rest of the pit crew, in one of the hotel's banquet rooms.

Now that Dante and I had "broken up," I was back to being a regular team member again. No more perks. Which was fine—preferable, even. The guys had accepted me back into the fold with only a few snide comments and snarky looks. Those, I could handle and ignore.

I stripped my jeans and T-shirt off and shrugged on one of the fuzzy robes I'd found hanging in the closet.

Maybe Dante would go to a club with Jack, like he had in Brazil. Maybe he'd visit me on the down low, like he had most nights since our official public "breakup." He hadn't slept over the two previous nights, but I'd chalked that up to pre-race concentration and his silly sex superstition. But even after he'd won the race, he hadn't mentioned anything about getting together, and he hadn't texted, which made me anxious.

I suspected he had team obligations because I'd seen him huddling with Tanya and Bronson earlier in the day. And since he was poised to become World Champion if he took one point in the final race in Dubai—essentially, came in fifth or higher—surely they'd want to show him off in some high-profile way.

As the water for my bath flowed into the big tub, I swiped on my phone, idly checking Facebook. I scanned the updates of my friends back in the States—oh, look, Brittany from college was getting married to her high school sweetheart—and my eyes flitted to the right side of the page, where the news updates sat.

Formula World Star Spotted with Mexican Model

I tapped on the link so hard I thought I was going to shatter the phone's glass screen.

The news item was from a tabloid, and it had been posted just moments before. It was about Dante: he'd been spotted in a trendy part of Mexico City earlier in the evening, walking into a swanky bar with a model named Iolanda. His hand was on the small of the woman's back, and at seeing this, I cried out. That was where Dante had always touched *me*.

The article was scant on details, but with each word, my guts felt like a fist was wrenching them tighter and tighter. It said Dante had broken up with his American fiancé and was likely with the model as a rebound affair. Iolanda had no last name apparently, and she was famous in Mexico. Famous for her curves and pillowy lips. Famous for her extremely long legs and bronze skin.

Iolanda had had a crush on Dante since she was a girl, one of her friends told the tabloid. Iolanda was eighteen and had recently signed a modeling contract for an Italian lingerie company. Io fucking landa.

I looked down at my pale legs and burst into tears. Sobbed until my nose stuffed up and snot was running down my lip. I set down my phone and shuffled into the bathroom, still crying, to blow my nose. Blubbering, I checked the tub. The water was scalding, the tub full, and I shut the faucet off.

I blew my nose again, this time making a little honking sound, but the tears wouldn't stop. Of course Dante was with Iolanda. Why wouldn't he be?

Then I heard my cell phone ping.

I padded back out to the nightstand and picked it up.

Amore mio open your door please

Why? I texted back, frowning.

Because I'm standing here and don't want to make noise by knocking. I think there are photographers around. Open.

I blinked at the phone several times. Why would he come here if he'd been with the model earlier in the night? What kind of game was he playing?

With a heavy feeling in my chest, I flung open the door, and there he was, cradling a bucket filled with ice and a bottle of champagne in one arm. He charged past me.

"What are you doing here?"

"I thought we'd celebrate with our favorite champagne. Veuve Clicquot Rosé? You loved that back in Belgium."

"No."

"Wait, did you like the Dom better? Let's call room service for that. And how about some chocolate-covered strawberries?"

I shook my head. "I'm not talking about the fucking champagne, Dante."

He set the bucket down on a desk and looked at me with a playful, coy expression. "Amore. What's wrong? Why does my little *gattina* have claws and teeth tonight?" He stepped forward to take me in his arms, and I noticed he was wearing the same outfit as when he'd been with *her* earlier this evening.

He narrowed his gaze. "Why are your eyes puffy? Have you been crying? Did something happen? Wait, I know. Did you talk with your mother?"

I squirmed out of his embrace. "Do you seriously think I'm stupid? Why aren't you with Iolanda?"

Dante groaned. "Dio. Is that what this is about?"

I snorted.

"Amore, amore, amore. Bronson's scheme—that's it."

I pressed my fingers to my temples, feeling a headache coming on. What was real with these people? What was fake? Who knew? I was two steps behind.

Dante cupped my face in his hands. "Come on, Savannah. I left as soon as I could so I could be with *you*. Celebrate with *you*. I couldn't care less about Iolanda. I think she actually has a boyfriend. What were you doing when I knocked?"

"About to take a bath," I mumbled as he kissed my forehead.

"Mm. A bath. That's a great idea." He picked up the bucket and headed for the bathroom. I stayed behind, trying to regain my composure. Maybe I should kick him out now. At some point, I would need to re-establish my dignity. If he didn't break my heart with the likes of Iolanda, it would surely happen eventually with another woman.

Or, more likely, he'd try to let me down gently after the Dubai race in two weeks. He wasn't a total monster, and I was sure he'd be as suave as possible when it came to our breakup. Then he'd fade away back to Italy, and I'd schlep back to my boring life in America until the next race season. Maybe he'd send me a Christmas card each year, but otherwise I'd keep up with his exploits by stalking him online.

I sighed. A miserable life unfolded before my eyes.

The unmistakable pop of a champagne cork echoed through the hotel room and snapped me into the present.

"Dante, what—?"

When I stepped into the bathroom, he was already naked and in the tub, the open bottle in his hands.

"I didn't see any cups, so we'll have to drink from the bottle. But we need to be careful about glass in the tub."

"For a guy who risks his life every couple of weeks on a racetrack, you sure are safety conscious," I grumbled. He was so cavalier with my feelings, and my heart. Was he being cruel, or insensitive, or was he just obtuse? It was kind of mystifying that he hadn't caught on that I was head over heels for him.

"Savannah, come. Join me. The water's perfect . . ."

His hard athlete's body did look tempting in the water. Dammit. I couldn't say no to him. Not now and probably not ever.

Shrugging off my robe, I couldn't help but smile as he lustily stared at my body. I stepped into the water and knelt between his parted legs, facing him. He offered me the bottle.

"Cheers."

"What are we toasting to?" I took the bottle in both hands, careful not to let it slip.

"Us."

"Us?"

"Yeah, to us. Drink up."

I attempted to take a dainty sip, but when I tipped my head and the bottle back, rivulets of the cold liquid ran out the corner of my mouth and down my chin. The champagne dribbled past my collarbone to my nipple, which tightened under the chill.

He laughed and took the bottle in one hand while cupping my breast gently with another. "*Saluti*. *Per la mia fidanzata*," he said softly, hoisting the bottle in my direction, then taking a long drink. He set the champagne on the floor and leaned forward to kiss me, trailing the backs of his fingers over my face. I wrapped myself around him, feeling his familiar, muscular body against mine.

I wanted this to last forever, so badly that I could cry.

DRIVE

◊

DANTE

Dio, I was exhausted. Between the sweltering temperatures of Mexico, the closest race of the season, my fake "date" with that ridiculous model whose name I couldn't recall, and the long and emotional sex session with Savannah . . . even I was shocked that I hadn't collapsed. For the first time, I felt every bit of my thirty-two years.

But it wasn't that I couldn't drift off. I didn't want to. Instead, I wanted to watch Savannah. She was curled up next to me in bed and breathing deeply, looking peaceful and gorgeous as she slept. A little smile tugged at the corners of her mouth. I still hadn't turned out the light in the bathroom, which cast a warm glow onto the bed.

There was no way I could give her up at the end of the season. What I'd said back in Amalfi—*I might keep you for myself*—I now meant with every fiber of my being. I'd been so tempted several times tonight to tell her my feelings. But I wanted that moment to be special, and first I needed to overcome my hesitation about uttering those three important words aloud.

It would help if I told her somewhere fitting and impossibly romantic, somewhere deserving of her. Maybe back in Amalfi? Would it be too cold in November to bring her to the grotto, where I'd first realized that she was more than a gorgeous face? Yes, the grotto was our sacred space. It was where I'd discovered she had goals and dreams of her own. Where I first recognized we could be a team, together. Where I felt like she was the first person to listen to me, really listen, and not give a damn that I was a rich athlete or a talented driver.

Where I'd truly fallen in love with her, now that I thought about it.

I kissed her forehead, letting my lips linger on her warm skin. Maybe we could go to Amalfi right after the final race. We'd bundle up in warm clothes, take the kayak into the cavern, and I'd ask her to marry me. Or I could wake her up and ask her right now. As if she knew what I was considering, she snuggled closer with a little coo.

"Can you shut out the light?" she murmured.

I hustled out of bed and to the bathroom, snapping off the light and then assuming my place beside her again.

No, I wanted everything to unfold neatly and precisely. Right now, there was only one thing I had to concentrate on, and that was winning the next and final race in Dubai.

Once I'd clenched a seventh championship for the history books, I'd pour my heart out to win my perfect woman.

Plus, I didn't want to screw up such an important moment, like I had when I took her virginity. Revealing that I was in love for the first time in my life would take extensive and detailed planning. I also didn't want to unsettle her right before the race. I knew that competition was important to her, too, and this was her first championship team. She'd want to focus on her job and revel in the win. Our time would come later.

I carefully tucked her into my side, pulling the duvet over her exposed shoulder. Another little moan escaped from her throat, and she pressed her face into my chest.

"*Dormi*, tesoro."

Yes, I'd wait until after we won to ask her to marry me.

Perhaps I'd propose for real, in front of the crowd in Dubai. That was another option. I sank into a deep sleep, my heart full with the fantasy.

CHAPTER THIRTY-TWO

DANTE

Savannah mia, what room are you in?

2217

I'll be right there

"What floor, sir?" The elevator attendant asked.

"Fifteen, thank you." I spotted two young guys snapping photos of me with their cell phones. We were staying at the Burj Khalifa in Dubai. It was one of the most luxurious hotels in the world, and the guests were among the richest on the planet—and on race weekends, we drivers were treated like gods.

"You looked awesome at practice and qualifying, Dante! Seven-time world champion," one guy yelled, and I flashed a victory sign, although that felt a little sacrilegious. I never counted on a win until it happened.

I rode the elevator to the fifteenth floor, got off, and wandered around, hoping to evade any stray paparazzi. Then I made sure I got in a different elevator and took it to floor twenty-two.

The ride to Savannah's floor was silent, and the attendant smiled as he held the door open. "Good luck tomorrow, Mr. Annunziata."

"Thanks. Have a great night." I slipped him a hundred-dollar bill. This whole day had been surreal, from the stunning desert view from the hotel to the realization that tomorrow would be my last race ever.

I made my way to Savannah's door. The hall was blissfully free of fans, photographers, *people*. Before we'd arrived, I'd asked Bronson to make sure my floor and Savannah's both had extra security to keep the media away. I pushed out a heavy, satisfied breath and knocked. It was a risk, going to her room. But it might be the only time before tomorrow that I could see her alone, and I desperately craved a few moments with her.

The door swung open, and my muscles immediately lost their tension at the sight of Savannah's gorgeous, freckled face. She wore her casual team outfit: jeans and an Eagle polo shirt.

"Hey, babe, how are you tonight?" I said in an exaggerated American accent while kissing her on the cheek and moving inside.

She shut the door. "Just getting ready for the party. Won't stay long, though. Big day tomorrow, you know?"

I sank onto the bed and flopped back. "Is it? What's tomorrow?"

She sat on the edge of the mattress, a foot away from me. "Oh, a little motorsports event. Nothing special."

"I'm worried, Savvy." I sat up and stared into her green eyes.

She frowned. "Why? Are you exhausted? It's been a long day and this heat—good Lord."

"Yeah, I'm beat. But my worries aren't due to that. It's general self-doubt."

"You never have that."

"I know. But this is it. This final race. It's over for me." I sucked in a breath and studied my hands. "What if I don't come in fifth?"

"No chance of that." She shook her head dismissively. "You've driven perfect races almost all season."

I didn't bring up the Italy race. "What if the car fails? What if there's a crash?"

"Dante." She put her hand on mine, sending warmth through my body. "You've got this. Trust me. You're the best in the world."

We studied each other, and I could've sworn she swallowed hard, as if she was about to say something difficult. Her eyes looked unusually pink, but that was probably from all the desert sand. I'd heard a guy on the team talk about how it affected him that way.

"Thank you, Savannah," I said softly.

"For what?" Her tone was shaky.

"For being my . . ." My gaze dropped to her lips.

"Fake fiancé?" Her voice was hardly more than a whisper.

I shook my head. "For being my friend."

Her lips parted, and I watched her bottom lip tremble. Dio, was this the time to tell her that I loved her? My heartbeat kicked up, and to stall for time while I decided, I leaned toward her mouth.

After a few seconds of slow, languid kissing, I eased away, pressing my forehead to hers. "Savannah, I need to tell you . . ."

"Shh," she said, putting her finger to my mouth. "It can wait. We need to go to that party soon."

I groaned. "It would be so much easier if we could just go together."

"I know. But Tanya wants us to stay apart. We can't attract attention."

"Maybe later tonight you can sneak up to my room." I nuzzled her neck, inhaling her sweet scent. If I could hold her in my arms tonight, I would tell her everything. "God, you smell so good right now."

She shook her head. "You need to be alone and sleep. It's too important of a race. And you always feel better after you get a decent night's rest. Don't stay at the party too late."

She was right, of course. Tonight wasn't the time to tell her. My emotions were too high right now. The best thing would be to return to my room and focus on tomorrow.

On winning.

We both stood, and I gathered her in my arms. "The last thing I want is to go to a party," I murmured.

She pulled away and again swallowed hard. We walked to the door, and she pressed her mouth to my cheek. "Don't worry about anything," she whispered in my ear. "You're going to win tomorrow. I know you will."

I squeezed her tight once more, then left. On my way to the elevator, I grinned big. Savannah would be so surprised when I asked her to marry me. I couldn't wait to see her expression.

A text from my father interrupted my thoughts. He was somewhere in Dubai; I'd met up with him earlier.

I'm at a party tonight, so I'll see you in the morning. I just wanted to tell you how proud I am of you. Good luck tomorrow, son. *Remember: focus on winning. That's the only thing that matters until you reach the checkered flag. Block out all the other distractions. Make sure you sleep well.*

Shuddering in a breath, I knew he was right. Savannah, and my big, intense emotions for her, would have to wait.

◊

SAVANNAH

When we arrived in Dubai for the last race of the season, it was as if the whole Eagle team was holding its collective breath, not wanting to inhale the scorching desert haze for fear it would steal the competitive edge from us. Dante needed exactly one point to win the drivers' championship. Max was in second, and the team was poised to take first in the constructors' championship.

All with a rookie team. The energy in the air crackled and popped. Everyone was trying hard not to be too excited, and we all spoke in quiet tones as we gathered at a private party on one of the terraces of the Burj Khalifa, the world's tallest building. Yesterday, we'd actually watched the sun set twice from this vantage point: it was so tall that the team stood in the lobby and watched the sun dip below the horizon and then took a three-minute elevator ride to the top of the building where we watched it set again. It was the only place in the world where this was possible, and even the normally blasé Dante and Max were impressed.

It was the night before the race and even though it was dark now, it was infernally hot. I was wearing jeans and a branded polo shirt like the rest of the team, and I was so uncomfortably warm that I longed to strip off my clothes and lie facedown on the marble in the lobby to cool off.

The hotel had set up devices on the observation deck that sprayed a fine mist on the guests, along with fans to cool the air. Which seemed kind of pointless outdoors in the desert. I'd seen a lot of wasteful luxury over the past six months during my time as a pit crew member, but this—a private party on the skyscraper's observation terrace overlooking the world's richest kingdom—was like something out of a surreal dream. The entire city of Dubai practically shimmered from the combination of its desert heat and its vast oil riches.

I'd grown up privileged, but tonight I felt like a low-country hick among these sheikhs and princes and others of the world's wealthiest people, all of whom wanted to be close to Dante, the star Formula World driver.

Regardless of the race's outcome, in only twenty-four hours, the season would end. And the real challenge would unfold: What would happen between me and Dante? I planned on having a talk with him, once and for all, after the race.

I'd almost said something when he'd snuck into my room to say hi an hour ago, but I'd chickened out.

He needed all of his focus on the race, and I didn't want to be a distraction. I needed to focus on my job as well—Jack had already assigned me to change tires at this final race of the season.

As I sipped my sparkling water, my eyes flitted to Dante. I'd been trying to catch his attention all night but hadn't been successful. I longed to ask him about Dubai and his thoughts about the city. He probably knew all of the landmarks, and I secretly hoped we could spend a few days here together after the race—although

I suspected that would be impossible, given the team demands once he won the championship. *If* he won, that is.

Of course, we couldn't chat in public because we were officially over. Bronson and Tanya told us to keep our distance from each other while others were around, even the rest of the team. So I circulated, snacking on shrimp cocktail and making small talk with the guys.

As I was getting another sparkling water inside, Tanya approached with a smile. "Hey, Savvy. How are you holding up? It's been a great season. Thank you for being so accommodating. Let's chat. Over there, where it's more private."

I followed her over to a high top table near a floor-to-ceiling window with a dizzying view of the desert city below. Unlike at the beginning of the season, I now considered Tanya a friend. "It's honestly been the craziest and best six months of my life. I can't thank Mr. Bronson enough. And you've been great too." It was true; I'd warmed to Tanya over the months, realizing that she was working hard and doing her best for the team.

"I've been in racing PR for ten years now, and I've never had such a wild ride as this. Between the scandal and your fake relationship with Dante"—Tanya blew out a breath—"you must be happy that it's almost over."

I shrugged. *Happy* wasn't the right word. I was anxious about what would happen next. As a pit crew member, I was scheduled to return to Italy with the team for post-season meetings. It was there that I intended to talk to Dante about us. I needed to find out where I stood with him, and I had to tell him how I felt.

I was in love. It was as simple as that.

I hadn't wanted to bring it up before the final race of the season.

It seemed too complicated, somehow, to broach the subject when he was on the cusp of a seventh, historic world championship.

"I'm excited for next season," I replied blandly.

"Oh, well, you should talk to Bronson about whether you'll be needed."

I tilted my head. "Hmm? I thought I was doing a good job. That's what Jack said."

"Oh, sweetie." She leaned in, while glancing around to see if anyone was close by. "I wasn't going to say anything because you seem like such a nice person. But this was all a publicity stunt on his part. He wanted a woman on the team. He wanted all of this controversy with you and Dante. It's kind of sick, but that's how it is in motorsports these days. It's all smoke and mirrors, and publicity."

Bile erupted in my throat and the contents of my stomach threatened to explode. I'd been duped.

"Of course, Bronson didn't want to hire just any pretty face. You did have experience, and that was important to him. And everyone agrees you were an excellent team member." Tanya followed up quickly. "Maybe he'll keep you on. We'll see. Or I'm sure you could get a place on another team. I'll give you an excellent recommendation."

I leveled an incredulous look at her. "I-I was set up? Used?" All those rumors about the way Bronson does business. I should have known.

Tanya shot me a sad smile. "That's a bit harsh, but yes. I shouldn't be saying anything, but I'm not in favor of how they treated you. And even if Bronson was serious about you being a team member, you would have been doomed with Dante anyway."

"What do you mean?" My brows pinched until my facial muscles hurt.

Tanya moved closer and lowered her voice. "He planned on seducing you to get you off the team. He told Jack when you first showed up in Italy. But Bronson changed everything with his scheme. It even caught Dante off guard." Tanya patted my shoulder. "I've watched Dante from afar for years and have never seen him so shell-shocked as when Bronson told him that you were going to be his girlfriend all season. I don't think Dante's ever been with the same woman for six days, much less six months. But who knows *who* he was doing while pretending to be with you. I hope you didn't take him seriously."

Oh. My. God. Dante had also manipulated me, in his own way. For his own gain.

"In fact," Tanya said, leaning in, "that paparazzi photo in the garage the week you started? Bronson set that up."

"What?" I gasped aloud, all pretense of composure gone. "Why are you telling me these awful things?"

Tanya lifted a shoulder. "I'm not coming back to this team next year. I'm taking a corporate job with a company in the US. I haven't been thrilled with the way Bronson operates. I can't say anything publicly because of the nondisclosure he had us sign. But I can tell you. I like you. Feel sorry for you, but I like you."

"I'd hate to think how you'd act with someone you disliked," I said.

She looked genuinely crushed. "Savvy, I'm sorry. Truly. I debated whether to warn you earlier, but you seemed so happy that you were getting the experience you wanted."

Nausea didn't bubble in my stomach; it boiled. Dante had lied to me. He'd schemed to get me off the team, and then when

Bronson had come up with his stupid plan, he'd gone along with it. He was likely never really attracted to me at all, and I'd totally misread him because of my inexperience. I sucked in several deep breaths to calm myself and each inhale was filled with hot, stale desert air. And the worst thought of all? Both he and the team had used me. They'd orchestrated all of this and I'd been merely a pawn. A stupid, young girl in a high-stakes world controlled by men.

Exactly what my mother had warned me about.

"Excuse me," I whispered, setting my glass on the tray of a passing waiter. I half walked, half ran out of the room.

I fled to the luxurious bathroom inside. Fortunately, the stalls were like mini-rooms, private and silent. The toilet handle was gold, and I wondered if it was real—then I vomited. I walked out to the wash area. As I was wiping my mouth with toilet paper, the bathroom door opened with an explosion of voices. Two blond women sporting tight, bright dresses and speaking in throaty British accents chortled. They were probably either VIPs, wives of some sponsor, or Formula World groupies—those were generally the three categories of women who snagged exclusive invites to parties like tonight's.

"Did you see him? I've never been around a sexier man. I swear, my panties melt whenever he's nearby. Do you think you'll get another chance with him?" one asked.

"I simply don't know, darling. We hooked up two seasons ago and he's been avoiding me all this year. Probably because of that American slag. Maybe now that he's cut her loose I'll have a chance again this weekend. Did you see how lost that little ginger girl looked? Poor thing. She needs to go back to the States and screw those fat stock-car blokes. Totally out of her league here. I wonder what Dante saw in her."

The women giggled more, then stopped abruptly when they spotted me.

I fled back into the stall, knowing I looked pale and sickly and unfashionable. Eventually, I'd have to face the world. But now, I only wanted a moment to collect my thoughts. I dabbed at my stinging eyes and hoped I wouldn't run into Dante on my way up to my room.

If I did, I'd have to be gracious. I couldn't ruin his last race. Part of me wished I had the guts to return to that party and start screaming at him and Bronson.

But I wasn't hardwired that way.

Life is about putting on a happy face and acting the part.

Once again, my mother was right.

Even though there was nothing in my stomach, I retched into the toilet again, wishing I was anywhere but Dubai.

CHAPTER THIRTY-THREE

SAVANNAH

The next day, I wasn't feeling any better, physically or emotionally.

But because I was a professional, I pushed it all aside. I shook Dante's hand before he climbed into his car from the right side, keeping in line with his superstitions. I acted like all the other pit crew members, serious and eager to help the man poised to be the world's champion racer.

Of course, I had on my helmet, so he couldn't see my watery eyes or the way my bottom lip trembled when he was near. Dante reached to pat me on the shoulder at the same time I reached to squeeze his, and we bumped arms awkwardly. It was all I could do not to crumple onto the floor of the garage at his feet.

A pat on the shoulder. Like one of the guys. He was definitely through with me.

I flipped up the visor on my helmet. "Good luck out there,"
I said, trying to put on a brave face. "Drive it like you stole it."

That made him smile, at least. But it didn't make me feel
any better.

Now that the race was underway, it looked like he was driving the best race of his career.

And I'd done my part perfectly, because that's why I was
here. To do a flawless job. In my mind, I was like a ballet
dancer, graceful and quick as I used my wheel gun to detach
and attach the car's front right tire. After that 2.8-second stop,
it was apparent that Dante was so far in the lead—by ten whole
seconds—that everyone visibly relaxed. I could practically see
the crew members' postures grow a little looser with each lap.
The grins grew wider too.

"Let's not get overconfident," Jack yelled into our team
headsets. "It ain't over till it's over, mates."

But when Dante's car was the first to soar past the checkered
flag, everything, everyone, erupted.

The crowd cheered lustily. A genuine smile spread across my
face as I pulled off my helmet. He'd clenched his seventh championship and a place in the record books. I couldn't help but feel happy
for him. Proud, too, for being part of the winning team.

Tilting my head upward to a Jumbotron screen, I watched
Dante drive a victory lap, pumping his fist and making the
number one sign with his index finger the entire way as the
crowd roared. Giorgio pulled me into a hug, then another
team member did, and then Jack followed. For that one perfect
moment, I was swept up in the excitement.

"We did it," I shouted.

Jack screamed something unintelligible in his accent and whooped.

"A spectacular final race for Dante Annunziata," the announcer boomed over the loudspeakers. "And a seventh championship has propelled him into the ranks of motorsports legends. Well deserved. An incredible season."

He was an unmatched athlete, and I'd probably never see the likes of someone like him again. Professionally or personally.

But within minutes, the toxic feelings of being used and humiliated had washed over me again. I'd pushed them deep inside during the race, but now they crested. I wasn't wanted here. This wasn't my place.

I'd spent much of the night in bed staring into the dark, thinking about this moment. Checking to see if anyone was watching—they weren't—I stole away to the ladies' room, away from the raucous celebration underway.

No one would notice. They were too busy cheering. And I didn't care about my future or the team because I didn't have one. Dante would be in the limelight, basking in the glow of being an even bigger celebrity with even more money now than ever before.

Neither the team nor Dante had any use for me. It was time for me to return home to Georgia, where I belonged.

There, in the calm of the team bathroom—there was a separate women's shower—I quickly washed and threw on a long black dress and a black headscarf. Also a pair of giant black sunglasses.

From there I grabbed my passport and a carry-on bag out of my locker, and wove through the crowds of jubilant racing fans to hail a taxi to the airport. In the back seat of the cab, I teared up as I typed two texts. One was to Bronson. I wanted to be snarky and angry, but the only words that came out were kind and polite. I was a Southerner, through and through.

Thank you for the opportunity, I wrote. *I wish you and the team all the best.*

There was no use in being mean now. I'd allowed myself to be used, by both Dante and the team. I should have walked away months ago and faced Bronson's wrath—or tried harder not to fall in love. Instead, I'd taken every scrap of affection Dante had thrown my way. I pulled up his number on my phone.

Congratulations on your win. You drove a perfect race. A perfect season. I wish you only the best in your post-race career. xo, Savannah

Thank God I'd saved money over the season, because the last-minute ticket back to America was insanely expensive, even for coach. I couldn't handle questions from my parents, so putting the ticket on their card was out of the question—Mom would have rung me within the hour since she monitored my spending like a hawk.

Her voice saying, "I knew something wasn't right," echoed in my head with every step. I'd have to deal with her soon enough.

I handed my passport to the ticketing agent, who mentioned something about how I'd gotten the last seat on a flight to Berlin because someone had canceled.

"The passenger must be having too much fun at the Formula World race," the agent said in dulcet tones.

"I'm sure that's it," I said, my knees shaky with defeat.

Mercifully, the flight boarded quickly. I shuffled down the aisle and threw myself into the seat, shucking off my sunglasses and headscarf. Minutes later, a flight attendant passed by.

"Magazine?"

Trying to distract my spinning mind, I accepted. Stuffing the magazine in the seat-back pocket, I forgot about it as the plane lifted into the air. I was in the window seat, and so I peered out at the Dubai skyline below, which shimmered in the sandy haze of the city. What was Dante doing at that moment? Probably celebrating. Giving interviews. Posing for photos with rich men and pretty women.

He'd almost certainly forgotten all about me. It would take a lifetime to forget about him.

"Look," said the man seated next to me. "There's the Formula World track."

I looked down to see the course, set amidst the tan desert landscape.

I sniffed. "I couldn't care less."

Scowling at my seatmate to prevent further conversation, I grabbed the magazine out of the holder. It was a men's fashion magazine, and I wasn't sure why the flight attendant had given it to me. I didn't want to see men, much less read about them. Still, I thumbed through, trying to take my mind off my anxiety.

"Oh, check it out," my seatmate said.

Lord, was he going to talk all the way to Berlin? He pointed at the magazine and I fought the urge to slap his hand away.

"It's the racing champion himself. The ladies love him, you know," said the man, tapping on the photo with his index finger.

I looked down at the glossy pages on my lap. There was Dante.

It was a fashion spread for an Italian designer. I recalled the day that he'd done the shoot, not long after our week in Amalfi. The photos were raw, arresting, black-and-white. One was a close-up of his face, and he wore only a hoodie. His eyes were closed and his lips were parted, and I recalled that he'd looked almost identical once when we were in bed together. Like he was in ecstasy.

I burst into tears because the full force of the truth slammed my senses.

That man had shattered my heart.

CHAPTER THIRTY-FOUR

DANTE

I sat at the long table, answering question after tedious question from the press. The race had ended an hour ago, and between the ceremonial awards show on the podium and the sponsor greeting and this interminable news conference, I was restless and anxious. I jiggled my leg, unable to contain the nervous energy in me. All I wanted was Savannah, and I needed to find her. Take her in my arms and kiss her until she couldn't breathe. In front of the whole world. And Bronson couldn't do a damn thing about it now.

For some reason, I hadn't seen her in the pits when I'd steered the car back to the garage.

"Can you credit any one thing to your success this season?" a reporter asked.

"Yes. My fiancé, Savannah Jenkins," I said into the microphone. Murmurs and laughter rippled through the press corps. "We've gotten back together. It was only a little fight, and we, uh, called it off prematurely. She's been more than a fiancé, more than a pit crew member. She's my teammate on the track and off. She's kept me focused and sane, and she's even taught me a thing or two about driving. And life."

"When's the wedding?" another reporter asked.

"As soon as possible, I hope. I'm actually trying to get out of here so we can talk about that. I was hoping for New Year's Day on a beach somewhere. Where is she, anyway? I'd like her to come say a few words. Savannah?"

Craning my neck, I looked into the crowd of journalists, hoping she'd be listening.

"Maybe she's in the gara—"

Bronson stepped forward and interrupted me, holding his palms up in the direction of the reporters. "Yes, Savvy's in the garage. She's not available to talk. I thank you all for coming to the news conference and celebrating this historic win with us. We'll see if we can make her available for interviews later."

The reporters grumbled as the news conference wrapped up. I rose and approached Bronson, clapping him on the shoulder. Had he cut the news conference short because I'd mentioned my love for Savannah? Whatever. Who cared what Bronson thought now?

"Great race," Bronson boomed.

"Thanks. Great season. And sorry, *dude*," I said sarcastically. "I think your plan backfired. I ended up falling in love with my fake fiancé. Where is she, do you know? I haven't caught a glimpse of her because I've been overwhelmed. Crushed with requests. Where is she? I need to see her."

Bronson rubbed his lips together.

Fear flooded my body. "What? Is she okay? What happened to her?"

"That's why I stopped the news conference. Savannah's gone, and I didn't want you to embarrass yourself."

"What? Gone?" My guts twisted into a knot. "Where? Is she okay?"

"She's disappeared. Well, not exactly disappeared. From the text I received from her, I gather she's flying out of the country and back to America. She didn't give an explanation, but I guessed she was upset since she left so abruptly."

I swore in Italian. This couldn't be true. *Why?*

Why would she leave now, when we had so much to celebrate? I ran to the paddock, where I knew the pit crew would be assembled. Everyone clapped when I busted in. I waved my arms.

"Guys, has anyone seen Savannah?"

They all looked around and shook their heads.

"Now that you mention it, we haven't seen her for a while," one said.

"I saw her go into the ladies' locker right after the race," said another.

I swore again in Italian, one of the foulest things I could say in my language, and went to my private dressing area. Pulling my bag out of the trunk, I pawed around for my phone. There. A message from her.

Congratulations on your win. You drove a perfect race. A perfect season. I wish you only the best in your post-race career. xo, Savannah

I felt like punching something.

Where are you? I typed.

No answer. I typed another message while a sinking feeling settled in my gut.

Where did you go? I need you.

I stared, dumbfounded. Always so attuned to my heart rate, I felt it climb as my chest constricted. I remembered all the passionate things she'd said the last time we were together. Were they all a fucking lie? I tossed the cell phone in my bag. Why wouldn't she want me?

This was supposed to be the best moment of my career. Of my life. A seven-time Formula World champion.

And all I could think about was a redheaded girl from Georgia. Where had things gone so wrong? What had changed in the past day? I smacked my palm against the locker, and the sound of skin hitting metal echoed in the room.

"Mate, I think I know what happened to Savannah." It was Jack, speaking in a tight voice.

I whirled to face him. "What? Tell me!"

"She had a talk with Tanya last night. And Tanya told her that her presence on the team was all a PR stunt."

I groaned and sat on a bench, cradling my head in my hands. Fucking Bronson. Fucking Tanya.

"That's why she left? She abandoned me because she felt used by the team? She didn't care enough about me to stay to celebrate our win?"

Jack shook his head. "That's not all. Tanya also let it slip that you were initially going to seduce Savvy to get her off the team. I think she probably assumed she'd been used by everyone."

"What? How did she know . . . oh fuck. You told Tanya."

"Pillow talk, mate. I'm sorry. Truly. I was going to update her with the latest but hadn't had time. We've been on and off for weeks."

I'm so wired from the race and this news that I feel like I've been shot out of a cannon. "Dio. I'm going to kill you. And now Savannah thinks I'm not serious about her."

"I'd say that's the case. My sincere apologies. I can try calling her if you'd like."

"No. This is my mess to clean up. I was ready to propose during the press conference if she'd been there. I'm serious about her. Serious as a heart attack. Which I'm about to have if I don't find her." I balled my hands into fists. "I've got to find her."

"I'd say that's true, mate, if you want a future with her. You've got to explain and grovel. And grovel some more. When you're done, I'll back you up and grovel my fair share too. She deserves no less, because that one's worth fighting for."

CHAPTER THIRTY-FIVE

SAVANNAH

It took two flights to get to Atlanta, and then a third flight on a tiny puddle jumper to arrive in Savannah. The sun rose and fell, then rose again, and I spent most of the trip tipsy from wine or sleeping. The trip seemed to take days, but in reality it was a thirty-six-hour journey.

Thirty-six hours of second, third, and fourth guesses, cramped seats, and food so bland and terrible that I'd stopped eating somewhere over Europe. There was crying in airplane bathrooms—lots of it. At one point, I threw a blanket over my head and tried to sleep but just ended up sobbing softly. My hurt was a raw, open wound, visible for everyone to see.

Not like I cared.

I was groggy and wrung dry of tears by the time I reached my hometown, and my phone had no juice since my charger was still in Dubai because I was an idiot and had accidentally left it behind. I'd meant to buy a charger on my stopover in Berlin, but I didn't have much time to catch my connection. So I'd used a stranger's phone right before takeoff to text my brother. Fortunately, he was at our family's home in Savannah, and I'd pleaded with him to slip the key under the mat of our family's beach cottage on Tybee Island. I needed the ocean and solitude, not the familiar trappings of my childhood home.

Please don't tell Mom and Dad I'm home. I'm begging you, I typed.

Fine, but you owe me, my brother typed back. *They're in Atlanta anyway, staying at the condo.*

I read his text and let out a breath. A nearby couple stared at me.

"Finally, some good news," I muttered, not caring that I was talking to myself in public.

My entire body was so exhausted that my teeth ached. Sliding into a taxi at the Savannah airport, I asked the driver to take me to Tybee. It was no small stroke of luck that my parents were in Atlanta. I couldn't withstand my mother's barrage of questions right now. After a few days of alone time, I'd call her and attempt to explain everything.

And if any nosy reporters were looking for Dante's fake-ex-fiancé in the wake of his championship win, they'd never find me here. Not that any would try; I was certain that Dante was back in Italy, soaking up the limelight. I was an afterthought, a footnote in the history of Formula World racing.

In the back of the cab, I allowed my head to loll back on the seat. Maybe it was the fact that I was so close to home, but I was more relaxed now that I was in the humidity and slow pace of the South than I had been the whole trip. I drifted to sleep on the hour-long drive.

"Miss, we're here," said the driver, jarring me awake. His Southern drawl was at once foreign and soothing after months of different accents.

"Thank you." I pulled out some cash and grabbed my backpack. I'd had most of my things in Dubai shipped home. The ball gowns, the souvenir race programs—everything. All I'd brought with me were a change of clothes, the diamond earrings Dante had given me back in Monaco, a pot of lip balm, and my electronics, which were now powerless. Like me.

I hoisted myself out of the taxi and scowled.

An unfamiliar car greeted me in the cottage driveway. It was a silver Toyota with Georgia plates. Maybe my brother's assistant? He was probably too busy to bring the key over, which made me bristle.

Shrugging it off, I inhaled and closed my eyes. The air smelled like salt water and jasmine. The welcoming yellow beachfront cottage was the first thing that had given me joy in days. I smiled, and tears welled in my eyes.

God, I was exhausted. And I was *home*.

Slinging my backpack over one shoulder, I made my way to the back of the house, which faced the ocean. I'd told my brother to make sure the key was under the mat by the rocking chair on the porch. Tybee was safe and small, and all the neighbors knew one another.

I rounded the corner and saw a figure sitting in the chair. What the—

"Dante?"

I stood at the bottom of the porch stairs, frozen. "What are you doing here?" I wasn't sure whether I should be angry or break down in tears. Why did I feel so dizzy all of a sudden? And how the hell had he gotten here so quickly? Before me? Nothing made sense.

Maybe I was hallucinating. That must have been it. Because otherwise, why would a rested-looking and gorgeous Italian man be standing on the porch of my parents' beach cottage, sitting in a rocking chair and staring at the ocean?

But would a hallucination walk up and hug me? Would a hallucination kiss me softly? The last time I'd seen him was two days before, in a race car, on a track in the Middle East. Maybe I'd stepped into some sort of time/space warp thing.

"I'm here because I love you," he said in a raspy voice.

I looked around, a flicker of hope alighting in my heart. "What did you say? Are you real?"

His near-black eyes positively blazed. "I am. And I'm here to apologize."

I stared at him, confused. It really was him. "Did you just say you love me?"

He kissed my forehead. "Mm-hmm. I did."

"Why are you here?" It would be better if I could sound angry, but I was too tired and suddenly too excited to adopt an edge to my voice.

"Because I needed to see you."

"Oh." My legs weren't able to hold me up any longer, so I sank onto the top step. He crouched in front of me.

"I'm sorry, Savannah mia. I found out what happened. And I'm sorry that Tanya told you all of those things in Dubai. It was wrong of her. She and Jack send their apologies." His eyes softened with an anguished expression.

"But were they true?" I couldn't stop the tears from sliding down my cheeks.

Dante inhaled and looked at the ground. "When we first met, I did tell Jack that I was thinking of seducing you in an attempt to get you off the team. It was an offhand comment, and I didn't mean it. It was a horrible thing for me to say, and I apologize. I was, as you would say, a jerk."

"You were a huge jerk."

"But I stopped wanting to seduce you for sport in Montreal—I wanted to seduce you for real. Because you were the most real person I'd ever met. I discovered that you are beautiful. And intelligent. And funny. And caring—and you know a lot about tires."

I was sobbing now, full-on snorting and snuffling. Dante sat close and held me, stroking my hair and kissing the side of my head.

"I discovered something else. That you are loyal. You gave more of your heart to me than any person's ever given me, Savannah. What you gave me was better than any championship."

I couldn't think of any words to say.

He tilted my chin upward. "I fell in love with *you*. And I realized that I want you to be my real fiancé. My wife."

"Oh my God," I whispered, pressing my face into his chest. "You're not a jerk at all."

He sank to his knees on the bottom step and took something sparkly out of his pocket. I stared at the ring, which wasn't the one that had sat on my finger during the race season.

This one was even more stunning.

"I had a Dubai jeweler deliver some rings to me so I could select one for you while on the plane to America. I chose this one. Sapphire and diamonds. The sapphire's the same color as the water in the Amalfi grotto. Our grotto. Where I fell in love with you."

He took my hand and looked up, a tear streaming down his cheek.

"Will you marry me, Savannah? Will you be my teammate for life? I need you."

I nodded through my tears. "Yes. I will. I will."

He slipped the ring on my finger and rose.

"I love you, Dante." I stared into his warm, dark eyes, and peace washed over me. I was home, and with him. He hugged me so hard that my breath squeezed out of my lungs. We both laughed.

"Sweetie, how did you get here so fast?"

"I'm the fastest man in the world." I pulled back and giggled as I sniffled. "No, seriously. How? I got a last-minute ticket, and it took me two and a half days. How long have you been here?"

"Such are the benefits of being the world champion. I got a business class flight, and it took just under twenty hours. I arrived in Savannah, rented an anonymous Toyota, and found your brother. Explained everything. Then came here to wait."

"You rented a Toyota? You told my brother everything?"

"Well, almost everything. I left out a few details."

I looked at him in horror. "I hope you left out *many* details."

"Don't worry. He was quite entertained. And he'd seen the news conference."

"What news conference?" I frowned.

"The one I gave after the race, where I told the world we'd gotten back together and that I wanted a New Year's Eve wedding."

"What?"

"Amore mio, if you don't want to get married that quickly, it's okay. It was only a thought," he said hurriedly.

"No, I . . ." My voice trailed off and I laughed, thinking of how my mother would simultaneously freak out about organizing a wedding on such short notice and be over the moon that her little girl was marrying the richest athlete in the world for real.

"What?"

"New Year's Eve is excellent. I can't wait to tell my parents. Maybe we can get married here. On the beach. It might be cold. But it could be perfect."

"You know what's perfect?" He held up the key to the house and went to unlock the door.

"What?"

He pulled me inside my own house, and I laughed.

"That we're finally together with no deadlines, no races, and nowhere to be."

EPILOGUE

SAVANNAH

FIVE YEARS LATER

My three-inch Louboutin heels clicked on the marble floor of the conference room at Annunziata Auto near Rome. I was wearing a sharp black sheath dress—even though I still preferred my coveralls.

I paused before I entered the room, looking to my husband.

"You ready?"

"Of course, amore mio," he said, brushing my lips with his.

Our one-year-old daughter, Gabriella, was in his arms and reached for my hair. I couldn't help but grin when I heard Dante correct Gabby in Italian. "No, baby. Don't mess with Mama's hair today, okay?"

The three of us walked in and stood near a lectern where Tanya, our old PR expert during our racing days, addressed the media as Annunziata Auto's media relations liaison.

"And here is Savannah Jenkins-Annunziata to make today's announcement," Tanya said.

I stood at the lectern and smiled. "I'm thrilled today to tell you that our company will be sponsoring a Formula World team next season. And I'm even more ecstatic to announce that one of the drivers will be a promising young woman who is already a star in open-wheel racing in North America."

Murmurs rose amongst the reporters and cameras fired rapidly. I continued, explaining my plan to recruit more women onto the new team.

"As one of the team principals, my job will be to bring more women into the sport. I'd like to open the floor up for questions now. Yes?" I pointed at a woman in heavy black glasses, someone I recognized from *La Gazetta dello Sport* in Milan.

"I've heard that since Team Eagle shut down due to a lack of money, you are hiring many of their engineers and crew members. Is that true, and do you have anything to say to your old team owner, Brock Bronson?"

I nodded and grinned. How sweet it had been to make offers to our former, talented teammates and rub it in Bronson's face that we were entering the field just as he was exiting it due to mismanagement. "Dante's winning season was the first and last for Team Eagle, and we're thrilled to welcome some of their best and brightest to our racing stable. Next?"

I pointed at a reporter from the *Daily Mail*.

"How will you juggle the demands of being a mother and a team principal?" the man asked.

Dante stepped to the lectern, still holding Gabriella. "I'll answer this. My wife is capable of anything. Unlike me, she's an expert at multitasking. We've also decided that I will be the primary caregiver of our daughter while Savannah manages the team. But all three of us will be traveling with the team during the season, and I'll be lending my expertise to the drivers."

Another reporter shouted a question. "Dante, you once famously said you didn't want women on the teams. What's changed? Was it Savannah?"

He'd changed so much since we met. And I had too. Never did I imagine that I'd trust anyone, or love anyone, as much as I did him.

"It was three women who changed me," Dante said. "First, it was my sister. She was a pioneer in motorsports. Then, Savannah. She showed me that I was, how do you say, a Neanderthal in my views on women and sport. She's opened my eyes to a lot of things. That's why I married her, because I adore her, and love her more than life itself."

"Who's the third woman, Dante?" another reporter called out. Dante laughed and bounced Gabriella on his hip. My little girl, who wore a white Annunziata Auto T-shirt and a pink tutu with pink sparkly shoes, wrapped her arms around her father's neck and buried her face in his shoulder.

"This one. I named her after my sister and want her to be anything she wants to be. No barriers for her."

"Even if she wants to be a driver?" a reporter shouted.

Dante beamed. "Even if she wants to be a driver."

I couldn't help the tears pricking at my eyelids. My husband had come so far since I'd met him.

"That will be all the questions for today," I said into the microphone.

The three of us walked out of the news conference and paused in the privacy of the hallway.

"Never thought you'd hear that coming out of my mouth, did you?" Dante murmured, leaning to kiss me. Our daughter giggled, which she always did when we were affectionate in front of her.

"Oh, I knew you'd evolve someday." I laughed softly.

"How could I not, with you on my team?" I gently placed my hands on his face. "I love you."

"And I love you. Kiss me again, Savannah."

I leaned in and grinned against his lips. I'd never get enough of his kisses, or his adoration. We were a team, a strong and unbreakable one, a family of three without judgment or shame. A family filled with love and respect.

I'd gotten everything I'd wanted, and more.

ACKNOWLEDGMENTS

All of my love goes to editor Deanna McFadden and the entire Wattpad team. They believed in this book and in me, and I will always be grateful for their support.

ABOUT THE AUTHOR

Tamara Lush is a Rita Award finalist, an Amtrak writing fellow, and a George C. Polk Award–winning journalist. She's a former reporter who writes contemporary romance set in tropical locations, and she writes mysteries under the name Tara Lush. A fan of vintage pulp-fiction book covers, Sinatra-era jazz, and 1980s fashion, she lives with her husband and two dogs on the Gulf Coast.

TURN THE PAGE FOR A SNEAK PEAK OF
BOOK TWO IN THE PRETENDERS SERIES

CRASH

COMING WINTER 2023

CHAPTER ONE

EVIE

According to one of my business school professors, internships are supposedly like planting strawberries. You nestle the seeds in the ground, diligently water the sprouts, welcome the sunshine, and then eventually enjoy the delicious, ripe fruit that bursts with flavor.

It's like love, she'd say. Cultivate it, nurture it, and reap the benefits.

Now, I know nothing about love. But this is my third internship, so I'm pretty knowledgeable in that department.

In reality, internships are like potatoes. After cultivating the plant, you dig in the earth, get messy, and eventually find a dirty, lumpy vegetable. Then you have to put in more time and more work until it turns into something edible. And even then, you might burn the spud while frying it in boiling oil.

My thoughts drift to french fries and my stomach growls—a Pavlovian response to my hunger. I shove aside a company brochure, check my phone, and sigh. It's seven at night, and I should be home. Instead I'm glued to my uncomfortable, gray office chair on the third floor of the Jenkins International building, staring at a stack of files on my desk.

For a second, I rest my head on my forearms in the hushed office, trying to will away the hunger, and yeah, the boredom. The sooner I finish proofreading these memos, the sooner I can get home.

Thanks for piling on during the last two weeks of my internship, Josephine. She's my boss, and normally, I proofread marketing copy, such as the kinds of blurbs and snippets that showcase the company's charitable side. Charity is in short supply on the intern level, though. Even though I'm only making twelve dollars an hour, the company treats me more like a junior public relations executive. All work and very little pay for the opportunity to be considered for one of the few PR jobs that come open each year.

Groaning, I lift my head and thumb through the files, my eyes feeling dry and scratchy from the harsh overhead fluorescent light. I'll never get home in time to make dinner, and I'll totally be too tired to work on that newsletter for the community garden in my neighborhood. Why did I volunteer to do that?

I pick up my cell and wearily tap a number listed at the top of my recent calls.

"Sabrina? Hey. I'm going to be late. You're on your own for food. There's one of those microwave pizzas in the freezer, I think." I cradle my cell between my ear and shoulder, opening the cover of one of the files on my desk.

"Um, let me check, Evie." I hear the sound of the freezer door open and my sister's melodic southern accent soothes my mood. "Oh, look at that. There are three pizzas. Want me to heat one up for you? I'll save the third for my friends who are coming over."

That we're related sometimes baffles me. I have an accent as flat and dry as Florida. "No, I'll deal with it when I get home from work. Eat yours. Microwave only on medium. Four minutes. And hey, no friends over tonight. You need to study for finals."

Sabrina's high-pitched whine fills my ear. "But, Evieee, I need to study with them and we were going to hang out and go to a—"

I don't have time for this tonight, so I snap at her. "No guests. No going out. Your butt stays home tonight."

"But the exam's hella simple. I was going to invite over Kris and Aiden and—"

"I don't care if the biology exam is easy. Keep studying. Alone. Love you." I tap the off button on my phone, cutting her off midsqueal.

Boys worship her (which is a little adorable). Men love her (which is gross). Hell, she's even confided in me that she's experimented with girls. (That's fine with me, whatever makes her happy). She's too smart to screw up her life with an unplanned pregnancy or a starry-eyed elopement. Studying should be her priority, while working to keep us fed and sheltered is mine.

She does a pretty decent job of keeping on task, but I'd never tell her that. I try to act like Mom and Dad would have, or how I think they would've acted, had they lived. Sometimes I try to channel their reactions, something that Sabrina hates.

But I'm now Mom, Dad, and big sister. Or, according to Sabrina, a jail warden. Our fights have gotten more frequent during her senior year with all the parties she's been invited to.

It's my goal to get her to graduation next week and to an elite science camp in Boston for the summer. She's been accepted and has gotten a scholarship for 75 percent of the cost. I'm determined to scrape up the rest. Maybe I'll take on an additional shift at the bar . . .

I don't even want to think about college in the fall. That's what loans are for. God knows I have enough of them. I might have to defer them for the rest of my life, but at least I have a business degree. I'd hoped to go for my MBA, but Mom and Dad's death killed that dream. Maybe someday.

Back to work, Evie.

Scanning the first page of the file and then a glossy brochure paper clipped to the folder, I spot the Post-it note left by Josephine. It's stuck to the brochure.

Proofread this marketing plan for spelling errors and then bring this entire file to Alex's office. Right away. He needs to sign off in person and wants to see the attached brochure as it's printed.

The second underline is a bit of an overkill, in my opinion.

I frown and flip the note over, hoping for more instructions. Alex's office? The managing director? I'm an *intern*. Interns *do not* casually drop off reports for upper management like that.

"Josephine?" I had her in my favorites on my cell, something she'd insisted on when I started. "Hey. It's Evie. Sorry to bother you. Can you hear me?"

There's clicking and a fuzzy response. Dammit, she must be on the MARTA, headed home to Sandy Springs. The line goes dead. I text her instead.

You want me to bring everything to Alex's office? Do you mean Alex Jenkins?

Already, I have so many questions. What if I find an error? How should I correct it? Do I go over the corrections with Alex? That can't be right. Josephine's usual micromanagement style seems half-assed tonight. Something is amiss, and all of the poop has rolled downhill and landed in my lap.

I rifle quickly through the file while I wait for Josephine's response and don't spot any errors. It's such an unusual request from Josephine because she always deals with him directly. Why can't I just email this? Does the managing director not know how to use PDF files?

The last thing I want is to bust into Alex Jenkins's office after hours. Just the thought makes me shiver.

Dale Alexander Jenkins isn't around much. Usually he's traveling the globe, running one part of the company or another. Jenkins International owns the world's largest tire manufacturer. The company was started by Alex's grandfather, according to a plaque in the lobby commemorating the older man.

But the conglomerate also recently acquired a line of chemical and industrial rubber products, a chain of sporting goods stores, and, inexplicably, a company that makes roofing supplies.

Rumor has it that Alex also wants to be the company's CEO—a job that's occupied by his eighty-something-year-old grandmother. She's opposing the move, I've heard. I try not to pay attention to the rumors. They're none of my business and likely aren't true.

I'm in the corporate communications department, which means I write feel-good stories for the company newsletter and copyedit press releases about Jenkins's "corporate citizenship."

Safety! Environment! Community!

Those are the company's three buzzwords, and they've been imprinted into my thoughts during my five months here. They're on the company letterhead, at the bottom of my emails, and in every news release. They're in my stupid dreams, ones where I push papers and type until my fingers bleed. I wonder if Alex Jenkins knows his corporate communications intern works unpaid overtime.

If those buzzwords float in my brain, Alex Jenkins is branded there too. Because good lord, he is gorgeous.

While I see him every day in our company literature, smiling and self-possessed, I've only seen him twice in person. Once during a company-wide forum where he'd given a presentation and once in the lobby of our building on a Saturday a couple of months ago. Both times I was shocked at how young he seemed—he couldn't be a day over thirty—and how he had the most extraordinary way of looking both earnest and wicked with his dark hair and intense eyes.

I glance down at my phone, shaking off those silly memories.

Why isn't Josephine texting me back?

I look outside the window to see the sun setting over Downtown Atlanta, then at the stack of files. I'll never get home if I keep daydreaming. I open the glossy brochure and scrutinize the words on the front. It's a trifold, full color, glossy paper thing, the kind that's given to recruits at job fairs and corporate conferences.

When Josephine found out I enjoyed editing, she'd unleashed me on all sorts of projects. If there's one thing I'm good at, it's details. I see the trees, not the forest.

My concentration is interrupted by my cell. It actually startles me enough to cause a yelp to leak from my mouth. Glancing at the screen, I notice two details: it's 6:52 at night, almost two hours after I usually leave the office, and it's Josephine.

"Hey! Thank God you called. About this brochure. You want me to bring it to Alex Jenkins's office? Do I have the right Alex? Or is it someone else? I just wanted to double check. Can't we just email it?"

"Evie! Holy shit! No, we can't email it. Alex is going to a meeting in New York in two days and he wants everything to be perfect because of some huge deal. You haven't looked over the brochure yet? It's going to print tomorrow morning. I put that first in the stack so you'd do it right away. Didn't you see the note? Alex said he wanted to see the proof by eight thirty. Get your ass up to his office NOW."

Shaking, I hang up. Yep. There it is. A second note on the inside of the file folder that says: *do this immediately!!!*

The three exclamation marks are the punctuation version of a punch in the gut.

I glance through the slick, colorful brochure again, a pit growing in my stomach because I haven't spent enough time proofreading the thing. It will only take me ten minutes to read through it, but normally I'd spend an hour on something like this.

As usual, I get caught up in the details—I find one small error where there should be a comma and wonder if anyone but me will notice. I look at the time and gasp. It's eight fifteen. Maybe I'll explain to Alex that there's a minor typo and let him decide if he wants the whole thing redone. Why he's even interested in this level of minutiae, I'm not sure.

The brochure's glossy paper practically slips through my fingers as I stuff it into the file and run for the elevator. Once inside,

I punch the button for the top floor. I hate elevators. Loathe them. Normally I take the stairs when coming and going from the office. But I don't have time to dash up several flights right now, so I suck it up. Right now, I'm more afraid of my boss and not getting this project to Alex Jenkins than the elevator.

I'm sweating with anxiety by the time I'm halfway to the top floor. I must think about anything but this little, confined box hurtling up twenty stories. Dinner? My stomach growls. Whether Sabrina's doing her homework? Gah.

Or . . . Dale Alexander Jenkins. That's something curious to ponder. As I'm whisked into the upper reaches of the building, I idly wonder why everyone calls him Alex and not Dale. Maybe because his father and grandfather were named Dale? Maybe because Dale's an old-fashioned name? I try to imagine him introducing his sexy self as Dale and almost giggle.

A soft sheen of sweat blooms on my upper lip as the elevator takes me up twenty stories. It dings softly, and when the doors slide open, I lurch into a vast, private office.

It's low lit, illuminated only by a green-glass shaded desk lamp and the twinkling lights of Atlanta's business district below. Thankfully, there's no one behind the desk, though the room has the aura of a place that was recently occupied.

I haul in a lungful of air. My sense of smell is strong, and I detect notes of spice and musk. A man's aftershave. My gaze sweeps around the room. I spot a closed door in the corner and a coat rack with a suit jacket, but otherwise, the few pieces of sleek, dark wood and black leather furniture are the only things in the room.

Hesitantly, I take a few steps toward the desk, figuring I'll drop the file and run.

When I reach the desk, I open the file once again. That's my downfall, because I feel a compulsion to read the first paragraph of the brochure one more time. Just to make sure everything is correct. I can't stand errors and feel terrible that I haven't proofread this file more.

Jenkins International is North America's largest—

"Thank God, you're here."

I gasp and drop the file at the sound of the growly, masculine voice. The brochure and the papers spill everywhere at my feet, like leaves in autumn.